To
Jewell a
Paul Sidhy

MW01234815

Next First Lady's Bad Twin

by Paul Sidhu

authorHOUSE®

AuthorHouse™
1663 Liberty Drive, Suite 200
Bloomington, IN 47403
www.authorhouse.com
Phone: 1-800-839-8640

First published by AuthorHouse 7/21/2008

ISBN: 978-1-4389-0215-9 (e)
ISBN: 978-1-4389-0218-0 (sc)

Library of Congress Control Number: 2008906260

Printed in the United States of America
Bloomington, Indiana

This book is printed on acid-free paper.

Next First Lady's Bad Twin

Part II

The Trial Of

Will be out on September 29, 2008

Next First Lady's Bad Twin.

Sunday August 31st 2008, and the time was almost 5:00PM in Denver. The day is perfect with the warm 70 degree weather. A Greyhound bus comes to a sudden halt at the main bus stand. The driver comes out first and holds the door for the passengers, who are coming out slowly. The last to exit the bus is a tall lady in a long dress, with large sun glasses and her hat pulled over her forehead, hoping she cannot be recognized. The woman is looking rather weary Woman is thankful that after eight hour journey she has reached her destination. She walks over to where .Bus driver standing by the Bags now. So no body takes the wrong bags.

"Could you please call any porter, so he can carry these bags to the taxi for me?" the lady asks.

Looking to the left "they are already coming" said the driver; about four porters were walking towards the bus. When they come close, they ask who needed assistance.

The driver tells one of them

"She does", pointing to the lady" A fifty year old man gets near her,

"Yes, Miss, where do you want to go?" asks the porter.

"I need a taxi, for two counties away, near Mr. Monroe's estate. It is about forty five miles away and I need a coolheaded driver, with a lot of patience."

The porter replies, "These city drivers don't like to go that far and come back empty handed, let me take you outside and I'll find you what you need."

"Which bags are yours?"

The lady points to her bags and the porter puts them on the trolley. "Follow me" said the porter, the lady obliges and they walk out of the bus stand, where some taxis are picking up passengers. Instead the porter takes her over to where taxis were dropping off passengers. The porter looks at the taxis and he sees a taxi with a different color than the rest, and he tells the lady to wait, and walks five feet to the taxi. He goes to the passenger side front window and asks the taxi driver

"Do you want a good fare going back to your county?"

"Yes, of course" the taxi driver replies.

"Give me ten bucks" says the porter, "Oh yeah, I'll give you ten bucks when I see a passenger. I can't give you the money before I know you aren't jacking me!" responds the cabby.

"Ok, wait here", the porter goes back to the lady

"Miss, this taxi goes back to where you want to go" and he wheels the two bags to the taxi. The taxi driver comes out of the taxi, when the porter comes close to the trunk.

"Good afternoon madam" says the driver and she replies the same. The porter opens the rear passenger door side and the woman gets in, the porter closes the door puts her little bag in the trunk. The second bag is too heavy so both men lift it and put it in the trunk,

"What does this woman carry in her bag, gold or something?" says the porter to the driver.

The driver hands the porter ten bucks,

"I have no idea what women carry in their bags" he replies. They close the trunk, and the porter comes to the rear passenger window, and the lady hands him a twenty dollar bill,

"You are a nice man". As the porter thanks her, she pulls out another twenty dollars, and gives it to him, and he thanks her many times. The lady closes the window, and the taxi moves off. When the taxi moves away from the bus stand, the driver introduces himself,

"My name is Paul, and I'm from India, what is your name and where would you like to go?"

"My name is Cassandra and I want to go near Mr. Monroe's estate, when I get near there I'll tell you where to go. Here's two hundred dollars if you can stay with me till I find my place."

The smiling driver looking at the money says

"I can stick to you with that kind of money"

"No I don't need you to stick to my body itself, but if you stay with me till I find my place, I'll tip you the same amount."

"Ok, Lady I will be with you all the way but exactly where are you going" the driver asks.

"Well tell me five minutes before we reach Mr. Monroe's place then I'll tell you" said the Lady.

He says ok and the cab picks up speed, after a few minutes the cab is on a two lane highway cruising at 50. The driver and his passenger start talking to each other

"You know when you said Mr. Monroe, I heard his speeches, and he is going to be our next president. What a man he is, so intelligent and a kind person too. He shall bring this country's respect back, oh and his wife she is so lovely and kind, she is going to be the next first lady. God must have blessed them personally.

"Have you met her Mr. Paul?" the lady asks.

"Yes I did, a year ago; I met her in church with my family. She was so kind, I could not believe it. I thought she was going to be big headed, being so rich and powerful. But she was so sweet and beautiful, what I call a complete woman."

"Oh really what did she do for you that made you respect her so much" the lady asks.

"You know, I was introduced to her by Father John at the church. I was having trouble getting our family's Green Card, so I was told to go see Father John on Sunday, which I did and one day he told me to come to church, so all my family went there. After service my family was introduced to Mrs. Monroe, she was so warm in welcoming people. She asks us in private what our family needed and I told her immigration was not releasing our Green Card, even though it was supposed to be due six months ago. She took our names and Guess what; our Green Cards were delivered in special mail with an apology. Since then we decided we are all going to vote for Mr. Monroe, and I am going to ask all the people I know to vote for Mr. Monroe to be our next president, and she will be our next First Lady. I hope I'm not boring you." the cabby said.

"No, no not at all, I like your accent and the way you talk. Anyway Paul, how long have you been here and do you have children?" asks the woman "what do you think about this country?"

"Well Miss, I have been here twenty years, this is a very good country if you abide by the law. Anybody can make a living in this country regardless of race or color. I have four children a good daughter and three good sons. They don't always agree with me but I still love them, my younger sons are identical twins" Paul replied.

"Oh what a coincidence, I am an identical twin too" the lady says, then she suddenly goes quiet, she wanted to keep it a secret and then changes the subject.

"What religion are you?" asks the woman.

"Dear Lady, I am gone off all religions, they make trouble in the world, I am just a human and I respect all humans. We come one way, we go one way. I don't know why humans fight each other; every body is going to die one day so why fight? So live and let live, and I believe in doing good things."

"Yes, I agree with you" The lady says.

"Anyway we are five minutes away from Mr. Monroe's estate. So where and which way do you want to go" the driver asks.

"Just take me to Mr. Monroe's house, and if they don't let me stay, I'll go back to the bus stand and pay you the same amount and tip." The lady said.

As their conversation kept going, the driver asks again "Do you have an appointment with them or are you related to them?"

"Yes, something like that, you'll have a surprise soon",

"Oh what kind of surprise?" The driver is getting curious, and he sees a huge board about forty feet high and twenty feet wide saying,

Welcome to Mr. Monroe's estate. The driver says "we are here; I hope they let you in."

The taxi comes off the highway, and there is a private road to the right towards the estate, four blocks ahead they see a big security gate and a high security fence going left and right covering the whole estate. Whole fence is barbed wire, as the taxi slowly approaches the security in the middle, and it comes to a halt. A white male in his late forties comes out of the booth, when he is next to the window he asks

"Good afternoon driver, who do you have here?"

"The lady says she wants to see the lady of the house" the driver tells him.

"But Mrs. Monroe did not tell me about any appointments this evening" the guard says.

The lady tells the driver "tell him to come to my window, and then he can decide" Before driver tells the guard.

"Yes I heard that"

And the guard starts walking to the front of the car, and goes around to the passenger rear window, the driver lowers right rear window all the way and the lady takes of her glasses and hat off, and the driver turns his face to the right to look at her, and he is shocked to see who it is. By now the security guard has come to the window, and his eyes open wide with shock and surprise and says

"Mrs. Monroe I did not see You leave, when did you leave?"

Cassandra smiles and says,

"No I am not Mrs. Monroe, I am her twin sister, and I have not seen her in fifteen years."

The guard starts walking to his booth and again he looks back at her, he could not tell who she was. Upon entering his booth he turned on the close circuit TV and said

"Mrs. Monroe please come to the close circuit TV, quickly."

His voice was heard throughout the whole house where Samantha was on the phone with her mother-in-law. The house has speakers in every room, Samantha hangs up the phone and rushes to the TV in their living room and she turns it on. She can see the guard live, and the guard can see her too.

"What is it?" Mrs. Monroe asks.

"Mrs. Monroe, there is a lady in a taxi here, she looks like you, your exact double, and I thought it was you." the guard says.

"Ask her what her name is", the guard pulls his head out of the door, "what's her name?" the driver says Cassandra.

The guard tells Mrs. Monroe, her name is Cassandra,

Mrs. Monroe tells him to send her in. The guard turns off the TV and comes out, and tells the driver to open his trunk. The guard looks at the trunk and closes it, he tells the driver to go in. As the driver puts his taxi in drive, he moves slowly. They both see a huge mansion about three to four blocks away. They see a nice road, and a two feet wide walkway on both side of the road All the way from the gate to the house, the grass was perfectly cut; the foot path had light red perfectly square bricks, all kinds of roses in many colors placed all the way to the house on both sides of the road. The driver and Cassandra look at everything, and how neatly it is done. The driver says

"Dear lady you did not have to hide your face until now, I don't harm nobody"

"No Paul, don't feel bad, I did not want to be recognized in public because my sister is going to be the next First Lady. I did not want to hurt her reputation that is why." Cassandra replied kindly.

"Well that is understandable" says the driver. They are very close to the house, which is a ten bedroom plus a variety of other rooms, and a huge parking lot on one side and a six car garage on one side. When they come near the house, Cassandra sees two of the garage doors open while the cab is still moving. Cassandra takes out three hundred dollars and gives it to the cabby, and says

"Paul can you back up your car next to the open garage I'll take the little bag inside and the big one, you could put it in the garage corner, so it's not visible from the outside. Once I go inside, if I wave to you, you can go. If I give you a sign of five, it means five minutes." That means I will be only five minutes.

"Ok, you made my day, I am glad you twins are together now, and you should keep it that way."

The driver stops the car and opens the trunk; she takes the carry on luggage and her hand bag. As she looks to the main door at the house, which just opened and she sees her twin standing there, and the driver says again

"God bless our next First Lady and you too". Cassandra starts walking away from the taxi; the main house door is thirty feet away. Both twins see each other, their eyes are glued to each other, as she walks slowly, next to Mrs. Monroe is the housekeeper standing. The driver looks at both twins wondering what a miracle. Cassandra comes close to the door and climbs two steps and the huge door that was open, and she stands in front of her elder twin and drops her carry on bag and her purse on the floor

While Mrs. Jones, the housekeeper, looks on. First both twins hold each others hands and stare at each other, then their eyes fill with tears and they both hug each other so tight, with tears running down their cheeks .after about a minute, Samantha breaks the silence, while still holding each other.

"I missed you so much, where did you go? Why did you go? I love you so much I always will. You won't believe how lonely I was without you."

Cassandra replies,

"When I left home I did not miss you or mom. But in the last couple of years I have felt lonely and like I had no body, and I started to miss mom too, where is she?"

The Samantha takes her younger twin to the sofa and asks her to sit down.

"She passed away a year and a half after you left home. Every night she would wait by the window waiting for you to come back, or your call, until she felt sleepy and went to bed. Then one day while coming home from work with me she had a major heart attack in the snow. By the time the ambulance came it was too late" Samantha again has tears in her eyes. The sisters both hug each other again, while Mrs. Jones is looking at them, and Cassandra feels guilty.

"Samantha it is all my fault, if I wasn't such a bad girl she would have still been alive, and lived longer, I'm sorry I gave both of you such a hard time."

"No don't worry, god forgives all" says Samantha. Then Samantha gets up and walks to the door, she looks at the driver and says,

"Let me pay the driver."

"No sister I already paid him", Cassandra gets up and walks to the door too, Cassandra waves to the driver. But Samantha says,

"I know who he is; his name is Paul, he came to church one day, asking for Mr. Monroe. He needed help getting his Green Card, which was due earlier."

"Yes, sister, he was thanking you and your husband all they way."

Then Mrs. Monroe waves a sign to the driver to come into the house. The driver walks over to the door and Mrs. Monroe says,

"Paul, come in, have some refreshment. I am not going to let you go from this house until you come have something to eat or drink. And did your family finally get the Green Card?"

"Yes Mrs. Monroe, I mean our next first Lady, we are all citizens now, and we will all vote for Mr. Monroe."

"Don't stand out there Paul, come in, you have brought me happiness, my sister" says Mrs. Monroe, "What will you have?"

As Paul walks into the house he sits across the twins, he can only tell the difference by their clothes.

"I like a cup of Indian tea please, Mrs. Monroe" says Paul, and Mrs. Monroe orders Mrs. Jones for a cup of Indian tea.

After five minutes tea is served to Paul, Mrs. Monroe, and Cassandra. After having their tea, Paul says goodbye to both twins. After the cab driver has gone, Mrs. Monroe closes the door. It is nearly 7 o'clock pm of August the 31st 2008, Samantha asks

Cassandra, while picking her carry on bag up, and Cassandra picks up her purse,

"Let me show you everything around the house", Samantha takes Cassandra around the first floor of the house and to her bedroom where there is a wardrobe, baths, and everything a guest might need. Then she takes her two the next few rooms which are many other guest rooms. Straight across are the children's rooms. Next to the children's rooms is Mrs. Monroe Senior's room. They come back to Mr. and Mrs. Monroe's room and Mrs. Monroe says,

"You know where everything is, have a shower and come back downstairs, and then we will decide what you want to do."

Again Samantha held Cassandra's hands

"Now you are here, let us not fall apart again, we are family, let us look into the future not the past, this home is yours as much as mine."

As the sisters let go of each other, Cassandra asks,

"Sister, I know you both don't drink, but I cannot go to sleep without a couple of drinks."

Samantha replies,

"Ok, Put everything here; let me take you to the guest bar."

As they walk out of the bedroom, Samantha takes Cassandra to the room which is next to Mrs. Monroe Senior's room, as both twins go to the bar Samantha turns the light on; Cassandra is shocked to see how well her sister is doing. In the bar room, Cassandra sees how nicely the bar is done, and even though her sister and her husband do not drink, the bar is fully stocked. Cassandra takes a bottle and picks up a nice looking glass and fills half of it with Bacardi and another half with coke. She gulps her drink in one go, while Samantha looks at her surprised, but wants her to be happy. After having one drink, Cassandra says

11

"Let me have a shower, I'll join you in the living room" and the younger sister goes to take her shower. Samantha goes downstairs in the living room, while she is sitting and waiting for her sister. The house keeper, Mrs. Jones walks in, as soon as she is in the living room Samantha says,

"Come and sit down, I am so happy that my sister is here. I thought I would never see her again. But the Almighty made my wish come true."

"Mrs. Monroe, you never mentioned you had a twin",

"I know Mrs. Jones, I am sorry I should have said something, but after my mother died I just kept it all to myself" replies Samantha.

"What would she like to eat?"

"I don't know, when she comes down we can ask her, but something homemade. When we were younger she was always an outsider about everything."

While Samantha and Mrs. Jones are talking for about twenty minutes, Cassandra comes down with Mrs. Monroe's nightgown. As she walks in the living room, both of them were surprised to see Cassandra looking like a carbon copy of her elder twin.

Cassandra sits across from Samantha and Mrs. Jones, and Samantha asks Mrs. Jones to fix some food with a drink. Samantha goes to the smaller bar next to the kitchen and dining room and comes back with Bacardi and a coke, as well as a bottle of champagne and two glasses. It is nearly eight pm on Sunday the 31st of August 2008, it is already getting dark outside, and the curtains have been drawn.

Now both sisters are sitting across from each other, Cassandra is waiting for her sister to ask her to have a drink. Samantha is very smart, and says first.

"Cassandra, don't be shy, go ahead and have your drink and I'll have one with you too."

And Samantha moves closer to the table between them, she opens the Bacardi and coke bottle first, and then she opens the champagne bottle. Now Cassandra doesn't feel shy, and she pours herself champagne too. As they both pick up their glasses and say cheers. This time Cassandra only takes a little bit of the drink and Samantha has a little bit too. By this time Mrs. Jones comes in with a trolley, with many choices of food like chips, peanuts, and little fruit salads, onions, cucumbers, and other natural foods. She puts it in front of the twins, and Cassandra looks at Mrs. Jones but does not say anything. Samantha is too smart and can read her mind as Cassandra looked at Mrs. Jones, then turned to pick up her drink and takes another large sip. And now Samantha knows Cassandra has to say something."

"Dear, sister you can say, asks, or do anything in front of Mrs. Jones. She is part of the family."

After hearing that, the younger twin starts eating a little bit, so does Samantha. Then Samantha turns to Mrs. Jones.

"Mrs. Jones, is everything done with in the kitchen? I want to eat with my sister; I'll take care of everything. Pour yourself your favorite and come join us, we three women will have our night tonight."

"Thank you Mrs. Monroe, I have mine in the kitchen, and I'll go get it." Mrs. Jones goes to the kitchen and comes back with her drink. She sits down on one side of the twins and starts listening to their stories.

After having a drink and a half, Cassandra is feeling better now. Unlike the younger days when she would have one or two drinks and go wild, today is the first time in her life she has had control over herself.

"Sis, please forgive me, I have to drink for a few days to go to sleep. I have to really cut down, but I came to this situation because he rejected me for someone who was not even good-looking, just younger. I was a fool; I should have listened to mom or you, but that was not meant to be."

Cassandra picks up her drink and has another sip, Samantha and Mrs. Jones do the same, and the three of them sit there listening to each other, and sharing their problems. They eat their appetizers, and time passes by as Cassandra has another drink while Samantha is making sure she is eating something at the same time. It is nearly 10 o'clock pm, Samantha knows Cassandra is tired and drinking to much alcohol, she needs to go to sleep. Samantha supports her shoulder and helps her to the guest bed; she puts a light blanket on her as Cassandra is fast asleep. Samantha sits in the rocking chair as her sister sleeps, about an hour later she falls asleep too.

1st of September 2008, Monday morning, it was a nice sunny morning. Samantha and Mrs. Jones are already up. It is 9 o'clock am, Cassandra is waking up slowly, and she has not slept like this in a long time. Lately she would either drink too much or not eat enough apart from nuts and crisps. Today however, she is waking up at her sister's house and not worried about taking orders from anybody. Her curtains are still drawn and she doesn't have any hangover because of the good home cooked meal she had last night.

Her bedroom door is partially open, and Cassandra sees what kind of place she slept him.

She slowly comes to her own, and sits in her bed and looks around. Everything in the room was so beautifully done. As the sunlight comes through the curtains, she sees a beautiful dress still in the plastic bag laid next to a clean towel and fresh under clothes, and a new toothbrush and toothpaste, everything she needs lying by her feet. After these years Cassandra is getting the love and affection she never had before. Now the time has come were she can start giving love and respect to others. Cassandra finds the bed very comfortable and does not want to get up; she finally takes everything from the bed and goes to shower. After half an hour she comes out feeling fresh wearing the new dress, with her hair still wet, she comes down the stairs to the dining room. Cassandra sees Samantha and Mrs. Jones watching TV, before she enters she knocks on the door, both turn around to see her. Mrs. Jones speaks first,

"Good morning, Miss Cassandra Domenici." As Cassandra is walking in she replies,

"Good morning Mrs. Jones, good morning sister, I have not felt this good for years in the morning!"

As Cassandra joins the other two, the TV is on with a low volume, it is showing the news with Mr. Monroe again and again. It is hardly ten in the morning on September 1st and Mrs. Jones gets up and says,

"What would our next First Lady like for her breakfast? And her look alike, well you could both be our next First Ladies."

The younger twin gets the message,

"No Mrs. Jones, don't say that, I am nowhere near becoming our next First Lady, I give that honor to my sister Samantha."

Mrs. Jones goes into the kitchen to prepare breakfast for both the twins. It takes about half an hour for breakfast, meanwhile both sisters are watching Mr. Monroe's campaign news. Cassandra looks around and sees Mrs. Jones bringing them their breakfast. By the time they have finished eating and talking it is nearly eleven am, Samantha tells Cassandra that by lunch they have to go to the hair dresser, then shopping for new clothes. Cassandra has no choice but to agree.

By eleven thirty both sisters are ready, with different clothes, shoes, and their hair done. They look the same, but with a difference.

About eleven forty five Mr. Monroe's family limo pulls up in front of the house with one security guard in the front of the car and one in the back. The limo driver is standing by the passenger door waiting for Mrs. Monroe to come out; he still does not know the Cassandra has come home. Only the gate security guard and Mrs. Jones know that Mrs. Monroe has an identical twin.

As the main door to the house opens, both security guards come out of the cars and come to stand with the limo driver. One of the twins comes out and the driver and the guards say at the same time,

"Good morning Mrs. Monroe."

As the twin looks at all of them and says "good morning gentlemen" and gets in the limo. Then the other twin is still in side about to step out side. But driver closes the limo door, because he did not know that one more twin is coming. But the twin quickly opens it from inside and says,

"Wait my sister is coming too,"

The driver asks "Mrs. Monroe, I did not know you had a sister."

"Oh I am not Mrs. Monroe, she is" and Cassandra points to the door were Samantha has appeared

All three look at the other twin who is now walking towards the limo, they look in the limo and then out at the other twin walking towards them. All of their eyes open wide and their mouths opened too, when Samantha is very close to them, all three say in unison

"Good morning Mrs. Monroe, are you the real Mrs. Monroe?"

"Yes, good morning, I am the real Mrs. Monroe, and that is my twin sister I have not seen in a long time, she arrived yesterday."

The security guards say "how is Mr. Monroe going to recognize you? Or are we going to give him the surprise of his lifetime."

"Yes"

Samantha gets into the limo, and tells the driver to go to the beauty salon first.

Security car, limo, and the other security car move off, and the driver starts talking to the twins by lowering the glass in the middle. Driving in the streets of Denver, Cassandra looks around at the town that has changed quite a bit. She recognizes some of the places but there are many new ones she doesn't. After about twenty minutes the cars pull up to a new top of the line shopping center, where everything is done with class, most of the cars in the parking lot were very expensive. All three cars pull up in front of the beauty salon.

As the cars come to complete stop, both security guards come out of their cars and stand guard to the limo's passenger door. Then the limo driver comes out of the car, the three men look around to make sure no foul play is about. One guard goes to stand by the salon door so he can open it for the twins. Before they arrive, an old lady about sixty five carrying a little white pup is approaching the door, when she comes close he opens the door and says,

"Good day Mrs. Wonderful, nice to see you to see you nice

"Yes, good day, and where did you learn these charming words and manners. I know they are not yours. And you have nothing else to do, other than opening doors for old ladies."

"Oh no Mrs. Wonderful, this is for our next First lady" as he looks toward the limo, there she is," as one of the twins is escorted by security guards to the salon. The guard says to the old lady,

"Those nice words came from an old English comedian who married a few younger women"

"That was not nice of him, anyway here comes Mrs. Monroe."

As the twin comes near the old lady, the door is still being held open by the driver and the old lady steps in to the salon followed by a twin. The lady stands in front of her and says,

"Hello Mrs. Monroe, how are you? Maybe I should be calling you our next First Lady from now on"

Taken by surprise, the twin just looks at her and replies, "Dear lady I do not know you. I am not Mrs. Monroe but she'll be here in a second."

The lady is now getting a little irritated, not too upset because she has known Mrs. Monroe for a long time and they both have a sense of humor. The lady finally comes up with an answer that Cassandra was not expecting

"Oh Mrs. Monroe you don't know me? I know you are moving into the White House soon, but you aren't there yet and you have already started forgetting your friends. A lot could happen between now and the election, I know once people get into the White House they get big headed. But you're already there. You know your husband is going to win, so you have already stopped talking to Mrs. Wonderful."

Cassandra starts to plead and say,

"So you are Mrs. Wonderful! I am Mrs. Monroe's twin sister"

By this time Samantha walks in, and comes close to Mrs. Wonderful and Cassandra. Samantha turns to the old lady

"Good afternoon Mrs. Wonderful, how are you today?" Mrs. Wonderful goes quite and looks at both twins, then turns to Samantha

"So you are Mrs. Monroe, how come you never told me you had an identical twin?"

"I am sorry; it is just one of those things that never crossed my mind. I don't know what I would gain by lying about my sister."

By now the whole salon staff stops what they are doing and start looking at the twins, because they never knew Mrs. Monroe had an identical twin before. Mrs. Wonderful is still not satisfied, and does not like to be the underdog.

"Mrs. Monroe I am sorry to say I spoke badly to your sister, but people who live in the White House have lied, and people going to the White House lie too, it really isn't a White House as much as a Lie House."

Samantha knows the old lady is being carried away by politics so she tactfully changes the subject,

"Ok Mrs. Wonderful, this is my sister Cassandra, let us take our seats and I'll tell you all about it."

All three ladies are shown their chairs and Mrs. Wonderful sits in the middle of the twins. The staff has been shocked by the sisters and start working right away. The sisters are both silent but Mrs. Wonderful can't keep quite anymore; she wants to know everything about Cassandra. Right before the Salon Staff starts working on them she turns to Samantha,

"So Mrs. Monroe tell me more about your sister"

"What would you like to know?"

"I mean where she was all these years? Is she married? Does she have any children? Or home? Is she going to move to the White House with you or what?"

"Well Mrs. Wonderful you can ask her all these questions yourself, she has the free will to talk to you"

Mrs. Wonderful turned to Cassandra on the left, but before she says anything else Cassandra feels that she must answer because she does not want her sister to be put on the spot.

"Well Mrs. Wonderful, I left home at twenty one with a man, I thought he loved me. We lived together for fifteen years, and it ended up not working out. So I gave everything up and decided to meet my sister before I decide to do anything else. But when my sister becomes our next First Lady, I will be near by, not in the White House however, that is made for them."

Listening to Cassandra's answer, Mrs. Wonderful replies "you are a very smart girl, like your sister too you know."

"Well Mrs. Monroe, both of you twins are good and it is nice to see you together, but does your husband know about her?"

"No he does not; we are going to give him a surprise on Sunday in the Stadium when he gives his final speech. We will both dress and do our hair and make up alike to see if he can tell who is who."

"Well Mrs., Monroe, good luck!" By now the beauty salon staff has been working on all three ladies, and again the old lady turns to Samantha.

"Mrs. Monroe, I like your husband too, he is not only good looking but a good man as well. A lot of women like him too. Many people are counting on him to turn this country around. Anyway you never told me how and where you found him."

"I didn't find him, he found me."

"Well Mrs. Monroe, you are lucky, if I had met him before you, he would have been mine."

"Oh yes I know."

All three ladies chat for two hours while they get their hair, nails, and everything done. Once they are finished Samantha asks the old lady if she would like to join them for the rest of the afternoon to go shopping.

"Yes of course, Mrs. Monroe I love your company. Now we have your twin sister too. I can spend this afternoon with you, what do you girls want to do?"

"Nothing much Mrs. Wonderful, just shopping for some new clothes for my sister"

"I am ok with that, but what shall I tell my husband I am doing all after noon" she says.

"Tell him you were with us, and I will back you up" says Samantha, you can leave your car here and pick it up on the way home."

She agrees, again the staff is just standing there not knowing which twin is which. Mrs. Monroe tips them very well, and they thank her. Mrs. Monroe pushes a button on her cell phone and the driver comes in,

"Mrs. Monroe are you ready, and what is you next destination?"

"Yes we are and Mrs. Wonderful is going to accompany us, we are just going into the next shopping center for some new clothes. Then we will drop Mrs. Wonderful here and go home.

The driver OK's this plan, and then goes outside to tell the security guards the plan. Then they guard the salon while the twins get into the limo along with Mrs. Wonderful. Once all three ladies are in they drive off to the next shopping center where they were dropped off with one of the security guards. They spend almost two hours shopping and it is nearly afternoon, they have only had a quick bite to eat and a short rest, afterwards they twins drop off Mrs. Wonderful at the beauty salon. It is nearly six pm by the time the twins get home.

It is the evening of the 1st of September, and only the twins are home with Mrs. Jones, who had been waiting for them as they walk into the house. The driver comes in with all of their shopping bags and lays them in the living room. As the security guards leave, so does the driver and they lock the front door? Both twins sit across each other on the sofa. Mrs. Jones asks them if they need anything, both answer no, and Cassandra goes and picks up a pile of bags from their shopping trip. She picks out one bag out of them, and then walks over to Mrs. Jones who is sitting on the dining room chair. As Cassandra gives her the gift she says,

"Mrs. Jones, this is a gift for you from me."

Mrs. Jones opens the present and pulls out a dress and jumper for the winter, and after looking at the clothing she knew that they were from top of the line stores, with joy she replies,

"Ms. Cassandra you should not have done this, this is much too expensive, I am going to look too good in this. Mrs. Monroe you should have told her not to buy this for me" she turned to face Samantha,

"It was her wish; she wanted to buy it for you."

"I want to thank you Cassandra, you have a very good taste in clothes just like your sister" Mrs. Jones says, and she takes the bag and goes off to the kitchen.

While both twins are getting to know each other better they start sharing moments of their childhood. It is almost 6:30 pm, Samantha says

"Let me talk to the children and their grandmother so you can see them, we have a live camera. Just sit here on the dining room chair so you can see them, but they can't see you. We will surprise them on Sunday."

"Ok, sister" and Cassandra moves to the dining room table chair and Samantha turns on the TV and live camera with there children turns on. She sees her daughter and son playing, with their grandmother and the Senator's sister's children at the Senator's sister's house. When they hear a beep they know mom is on the live TV. When they see their mom on the other side, Samantha's son and daughter run up close to the TV and say together,

"Hi mom, do you miss us?"

"Yes I do, do you miss me?"

They look at each other and say, "No, not yet grandma is great. She gives us what we want and lets us eat anything, not what you want us to eat."

Samantha sees her mother-in-law sitting in the background with her husband's sister's children.

"Hi mother, how are you?"

She waves and says,

"Hi Samantha, I am fine are you feeling lonely?"

"Yes mother, but I will see you Sunday; I hope the children are not giving you any trouble."

"No they are not; when they do we take them to a fast food place. They play more than they actually eat."

The children come to the screen again, now one of the Senator's sister's children joins them.

"Hey Aunt Samantha, when are you going to join us?"

"Sunday evening, when we all get together in the stadium, I love you all; don't give your grandma a hard time. Ok guys, goodnight, and mother goodnight." And her mother-in-law says the same.

As Samantha turned the TV off, Cassandra had enjoyed every minute of it. It is nearly seven o'clock pm and Cassandra moves close to Samantha and sits across from her.

"Samantha you have a nice mother-in-law and beautiful children. I am dying to see them I hope Sunday comes very soon."

"Yes Cassandra, I have a very nice mother-in-law."

Samantha gets up; she knows it is seven pm and time for Cassandra to have her drink. She goes to the bar and comes back with the same drink, and puts it on the coffee table in the middle.

Cassandra helps herself to a smaller drink than yesterday. Then she says, "Let me go and have a shower, I will put these bags away."

"Let me help you"

And they both pick up all the bags and go to Cassandra's bedroom. About seven thirty pm, and Cassandra come out of the shower with her new dressing gown. She comes out to the front of the room to go to the living room, when she is coming close to her sister's room; she hears that Samantha is talking to somebody. She comes and stands by the doorway and sees her sister sitting in front of a small live TV, talking to her husband. Her husband could not see Cassandra because the angle was set only on Samantha.

But the speaker was loud enough for Cassandra to hear everything, she hears Mr. Monroe saying to Samantha,

"Honey, not only do I miss you and the children's company, I miss your food too! You know I've been here three days and I'm beginning to have an upset stomach, and you know what else?"

"Frank, do you want me to come tonight? I'll bring you some homemade food. Plus I miss you too" says Samantha.

"No you said something I wanted to hear, I'll be Ok it's only five more days. By this Sunday I'll be home, and then we will just have to wait for the election results and wait until you become the next First Lady."

"Oh honey, you are as sweet as ever! Will you love me even when I am an old lady with wrinkles?"

"Samantha, real love does not wear out with wrinkles or dentures. I fell in love with you the first day I saw you and that's it."

"Are you going to blow me a kiss Frank?"

"Yes, I can but what would the media do if they saw that?"

"Women in the USA would love to see that, you love me dearly. You will get more votes from women."

"Oh you talking about women, there were two of them here at the conference and I cannot describe, they both wanted to spend time with me" says Frank.

"What did you do honey?"

"I told them I have beautiful wife at home, then they got a little upset and said they can be better than you, but I told them not in the next million years."

"I knew honey, you are mine forever. It was probably set up by the opposition party."

"So what else are you doing honey? With the children at my sister's with my mother, and you alone with Mrs. Jones, what do you do? But you look a little extra happy today, I have not seen that in you, this is the first time I am seeing you differently.

"No honey, there is no difference. I have been shopping for you and the children, for your major speech. I bought you some nice clothes for it, some for everybody including your sister Sarah and their family. I bought a new suit for you and your final speech; it will be delivered to you that day."

"Honey I don't want to say it, but you are going to be our next First Lady, the most loving First Lady."

"Yes Frank, I will love you the same even when I am the next First Lady. Ok honey I'll let you go, I have a lot of stuff to do."

Frank is surprised; Samantha has never been in a hurry to part from him before, so he says,

"Honey, I told you there was something different about you today, you have never left me half way through our conversation before, you are hiding something."

Samantha tries to pretend and act that she is not hiding anything, and says casually

"No Frank, you know me better I would never hide anything from you. Mrs. Jones is just waiting for me in the kitchen."

"Ok honey, I believe you, I love you, and I'll call tomorrow." says Frank, and then they both turn of their live TV's.

Samantha still sitting her back is too Cassandra in the doorway and she says,

"Cassandra come in, don't stand there, it is all a family affair"

Cassandra walks in and comes close to her sister,

"Sister how did you know I was standing there?"

"I heard your footsteps; they did not go past this room, so I knew it was you"

Now both twins are face to face, and Cassandra is standing in the front

"Yes sister, you have very good judgment. I hope I was not being nosy listening to your conversation. You have a nice husband; Sister God blesses nice people, with nice people."

"Yes Cassandra, Frank is too nice of a man, we will discuss everything this week and we can tell each other everything. Let us go to the living room."

Both sisters go to the living room where Mrs. Jones is waiting for them. As they make themselves comfortable, Mrs. Jones is sitting next to the dining room table, and Cassandra helps herself to a drink which had been brought out for her. She takes a little sip, slower than before and Mrs. Jones goes in to bring the appetizers. It is around eight pm and Cassandra is feeling very comfortable with her sister. She knows her sister always had a big heart even when she was young, and after all these years she is still standing by her. That question is bugging her again and again, she doesn't know how to open up to her sister, the next First Lady.

After finishing one drink, she pours another, and Cassandra knows she cannot stay here forever so she must decided what to do. As she is drinking and eating, she asks her sister,

"Sister can I ask you a question?"

"Yes Cassandra, ask me anything."

"I cannot stay here forever, you have your family and I will have to decide to do something for myself, I do not want to be a burden on anybody."

"Cassandra you are not a burden on anybody, you are family, my children's aunt. I told them many times I had an identical twin sister, and they always ask, when you are coming back and now you are here. We are not going to let you go, you can stay here forever, I already told you. Frank and mother-in-law will agree with me. Until the election is over you won't make any plans. God willing we will move into the White House and we will decide then. Why, do you feel like an outsider at your own sister's house?" Mrs. Jones then puts her hand up,

"Mrs. Monroe, may I say something?"

Samantha says yes,

"Ms. Cassandra Domenici, I know what is on your mind, this is not an ordinary family. You are talking about a man, Mr. Monroe, you just don't know how big his heart is and he will be so happy to see you. I have been here thirteen years and we don't want you to leave. If you do not feel comfortable here, live near by but keep in touch.

Now Cassandra feels more comfortable, she picks up her drink and has another sip then bows her head down and takes another large sip. After a few moments and eating a few more snacks. The alcohol is setting in by now and Cassandra says in a broken voice,

"I want to be forgiven, I want to be forgiven." and she goes silent for a few minutes and then asks

"Sister, is Father John still around? I want to see him."

"Yes he is, he is quite old but still active." replied Samantha, "we can surprise him tomorrow around two, when he is on is own."

"Do you think he is still mad at me? I upset him many times when we were younger. Do you think he still remembers those things, oh will he forgive me? I want him to forgive me, yes I want to see him tomorrow." says Cassandra

The drink has started to get to her head, "I am sorry sister I need a few more days with you, I'll give up everything and I need someone to love me." Then she gets more serious "I did everything for Randy, but he never loved me from his heart, he was just using me and I was a fool. Why did it take me years to learn that he was a user? I made him and he deserted me.

Then she looks down and tears start pouring down, quickly Samantha gets up from across her and sits on the right of Cassandra, and hugs her and puts her head on her shoulder. Mrs. Jones also gets of her chair and sits on the left and holds Cassandra's hand. She runs her other hand on her back and says,

"Ms. Cassandra Domenici,

"It is better to forgive and forget, just think of it as a bad dream. Now you are home, this is your real home. Try to put everything behind you and start fresh. Your sister has been waiting so many years for you. She had tried so hard to find you, and she was always wondering and hoping you were alright."

After hearing those nice words from her sister and Mrs. Jones, Cassandra stops sobbing and Samantha helps her wipe her tears. She still cannot be herself, because she is so full of anger against Randy. But she tries to control herself again,

"I am sorry sister and Mrs. Jones, I did not mean to spoil your evening, and I won't act like this again I promise."

Cassandra starts calming down, and gets up and tells Samantha and Mrs. Jones that she wants to wash her face. She goes to the nearest bathroom and comes back with a smile on her face. She goes and sits next to her sister again,

"I am sorry again sister, I want to eat something and then go to bed."

Mrs. Jones goes to the kitchen to prepare both twins meals. Cassandra takes one more drink then she goes over to the dining table to eat with her sister. At the same time she is trying to shake away some of the misfortunes of her life. After eating, both sisters go too bed.

It is September 2nd 2008, Tuesday morning, very nice and full of sunshine. Mrs. Monroe is already up. It is already nine am, and Cassandra is waking up slowly. As she comes around she cannot get over how clean the house is. She has no responsibilities or duties here, so she takes her time getting out of bed, after having a shower she comes down to the dining room. Samantha and Mrs. Jones are watching the news report about Mr. Monroe's Campaign, as Cassandra comes closer,

"Good morning, ladies."

Samantha and Mrs. Jones turn to look at her; she is looking clean and fresh.

"Good morning sister,"

"Good morning Ms. Cassandra Domenici, did you sleep well?"

"Yes Mrs. Jones", as Cassandra sits on a sofa next to her twin, I slept too well Mrs. Jones, did you and sister sleep well too?" and she looked at them both in turn.

Cassandra asks them both, what had never crossed her mind before that she should try to control herself.

"Sister did I make any mistake last night?"

"No you did not, what would make you think that. You, Mrs. Jones, and I were here last night and you had your lunatic juice, and you ate and went to bed."

"I know I did do something wrong but I cannot remember, I want to know what I did after having alcohol."

"No Cassandra, you did not do or say anything, you were a little sad that nobody loved you. But I love you, and so did mom, just wait until you meet the rest of my family and we will show you that you are part of the family" Samantha tries to comfort her by putting water on fire not fuel on fire, and Cassandra feels better.

"Ok sister, what is the plan for today?" Cassandra asks, "First let us have some breakfast and we can discuss it then, what would you like?"

"I don't care I will eat whatever you eat."

"No, Cassandra we will give you what you want to eat."

"You are right; today I will ask Mrs. Jones too make me something that our mom used to make for both of us, let us go into the kitchen with Mrs. Jones and cook what we want."

"Ok Cassandra, you got it, I love to cook for Frank, but today you are here, so we can do it." All three ladies go into the kitchen to cook and eat. After eating they come to the living room, Cassandra is more relaxed.

"Cassandra," says Samantha

"Yes, Samantha?"

"You said last night that you wanted to see Father John?"

"Oh is that what I said last night? Lately in the mornings I have forgotten what I have said the night before because of the alcohol."

Samantha and Mrs. Jones make eye contact with each other, but don't say anything, and Cassandra does not notice it.

"So Cassandra, what time do you want to go to church to visit Father John?"

"Oh anytime Samantha" Cassandra replies,

"Ok, we will go around two, that's the time Father John always has to himself, plus it is a weekday, so not too many people will be there."

Just after midday, both twins get ready and about twenty minutes before two, the security cars and family limo have pulled up to the house. Both twins get into the limo and they are driven to the regular church. During the trip they share more memories with each other. The cars pull up to the church just before 2pm. The security guards look around outside, and there is nobody else there, so they tell the limo driver that it is safe. One of the guards goes inside the church to make sure. After everything is cleared the guards tell the twins that Father John Is sitting on the left side of the stage by the tall curtains. Both twins step out of the limo and walk to the door, half of which was already opened. They see Father John on stage reading, the two of them had already discussed who would go first. Father John cannot see very that far, the hall is huge at least one hundred to two hundred feet. His hearing is now compromised too. Cassandra says,

"Samantha I shall go now, you watch."

"Ok, go ahead."

Cassandra steps in, there are two isles on both the left and the right and all carpeted, in the front of the stage is a twenty foot hardwood floor for the young children to dance and put on plays. As Cassandra starts walking on the carpet, Father John lifts his head up. With his glasses still on his lower part of nose he sees a female coming. He cannot recognize who it is from that far. Cassandra comes onto the hardwood floor and her high heels make noise on the floor, Father John however, has not heard tapping like that in a long time. Cassandra holds her purse in her right hand and she crosses the hardwood floor. Father John stares at her, and she at him, wearing an ankle length dress. Father John is still looking at Cassandra as she steps on the stage which is only a half foot higher than the main floor. She walks slowly and stands in front of Father John, They both look at each other. Cassandra has not seen him in many years but she can still recognize him as the man who tried to correct her mistakes many times. Cassandra stands in front of Father John and Samantha is still standing by the door waiting to see what happens. Father John takes his glasses off and looks at Cassandra, thinking for a few seconds he says,

"Well I don't know what I can say, Mrs. Monroe, you have never walked like this before. I feel that there may be something wrong with your feet or you ankles or knees. Only your sister Cassandra used to walk like this. I remember her well; I hope she is doing fine."

"Yes Father John, you are one hundred percent right, It was her that walked like that, but do you remember something Father John? It is very quiet in here."

"Oh my Lord," Father John is surprised and shocked; he puts his glasses back on and stands up.

"Oh my Lord, you came back!" And then he walks around the table and comes and hugs her. By this time Samantha has started walking towards them, and she comes and stands next to the stage. Father John lets Cassandra go, and her eyes fill with tears.

"Will you be my real father until I die, so I can live a better life?"

"Yes, I will" Father John replies.

Samantha has come up on the stage and stands next to Cassandra and Father John is standing in front of both of them and he knows which one is which, but only at this moment because Cassandra has said something that he has remembered for years. He goes back to his chair and Samantha pulls two chairs from near the piano and the two of them sit opposite to Father John. Samantha is sitting on the right, and Cassandra on the left, both of them don't say anything.

"Mrs. Monroe, when you called me an hour ago you said 'we' are coming to see you, I was very puzzled, as to why you would have said that. Mr. Monroe, Mrs. Monroe Sr. and your children are not with you. So this is what you meant, that you are bringing you sister."

"Yes, Father John, I wanted to see if you could tell us apart, but you know the difference."

"Yes I do, I've noticed this since when your father died, when you were little, and your mother went to the hospital in shock and I had to take care of you both for two days.

During those two days I noticed the differences. Later on, I saw you two here and there; it is the only thing that is different between you. Most people cannot figure it out.

"But Father John, how come you have never mentioned it for all these years, we come to church every Sunday, and you have come to our home many times, but you never said anything about how we walked differently, that is how our mother could tell us apart and knew who was coming into the house."

"Yes Mrs. Monroe, you are right, the reason I have not mentioned it before was that Cassandra was never here. Second I did not want to be accused of looking at women with a bad intention, so as you already know there are enough church scandals. But you two do not need to hear about them. I am so happy to see you two together; does your husband and family know that your sister is here?"

"No Father, not yet, we want to give them a surprise Sunday."

"We will go together with you too, to give him a shock and see if he can figure out who is who" says Mrs. Monroe.

"What a good idea" says Father John?

"Father John" Cassandra asks, "I would like to confess that I have made a lot of mistakes and I am very sorry I gave my sister and mother a hard time, I know my sister has a big heart and she forgave me, but I need to confess."

"No you do not have to confess dear child, you have begun a new life. Try to forget about the past, God will forgive you when you start helping others." Father John replied. "So what is your plan? Are you going to stay here?"

"Father, I do not want to leave my sister she is so kind, plus you are here. I want to get married and settle down."

Samantha gets very happy and turns to her sister,

"I am so happy for you Cassandra, who is this lucky man? And you should have given me this news before; Frank and I are going to give you an amazing wedding. And Father John can conduct the ceremony like our wedding."

"Well dear child, I am happy for you, you need to tell us about this man because he is going to be the brother-in-law to our next President and First Lady."

"Yes, Father" Cassandra turns to Samantha, "Yes sister, he is very cool, I do not have his picture but he is the only one who turned my away from Randy and his crime life. I have his information at home; I'll give it to you when we get home."

Father John is now even happier, and he says laughingly "We are going to have Mr. and Mrs. Monroe's daughters as bridesmaids."

"Yes, Father John, I will be coming here more often, through the front door. You remember when I was younger I slept here now and then, because I was afraid of my mom, wearing short clothes, so I broke in through the back door."

"Yes, I remember everything, even when I sprayed you with holy water, when you mother first brought you here, and you asked me why I got you wet."

"Father John, you have a very good memory, I still have good memories of my younger days. But now when I have a drink at night, I cannot remember anything the next morning, I need more time to control my drinking and give it up."

"Yes, child too much drinking is not good for people." He turns to Samantha,

"Well Mrs. Monroe this is the first time you are hiding something from Mr. Monroe."

"I know Father John, I wanted to tell him but he is doing so well in the polls all over our country, and we want to surprise him Sunday. We are both going to dress exactly alike, and be on TV that might give him a boost with women voters. Oh I forgot to tell you, I bought you a nice suit for Sunday, it will be delivered in the morning tomorrow."

"You should not have done this Mrs. Monroe, you are too kind, and I still have the other suit you bought me."

"Father, I am no where near as kind as you were when our father died, and again when our mother died, if you were not around God only knows our fate."

Father John tries to make them comfortable by saying "it is all in God's hands and I did what I was told to do by the almighty, since then your family has been so kind to me."

All three sit in the church discussing what happened in the past, it has been almost two hours and they are still talking. They sit for a long time, and then both twins leave happily, and Father John sits in the church also very happy to see the sisters together.

The twins come home at around five pm and they are both hungry. Mrs. Jones is waiting for them too; her day normally passes very quickly with the children. As both sisters walk in Mrs. Jones is standing in the living room.

"Good afternoon ladies, you both look cheerful."

"Yes Mrs. Jones we are very happy, Cassandra gave me the news that I have been waiting for. She is going to get married and settle down near our home."

Mrs. Jones gets very happy as well when she hears this. And all three of them go to the dining room, and Mrs. Jones asks

"Before we talk about the wedding, what shall I get for you both? And don't discuss anything before I get back, I do love weddings."

Cassandra says,

"I'll have anything without alcohol."

Mrs. Jones goes into the kitchen and comes back with a tray of foods and puts them on the table and joins the twins as they eat some of their food, and pours some coffee. Again they start sharing some of their family situations.

"Ms. Cassandra Domenici, can I ask you a question?"

"Sure, Mrs. Jones anything"

"Who is this lucky man you are going to marry and are you going to ask him to visit?"

"Mrs. Jones he is very nice, he does not drink or smoke or do drugs, and he only has a mother. He is the one who turned me away from my bad life, which I thought was a good life, but more about that after Mr. Monroe's speech, let us talk about Father John"

They all agree to this, and they sit there talking to each other, sharing more of their past stories with each other, detail by detail. After seven pm Cassandra has her drink or lunatic juice, thankfully she is having less and eating more homemade meals.

They go out and about, and Cassandra watched her sister's children on the live TV every day.

As the time is flying, Father John has visited them a few afternoons, he is joyful too. And finally comes September 7th, a Sunday. The sisters wake up as usual and get ready. They come down to the kitchen for breakfast and Samantha has a conversation with her children and mother-in-law and Mr. Monroe. Today they are going to church for the eleven am service. It is a nice clear day with a lot of sunshine. At ten forty five, security and the limo pull up. Mrs. Jones is joining the twins to church wearing the beautiful dress Cassandra bought for her. In church on Sunday there were a lot of people who know Samantha as an only child, when Cassandra arrives too, they get a shock, and all the families come and meet her.

"How do we know which one is our next First Lady?"

"Well if I call you by name then you will know it's me."

Some of the families are also attending the speech and will get to see Mr. Monroe surprised, after the service is over the twins go over to Father John, and he tries to find a spare moment for the ladies. When he is free he comes over to them,

"Yes, Mrs. Monroe, what is on your mind? I am sorry about the delay, I was very busy."

"I know Father, there is no need to apologize, and I was just going to ask you if you would like to go with us to the stadium, you should not drive in the dark and we can take you."

"Sure Mrs. Monroe, that would be very nice, then I can have the company of you and Mr. Monroe on the way back."

"We are leaving home at seven pm and we will pick you up about fifteen minutes after at the church, after the speech there will be a small party at our estate and I have set aside a room for you to stay. Everything you need, will be there, and then you can have breakfast with us sisters and our family."

"Ok Mrs. Monroe, you are doing too much! But I agree I will be here at the church all day, I'll be seeing you at seven fifteen."

Cassandra replies,

"Father John, it was my idea that you spend the night with us, I have a lot to talk to you about. I won't drink either even though I cannot do without it. After seven I want you to be with me so I can have some will power like my sister, she will be attending to all her guests and I will need your support. After tonight I want to give up alcohol in the future."

Father John smiles and says,

"That is a wonderful idea, I'll be with you and so will God"

Samantha and Cassandra say goodbye to all the people in the church and they along with Mrs. Jones make it back home. Samantha spends her time talking to people who are attending the speech. Cassandra is continuing her life stories with Mrs. Jones.

As time passes, Mr. Monroe is busy with his party members at Denver Headquarters; the speech is to be made at eight pm prime time on Sunday the seventh of Sep 2008 in the stadium. About forty to fifty thousand people are supposed to show up to listen to Mr. Monroe's last speech. Before the elections, he is ahead in the polls by 20%. All of his supporters were counting on him to turn the country around. This country has lost a lot of respect around the world, plus the problems at home. He has already made his campaign promises once he moves into the White House. All of his supporters have decided that this is the man that is going to point the country in the right direction. At about seven pm, Mr. Monroe and his party members are supposed to leave headquarters and go to the stadium so they can welcome everyone attending.

Meanwhile the twins stay busy for a few hours after coming home from church, and they have an appointment at the salon. Normally the salon is closed on Sundays, but because of the speech they are making an exception for the twins. They manage to get home from the salon by five thirty and the day is still clear and sunny. As soon as they step in they see that the house is situated to sun, where the front door faces the sunrise, and the back faces the sunset. By six o'clock it starts to get cloudy, even though no rain was predicted for the day. The dark clouds are making there way from the west to the east and are covering most of Denver. All the newscasters were looking foreword to Monroe's speech. The twins and Mrs. Jones are slowly getting ready, but they know that they must leave at seven sharp. Samantha has already laid out 2 beautiful expensive dresses that were exactly the same for her and her sister.

Slowly the clouds are moving over Denver, and the sky keeps getting darker and darker, why the dark clouds, what is going to happen? God only knows. The weatherman had predicted clear skies, but the darkness has come only on the west side, it is as if one of God's angels is angry, but why? What is going to happen on this glorious day for America? Especially with the country in debt and the problems arising in the future, why does God have to make it rain and spoil the evening for a good and decent family? Only God knows why the angels have made it darker evening,

By six twenty, Cassandra was talking to Mrs. Jones in the living room and Samantha was in her bedroom having many short phone conversations.

Cassandra goes to her bedroom, and takes the dress that Samantha has laid out for her and puts it on. Both sisters have the same makeup, shoes, and hairstyle. She comes out of her bedroom and goes down to the living room. On the way down is her sister's room when she looks into the room and stands in the doorway and sees her sister is on the live TV with her husband and hears her sister saying,

"Honey send me a loving kiss"

"Yes, Samantha I can send you a kiss, but what if someone is bugging the TV" says Frank, "our pictures will be all over the world."

"Well you will get votes from married females once they see you sending me a kiss on TV."

"Why do you need an artificial kiss? Come here and I will give you a real one on national TV."

"I will get that too after your speech anyway, this one is for my inner feelings"

"How come you have two feelings now? Before you used to only have one feeling and it was for me."

"I just want to see how you feel about me, now everybody knows you are going to be the next president I wonder what it will be like to be the next First Lady."

"Ok, Samantha, I love you forever"

And Frank kisses the camera, when Samantha sees it she does the same.

"This one is for the next President, I love you forever"

"God bless your tongue for those kind words, my Samantha."

"No honey, God bless all," says Samantha,

"You know you should be the next President you are so sweet."

"No honey, I would be lost without you, anyway we are leaving at seven. Father John is going to join us, and you won't have to call us, we will be there about seven fifty. I know we have to go through the back door."

Cassandra knows that Samantha's conversation with her husband may last forever, so she slowly goes to the living room where Mrs. Jones is waiting for her in a new dress. When Cassandra steps in, Mrs. Jones cannot believe her eyes,

"Today I have to ask which one you are." Mrs. Jones just stands there quietly for a while, and then she makes a sign of guessing and shakes her head. Cassandra walks over and sits next to Mrs. Jones on the sofa facing the front door. It is just after six thirty pm, and the dark clouds had almost covered Denver. Mrs. Jones asks Cassandra,

"Do you want anything to eat?"

"No Mrs. Jones I'm fine, I do not need anything, and Samantha is still on the phone with Mr. Monroe. She said we are leaving at seven sharp so we can sit and watch Mr. Monroe's campaign. Both of them are watching TV, and the clouds are all over the house, going east. Suddenly it has become a little darker outside, the clouds are moving faster over Denver. There is still no rain, and the visibility is still good. Everyone turned there lights on and were very surprised to see the clouds when the forecast predicted a clear day. The whole estate has been covered by the partial darkness. Samantha had still been talking to her husband and the other sister had been watching TV with Mrs. Jones. Mrs. Jones breaks the silence,

"Ms. Cassandra Domenici, I don't like this, you know the sudden darkness. God is up to something, I know I should not be negative or suspicious but something is up. I hope God willing, everything will be alright."

Cassandra brushes it off as just a change in weather,

"No Mrs. Jones, it is just a few clouds, they come and go. Just relax, everything will be fine."

"I know it will be Ok, Ms. Domenici, but I have heard stories, when God gets angry and wants to have his way, and he will do things that we don't think or feel."

"Yes, I know what you are saying Mrs. Jones, my mother used to tell me lots of stories like that when we were little. I never believed them anyway Mrs. Jones lets change the subject. Death comes to every body one way or another so why discuss it?"

"Yes, you are right Ms. Cassandra, because I don't have anyone after my husband died. I fear the dark now and I don't know why. But I believe you; death will come sooner or later."

The clock is ticking six forty five, and Samantha was still on the live TV with her husband. Cassandra and Mrs. Jones are still talking in the living room.

At the security gate of the Monroe estate, two guards are on duty. Both men in their mid forties, ex cops, and live near by, which is very convenient. The limo driver is with them too, they know that the limo has to be ready to go at seven. The men are talking and joking with each other. It is getting darker in Denver and people can only see about twenty to thirty feet away. A few seconds after six forty five a dodge van with black stripes, pulling into the security gate.

The senior security guard stands in the door of the booth, as the van slowly pulls up next to him. He sees two white males sitting in the front seats, and Black man, and a Hispanic man in the back.

The driver of the van opens the window and the security guard is standing at the door looking at all of them, one by one. While putting his hand on his gun, the guard asks,

"Gentlemen can I help you?"

"We have come to see one of the twins" says the driver. The security guard is getting irritated,

"Back up and leave, there is no one home, they have all left."

The driver tries to lie to the guard, "well, one of the girls called us and said that they are still home, we have to see her."

Now the guard puts the whole hand on his gun, and the driver of the van can see it clearly. The guard says,

"Back up your vehicle now or you are dead"

The driver is getting scared; because none of his friends have their guns ready. The man puts his hands up and puts the van in reverse,

"Ok chief you have made your point, we are leaving."

As the van is about to move back, the man in the passenger seat says,

"Number two, back up twenty feet and stop."

As the van is reversing, the guard goes back inside the booth and the other guard speaks,

"I wonder who those men are, why would he say one of the twins called him? Do you think something is wrong?"

"Yes I do, they had no reason to come here tonight. They must have known they were not leaving until seven."

When the van has backed up twenty feet it stops, both guards and the limo driver sense something is amiss, they wait looking at the van The white man who was sitting in front passenger seat, about 6'2, steps out of the van, a similar looking Black and Hispanic man come out too and start walking about eight feet apart. Their hands were not in any pockets, so the guards did not suspect they had guns. As they walk slowly walk towards the security booth, the guard comes out with his hand on the gun, he sees that none of them have guns.

"Now this is it, stop, you are not going any further." and he is pulling the gun out of the holster. The Hispanic man is very quick, when he sees the guards gun come out, he knows someone may die and it could be him. He doesn't take any chances and wants to save himself; he very quickly shoots the guards. As the guard is starting to fall, the other guard pulls his gun out, the limo driver decided to go out of the back door. The Hispanic man was known as a sharp shooter, when the first guard had fallen he sees the second one pulling his gun out, he shoots him through the glass window of the booth. As he is falling, the limo driver sneaks out through the back, but one of the gang sees him running and shoots him too.

It is six fifty pm, things had gone very wrong. With all three dead, and they get in van and the Black guy says to the front seat passenger.

"Number one, lets get out of here quickly, I do not want to deal with this senator."

"I know, let us go inside and get the slut and the money" Number one says to black guy, you drive the van to the house.

"Number two, you stay here in the booth, if you see anything wrong, call us. We three are going to pick up the slut and the money."

He gets out and goes to the security booth, and the other three men already in the van and drive toward the house. The time is now six fifty three.

Mrs. Jones and Cassandra are sitting in the living room, they look toward the front of the house, and the limo should be pulling up now.

At six fifty five, Samantha is still on the phone, and the van is coming at high speed with high beam on. Both Mrs. Jones and Cassandra think it is the limo pulling up. When the van comes to a halt, they turn the lights off and Number one comes out of the passenger seat. Cassandra recognizes him and tells Mrs. Jones

"Save your self, I do not know how they found this place."

Mrs. Jones runs into the kitchen and locks the door from inside, turns all the lights off, and stands in front of a small window. She slides the glass to open it slightly, Which is between living room and the kitchen? So she can see what is going on. Cassandra runs into the room on the right side.

At six fifty six, all three men enter the house living room which had not been locked. They see that nobody was there; they look at each other and see the three staircases on their right leading to other room. One of the twins appears on the top of the staircase and in the doorway wearing an ankle length dress, a tight fit on the top and baggy on the bottom. In her right hand she is holding a gun, but it is not visible to the men. As they move apart about four feet from each other, the Hispanic man is on the right, closest to the woman. Number one stands in the middle and the Black man on the left. Mrs. Jones also has her gun ready now, which she always keeps in the kitchen cabinet. Mrs.

Jones stands in the small window in the kitchen, it is partially opened just enough for her gun to fire. If any of the men lifted their hands upon any of the twins she would kill them to save the twins and her self. She sees one of the sisters standing on the left in the door way, she doesn't know which one. And the white guy says,

"Come on slut, Randy wants you. Where is the money?"

The woman replies in a cool manner,

"Money, what money? I don't know what you are talking about. Leave now, you do not know where you are, this is not Randy's house."

Six fifty seven, Sunday

"Look tell us where the money is. If we do not get the money you are coming with us."

"Over my dead body", she starts moving her right hand in slow motion.

The Black man and Number one are standing on the left of the Hispanic man; they can see that the woman has the gun in her hand. The Hispanic man was known as a sharp shooter, was the only one who did not see the gun; however he is a panicky man and always had his gun handy. His motto was to kill rather than be killed. The woman lifts her hand four to five inches away from her hip, at the same time Mrs. Jones is watching the situation and feels like she has to protect both sisters and herself. At six fifty eight Samantha hangs up the phone with her husband.

As the twin brings her arm up 30 degrees, she first points her gun toward the Black man, then the White man, and lastly the Hispanic man. The sharp shooter looks at her gun, he knows that she could kill him so he quickly shoots at her, and Mrs. Jones shoots at him. Within a split second both the woman and the man are falling, Number one and the Black man run and jump over the sofa and hide behind it. The Hispanic man is now dead, and one of the twins is still falling down three stairs in the living room. Her sister hearing the gunfire comes running and sees her twin lying on the floor in a pool of blood, but still breathing. She picks her up by the shoulders and holds her tight. The dying sister whispers

"I love you, I love you, forgive"

Before she can finish her sentence, her eyes close and her sister holds her close to her chest.

"Please don't leave me, please don't leave me. I missed you so much" she says while tears flow from her eyes.

The live twin is still holding her tight to her body, "why god, oh god why. We were so happy" she cried.

She sits there holding her dead sister for about five minutes; meanwhile Number one and the Black man look up from behind the sofa and make sure she does not have a gun too. The men see her sitting on the floor, and start walking towards the twins. Mrs. Jones checks her gun in the dark to make sure she had more bullets. she opens and feels the barrel with her finger, She only had one bullet, so she keeps quiet and still looking through the gap in the glass window. The gangsters cannot see Mrs. Jones because it dark in the kitchen and continue to walk closer to the twins, live twin gently puts her twin on the floor. When she sees white guy come near her and she stands up in anger and frenzy and lurches at the White man. He holds her both hands. But she kicks him on the front of his right leg below his knee with her sharp front of her shoe. The shoe digs into the man's skin and he mouths back to her but still has her hands held by her wrists. She hits the other leg as hard as she could.

"Why did you kill my sister?"

Number one knows that she is stronger than he thought and tells the Black guy to do something. The black guy takes a handkerchief out of his pocket and spills something on it. He puts it in front of the twin's nose and holds it there until she passes out, both men lay her next to the dead twin.

Both of the gangsters are panicking, the Black guy says "I am leaving; I did not know this was going to happen, too many murders.

Number one tries to assure him to stay calm,

"Don't panic; call Randy on your cell."

The Black guy pulls his cell phone out and sees no signal, "Try yours I have no service here."

Number one pulls his phone out, and also has no signal. They look around and see a home phone and dial their boss's number.

"Hello?"

"Boss this is Number one, everything has gone wrong."

"First of all, where are you calling from?"

"We are calling from the Senator's house, we had no choice, and our cell phones have no signal."

"You both are stupid fools, but we can worry about that later, what happened?"

"Boss, your so called sharp shooter got shot. First he shot both security guards and driver in panic, and then in the house he shot one of the twins and the twin shot him. Then other twin came out looking exactly like her sister, we couldn't tell the difference. Now one of them is asleep and the other is dead."

"Just find the money and leave."

"Boss this house is so big, it will take two days to go through the whole house and we don't want to stay a minute longer. You can't help us here so what should we do about the bodies?"

"Bring the live girl with you, dump the sharp shooter's body somewhere on the way, and steal another van. Leave this van somewhere in that state. If you see any cameras anywhere in the house smash them all, make sure there is no evidence left behind."

The phone disconnects and the man pulls the cord from the home phone.

He then smashes the phone and tells the Black guy too drag the sharp shooter's body and put it in the back of the van.

"I'll go into the other rooms and make this look like an ordinary robbery."

Number one goes into the other rooms and checks for cameras and pulls out the wires from all of the sockets. By this time the Black man has gotten the body into the van. Both men meet again in the living room. All this time, Mrs. Jones has been watching through the window and is horrified.

It is seven fifteen and Father John is still waiting at the church for the twins to arrive in the limo, he waits for another five minutes and starts getting restless, they should have picked him up by now.

Father John calls the Monroe estate house phone but gets no answer he tries Samantha's cell phone but there was no answer. He wonders what is taking so long and then he notices the dark clouds. He has an eerie feeling something is wrong so he gets into his car and starts driving to the Monroe house.

Just after seven twenty, Number one picks up the live twin by her hands and then her body and flings her over his right shoulder and carries her out to the van. He lays her on the row of three seats in the back. He goes back inside and both men shoot out all of the lights. They get back in the car and drive off. Mrs. Jones sees them leave and get out from behind the window.

Father John is driving towards the house slowly, because of his weak eye sight, and is only a few blocks away. The van pulls up to the gate and the Black guy tells Number two to get in quickly. As he gets in he says,

"What took you so long? I was worried something had happened."

"We'll tell you everything, just sit down. Everything has gone wrong. Randy's 'sharp shooter' has got us in a lot of trouble."

"I don't see him, I only see the slut."

"He was stupid; he shot one of the twins and then got himself shot by the same twin

The van comes to a complete halt at the stop sign in front of the Monroe estate to the main road. They see another car getting ready to turn into the estate, the driver of the van immediately turns right quickly as the car is turning in. Father John sees the van turning out of the estate and turns his high beam on but cannot read the tags.

When the van accelerated sharply Number one says "keep the speed to a minimum we don't want to be caught speeding with these bodies. When we get out of the area find a spot for us to dump the sharp shooters body.

"Where is his body?" asks Number two.

"He is in the back"

"But where is the money? And is this the real slut? You said they were twins and they looked exactly the same."

"We don't know; let's just get out of the state first."

"Wait what about that other car turning in; what if driver took our tag numbers? Should we go back and take care of him?"

"By the time we get back he would have called the police, we better keep going."

While the van disappeared from father john's sight, meanwhile Mrs. Jones turned the kitchen light on and gets a flashlight from the cabinet. She shines it in the living room and sees the dead twin on the floor and starts crying. Just few minutes ago the estate was a happy home, now only god knows what is going to happen. Mrs. Jones searches her pockets for her cell phone but could not find it; she searches in her purse on the dining room table as well. She finds her car keys and decides it's better to call the police from the nearest convenience store. With purse and keys in her hand she leaves the house and forgets to lock the main door. She was still shaking from what happened as she walks to the car. She is still crying and shaking as she backs her car. She presses accelerate a little harder and the car goes out of control and hits one of the family cars. She tries to start it again but the car does not start, because fuel cut off switch got deactivated, and she starts to panic. She goes back into the house and searches it with a flashlight but cannot find a phone or light switch.

As Father John sees the van speeding away from the estate and he has a feeling something is wrong. When he pulls up to the security booth .father john comes out of his car with his high beam still on. And he sees the guard's and driver's bodies are laying there dead. He looks no further and pulls out his phone and dials 911, within two minutes the police show up. Four cops come out of their cars and see Father John standing next to the dead body.

"Are you Father John, did you call 911?"

"Yes, I did"

"What are you doing here?"

"The Senator's wife was supposed to pick me up from the church around seven fifteen, so we can all go to the stadium together to hear her husbands final speech. When they did not show up I decided to drive down here, Mrs. Monroe is never late. When I got here I saw all these dead bodies, which is when I decided to call you."

The police officers listen to his story and one of them looks around outside, while a few others investigate the booth. The men in the booth find another body, and all of the other officers join him. The police chief is getting very suspicious and anxious so he calls for back up and an ambulance.

The gangsters have been driving for just over ten minutes and are now about five miles away from Mr. Monroe's house and the crime scene. Number one is getting very paranoid and they are finally out of the city limits. He tells the driver

"If you see any side street on the right, pull over there."

About a minute later they see a dead end sign to the right, Number one carefully looks for a spot to dump the body.

"Pull up here and stop! We will make a U-turn here, keep the parking brake on or we will all end up in the ditch."

Number one and two get out of the car and guide the driver. The men open the trunk of the van and pick up the body. They throw him into two feet of grass, and it slips down, the men throw his gun next to him so it looks like a suicide if anyone were to find the body. After dumping the body the men feel much more relaxed.

It is around seven forty five and Number one says,

"Now find a large gas station, and we have to get another van too."

They drive for a while before seeing a gas station, the driver pulls in and the men scan the area looking for another van. They pull over to the side of the station in order to see the vehicles pulling in. They see a similar sized van pulling in a few minutes later and an elderly man pumping gas into it. The old man walks into the store of the station with his credit card and as soon as he enters, Number one says,

"Pull up to the van; I am sure Number two can break the ignition lock."

"I have my stuff ready, just pull over there and I'll follow you in ten seconds."

Number two jumps out with a little bag and goes over to the new van, surprisingly the driver has left the key in the lock. He jumps in and drives of to follow the other van.

Meanwhile at Senator Monroe's house, the police are arriving. Mrs. Jones is still looking around the house with her flashlight; she starts panicking again and runs to the kitchen. When she hears the cop cars arriving and cops runs to the living room,

"Put, you hands up!"

"No, no please don't shoot, I am the housekeeper" It is dark in the living room, cop turn on their flash lights, where they see a body that looks like Mrs. Monroe. Father John slowly enters the house and stands in the doorway and hears Mrs. Jones sobbing near the kitchen.

"Oh god, why did this happen?"

Father John cannot make anything of the situation, and then one of the sheriffs asks if there are any light bulbs.

Mrs. Jones goes to a cabinet in the kitchen and brings out a pack of light bulbs, the sheriff instructs three of his officers to put the new light bulbs in. When the lights turn on Father John is horrified at the scene, he sees one of the twins drenched in a pool of blood.

"Oh my Lord, which twin is this?"

Right as he is approaching the body one of the cops holds him back

"No sir, you can't go near her, we still have to investigate the crime scene."

Mrs. Jones starts walking towards Father John and falls into his arms,

"Father, we were all so happy! Why did this happen?"

"It is God's will, but which twin is dead? And where is the other?"

Father John leads her to the sofa,

"Try to stop crying, and tell me what happened."

"Well, right as we were about to come pick you up, Cassandra and I were here in the living room while Mrs. Monroe was still getting ready and then this white van pulled up. These men came inside with guns and Cassandra recognized them and then ran upstairs. I locked myself in the kitchen when they weren't paying attention. Then one of the twins steps out with a gun and shot one of the men, while one shot her. While she was falling the other twin ran out but they drugged her. The men took her with them when they left, although they smashed all the lights first."

Mrs. Jones is out of breath and still crying, and Father John tries to calm her.

Meanwhile at Denver headquarters Senator Monroe is ready for his final speech. In the backroom are all is friends, family, and colleagues. About fifty thousand people showed up and the dark clouds that had appeared earlier were slowly moving east. The Senator is about to move from the backroom to the main stage

While the police are investigating the crime scene at the Monroe estate, Father John tries to make a call to the Senator, but his phone is turned off. He manages to get through to the Party headquarters but the Senator and all of the senior members had already gone on stage. One of the workers at the stadium answers the phone,

"Who's calling?"

"This is Father John; I need to speak to Senator Monroe or the Party Chairman this is a real emergency!"

"Sorry sir, but Senator Monroe has already gone on stage, but I can try to find the Party Chairman."

About a minute later the Party Chairman comes to the back room and answers the phone,

"Hello, this is Sean, Senator Monroe's Party Chairman."

"This is Father John, a friend of the Monroe family, I must talk to him there has been an accident in the family, someone has killed his security guards and driver, and I believe his wife too."

"I know who are, Sean says in very aggressive way, probably a dirty trick by opposition, I am not buying this stuff, Mr. Monroe is about to make his final speech and cannot be bothered now."

Mr. Monroe has started his speech and looks at his family cheering him on but he does not see his wife. She is always at his speeches. And he figures she is just running late and carries on with his speech. He receives a standing ovation now and then,

At the Monroe house, more police and medics have arrived. One of the officer's wife works at the local news station and calls her to tell her boss about the murders at senator's house, And she calls her boss,

Recognizing her voice he says,

"Ah, you decided to call after all my advances? How much do you need?"

"Thirty thousand in cash"

"I wouldn't even give you three, never mind thirty.

"But today you will, I have news for you. Which will give your TV company excellent ratings. There are four murders at Senator Monroe's house and one of the dead might be his wife."

"And you're serious who told you that?"

"Yes, make a commitment for thirty, my husband is a cop and he called me from the crime scene."

"Alright, I'll give you twenty thousand, that's it! And if this isn't true you're fired."

"And if you make a pass at me again, my husband will kick yours you know what."

"Alright, alright, I'll send a reporter down there", her boss calls one of the best and cheapest reporters in town.

Jody is coming out of the shower when the phone rings, she chooses to ignore it. The answering machine picks up the message,

"Jody, this is your boss. I am sending you a company chopper right now, there were four murders at the Senator's house and one may be his wife. I need you there before he finishes his speech; we need to be the first newscast to broadcast this."

Before he finishes the message she presses speaker on the phone.

"Hello Alan, what's up?"

"Thank God you picked up, I've been calling you, and a full TV crew will be accompanying you. We need to break this story before anyone else."

"Boss, I am not ready or dressed to do a news cover, would you like me to go as I am?"

"I don't care! Just get dressed and go. If you get this story I will double your salary this month. The country is going to be more interested in the news, not your looks Jody,

"Thank you for your remarks, clearly good looks isn't important to you, looking at your wife."

Jody was tired of her boss treating her this way, and she made up her mind to quit the company after reporting this story. She runs into her closet and grabs the first dress she sees and her best fits. She gets into the elevator and it takes forever for her to get down. Her copper is waiting for her in school ground next to her street, and she runs as fast as she can, and get in the chopper quickly.

At the stadium Senator Monroe's speech is eaten up by the audience.

Ten minutes later, Jody has reached her destination and is running to the senator's house and getting ready at the same time as best as she can.

The camera man and the engineer are trying to fix the stuff at the same time, so that the camera can be connected live to their TV station. Jody's boss is waiting anxiously to get this news on the air before some other TV station does it. It is 8:25 PM, and the sky is clear now, all the clouds are gone. Jody is standing twenty feet away from the yellow police tape. The crew is now ready for live TV and Jody is trying to look calm and relaxed. She knows that if she plays her cards right today, she will be picked by bigger TV channels, maybe internationally. So, when everything is connected, the camera man and the engineer give a thumbs up and say hit it, Jody changes her facial expression to appear sad as this is very bad news and says,

"America, I cannot say good evening today because I am here, at Senator Monroe's estate by the security gate. Our channel was informed earlier, that there have been three murders at Senator Monroe's security booth. As you all know, he is in the middle of his speech to the nation, so let me get close to the gate and ask one of the cops"

As Jody walks towards the booth, she is on live TV and she comes face to face with a cop. She asks him "Officer, what happened here? Can we look further?"

"No, you cannot. The only thing I am allowed to tell you is that two security guards and a limo driver were found dead here. The police have gone inside the house. Our Chief should be back any second to tell us what is going on" the officer replies.

The time is 8:30 PM.

Jody moves away from the cop. She starts talking again to the live audience,

"Before I say anymore, my boss has informed me that he talked to the Police Chief himself and that there is a female body inside the house. He confirmed to my boss that it is Mrs. Monroe's body as the Chief had met her many times before. So, all we can do is just wait".

While she is on live TV to the nation, a cop car speeds towards the booth and stops by the yellow tape. Two cops come out of the car and when they see that there is a TV crew, they are shocked and walk over to Jody.

"I know you Jody, how did you find out about this?" the cop asks.

"My boss found out, he told me to cover this house. What happened? Can you give us any news?" Jody asks.

"Jody, I do not know what happened here. We were called by Father John about three murders at the gate. Then we went inside and we found another body which is Mrs. Monroe. That is all I can tell you. Now, please excuse me, we have a lot of work to do tonight".

Now Jody is sure that the next First Lady has been murdered.

The time is 8:35 PM.

Senator Monroe's speech is so strong, that every time he sets an agenda for this country.Senator was given standing ovation many times. his ratings go up. In the back room, some of his colleagues are watching opposition channels to see their reactions.

The Party Chairman, Sean, has been running around attending to the details. Sometimes, he comes and stands next to Senator Monroe and claps with the public and sometimes he goes to the TV room to check that Senator Monroe's speech is reaching the world. It is just about 8:40 PM and the speech is supposed to end in ten minutes. One of the Sean's close colleagues comes running to Sean as he is standing next to Senator Monroe.

He pulls Sean's arm to get him away, but Sean shrugs it off since he is being watched by millions of Americans as Senator Monroe's right hand man. But, his colleague says something in his ear and the Party Chairman runs as fast as he can to the TV control room. Once they are there, the Party Chairman goes to the channel where Jody is broadcasting live. All the people in the TV control room are hooked on

Jody. Jody again repeats the news of the murder. Sean, gets aggressive and says to the TV engineers,

"How long will it take to turn America off from Senator Monroe's speech and broadcast Jody's channel? Come on, come on…" One of the engineers says "one minute".

"Do it now. Turn the Senator off and broadcast Jody and make sure she is on all our channels. If there is any political problem, I'll take care of that. I am the Party Chief" says Sean showing off. Within a minute, Senator Monroe's speech is cut off in the stadium and in the USA.

All the large TVs, which were showing Senator Monroe's speech is suddenly switched off and live TV news is broadcast on the TV screen in the stadium. The 50000 people who came to listen to his speech are stunned when they hear Jody on live TV,

"America, I can only say that this is a very sad day for the USA. I am standing here in front of Senator Monroe's house. Around seven p.m. three people were killed here, two security guards and a limo driver. We also learned from the police that there is a female body inside the house which the police are saying is Mrs. Monroe. Here body is lying in the living room. Nobody knows who did it or why. Forensic experts are here. But we have confirmation that it is the Senator's wife. Her family, friends and other people who knew her, were already calling her our next First Lady. From what we have heard, Mrs. Monroe was warm and a really wonderful person."

As Jody looks towards the security booth, she sees the local Police Chief coming towards her. The camera man turns the camera to the Chief and Jody asks the Chief,

"Could you please tell the nation what happened?"

"Yes, Father John called the police around 7:20pm about the security gate murders. And when we went inside, we also saw Mrs. Monroe's body. She was shot in the heart one time. It looks like she died instantly" the Chief replies.

As soon as he says that, all fifty thousand people in the stadium stand up with shock. Some say "Oh, my God, Oh, my God, why?" Everybody looks at each other and whisper to each other as Jody carries on with the news,

"But, Chief, do you have any clue? Why this happened today, especially when Senator Monroe was making his final speech to the nation and the world?"

"Jody, I have no clue. We looked inside for evidence. But, there is no evidence. It is going to take some time. At this moment, I cannot say anymore. My sympathy goes to the guards and driver's families and to our next President, Senator Monroe's family" the Chief says.

Meanwhile, as this is on live TV, Senator Monroe is shocked. He just stares at the large TV near him. His mother, his children and his sister come running. His children cling to his legs while they all watch the TV news and the Senator's daughter starts crying and says,

"Daddy, is mommy really dead? Are we not going to see her again? Please daddy, tell me what happened?"

"Senator Monroe picks up his daughter while his son is still holding his leg. He kisses her on her cheek and wipes her tears and says "Be brave". He hugs her tight, then gives her to his sister and tells his mother while still looking at the TV,

"Mother and sister, you take care of the children and sister, tell your husbands to be with them at all times. I need the support of my family."

63

By now, lots of senior party members are getting close to the Senator. They are all showing as much respect as they can. Meanwhile, the party chairman orders a helicopter. Most of the close family members are gathering in the back room. Five minutes later, a chopper lands on the roof and the pilot calls the part chief,

"We are here."

"How may seats you have in the chopper?" he asks

"Twelve seats" says the pilot.

"Ok" says Sean. He asks the most senior members to join Senator Monroe and they all get in elevator and start going to the roof. After a few moments, they all get in the chopper and fly towards Senator Monroe's house. As the chopper lifts off, people in the stadium watch him go. Suddenly, Jody's channel is turned off and one of the senior senators of Senator Monroe's party comes on the microphone and makes a speech.

"Ladies and Gentlemen, fellow Americans, what we heard and saw today is a tragedy. A tragedy that somebody, someone or some party is trying to break Senator Monroe's will to be our next President. They, who or whatever, they can try it, but nobody is going to bring Senator Monroe down. He is a man of principal and he has guts to stand by this country. We are all behind him. Today, this party is offering one million dollars in cash to any person who can lead us to the killers." The speaker moves away from the microphone after saying "God Bless all" and the people in the stadium who came to listen to Senator Monroe, the future of America, slowly start moving and head back to their destination. Lots of women have tears in their eyes and everybody starts leaving the stadium slowly wondering what is going to happen next.

Senator Monroe and some of the most senior senators are sitting in the helicopter, discussing in hushed voices why and who could have done this and why his wife was not with him. After about 20 minutes they land on the helipad at Senator Monroe's house. All the lights in the house and the grounds have been turned on, while in the helicopter; many thoughts go through his mind. He wonders how he is going to go on with his love being dead. But, his mind refuses to accept her death and he keeps telling him that she is alive. Why would she leave him half way through his life? He needs her, the children need her. He walks in the front along with the Party Chairman and all the senators follow behind. When the Senator comes to the front door, the two cops standing guard recognize him and bow their heads a little bit and say,

"Senator Monroe, we are very sorry for your loss. This is a very sad time; we don't know what to say…"

Meanwhile the Police Chief, who is in the living room, notices a group of men walking towards the room. He comes out of the room just as the Senator is about to step in and says,

"Mr. Monroe, I need to talk to you for a few minutes, please have the men accompanying you wait to the next room".

The Party Chairman, Sean, says "I'll take care of them" and Sean indicates to the other men to follow him. Having been to the Senator's house many times before, Sean leads the men to the library.

The Police Chief and the Senator step into the living room. The Senator notices Father John and Mrs. Jones standing on the left side of the room. By the two step stairs on the right side, he sees four men surrounding the body checking for finger prints. When the Senator sees his wife, Samantha's body lying on the floor between the four men, he is unable to control himself and rushes towards the body. The Chief, knowing that the Senator is going to pick her up, runs behind him. The Senator gently pushes the men aside and in a very sad voice says,

"Honey, why did you leave me?"

As he bends down and is about to pick Samantha's body, the Chief and another cop hold the Senator back by his arms and the Chief says,

"Senator, please. Please don't touch. We need more time. I know what you are going through".

The Senator continues to push forward towards his wife's body, but both the Chief and the cop restrain him and the Police Chief pleads with the Senator,

"Please Senator, please come away. We cannot let you touch her."

As the Senator bends down over the Samantha's body, tears fall out of his eyes on her dress by the ankles. Slowly and gently, the Chief and the cop pull the Senator away from the body and walk him to the sofa. Father John and Mrs. Jones walk from across the room to sit by the Senator. Father John sits on the Senator's left side and he puts his right hand on the Senator's back to comfort him and says,

"Senator Monroe, you have to accept God's will. We are all his children. He brings us all here and then takes us back one day."

Senator Monroe puts his head in the palm of his hands and bows down and closes his eyes and does not say anything.

The Police Chief, who is standing in front of Senator Monroe, says sympathetically,

"Senator Monroe, I am sorry for your loss. I know what you are going through. But I have to ask, do you have any suspicion as to who could have done this? Did your wife say anything to you when you spoke to her before seven p.m.?"

"No, I don't have any suspects. But, my wife told me that she had a nice surprise for me. I did not know that this was her surprise! I should have kept her with me like always…she would be alive now" he replies.

The Police Chief asks again,

"Is there anything else you can tell me that can help us with our investigation?"

"Yes" the Senator replies "We have a hidden camera in every room and on the outside by the security gate. Even the guards did not know about the secondary cameras. There might not be any sound present, but the picture should be clear. These cameras are hidden in the ceiling. I'll call the security company tomorrow and get the DVD for today."

"Senator Monroe that will be very helpful" says the Chief.

The forensic experts are done with their work and the body is put on the stretcher. Senator Monroe has his back turned to the body and once again the Chief addresses the Senator,

"Senator Monroe, we have to take her body for examination. We are ready…"

The Police Chief comes close o the Senator and hold his right hand with both his hands and in a somber voice says,

"America lost a golden hearted lady who would have been our next First Lady."

The Chief walks towards the body and he tells them to take it away. It is almost 10 PM. The medics zip the body in the bag and start to head out. Before they reach the door, senior Mrs. Monroe along with the Senator's children, Senator's sister with her husband and children walk in with other close family. When the children see the body bag being carried out, Senator Monroe's daughter starts to cry and gets hysterical. Senator Monroe immediately stands up and his daughter runs to him upset and says,

"Daddy, daddy, they are taking mom away!! Stop them! Why are they taking my mommy?"

The other children start to cry too. The Senator picks up his daughter and holds her close to his chest and turns her face away. The medics quickly take the Mrs. Monroe's body out. Hearing the children crying, the other senators rush in from the library and try to calm the children by hugging and soothing them. The Senator continues to calm his daughter and then walks over to his sister's husband and asks him to take care of the guests.

The time is 10:10 PM. The police are still at the security gate. The Senator stays with his mother, sister, Father John and Mrs. Jones in the living room while his daughter joins the other children. By ten thirty all the people who have came with the Senator start to live and by ten forty five the helicopter flies those all back to the stadium where they have their limos waiting.

Meanwhile, the pizza Mrs. Jones ordered for the whole family arrives and the kids gets busy eating and talking about how to get revenge on the killer. The Senator who was in the living room suddenly gets up and leaves. When the Senator's sister notices him going into the next room, she tells her mother. Both of them worry about the Senator being alone in the room since he is grieving for his lost love. They decide to wait for a few minutes before interrupting him.

When the Senator does not return soon, his mother and sister go to the next room looking for him and pause at the door. The Senator has his back to the doorway and they see him looking at a photo of his wife which was taken just after their wedding. His mother and sister are very worried because ever since they heard the news of Samantha's murder, the Senator has become very quiet and they have never seen him so sad and upset. They both know how much the Senator loved Samantha. Even they had been charmed by Samantha since she was such a good person.

Though he hears his mother and sister walk into the room and stand besides him, he keeps looking at his wife's picture and does not speak. Finally, unable to keep quiet any longer, his mother pulls him in an embrace and with tears streaming down her face says,

"Son, I know you loved her very much. I did too, but I cannot see you break down like this. After your father died, you are the only one we have in this family"

The Senator tries to pull himself together and puts on a brave face in front for them and says,

"I'll be ok, mother, I need a few minutes to myself. Please go and be with the children. I will be out soon."

But, his mother does not want to leave him alone. So, his sister goes outside and whispers something to Father John. He immediately gets up and joins the Senator and his mother. He tells the senior Mrs. Monroe

"I'll stay with him and give him company". When the Senator's mother leaves the room, Father John starts the conversation with a slow, soft voice. Father John reveals to the Senator the arrival of Samantha's younger twin sister. While the Senator is surprised and listening to all this information, the Senator's sister and her husband interrupt them to ask if they want anything to eat. But they refuse since the Senator gets more and more intrigued by the information about his wife's twin. Listening to Father John, the Senator starts wondering if perhaps that it was his wife's twin who was killed and that his wife, Samantha may be the one kidnapped. He feels hopeful that his love might be alive and starts questioning Father John about every single detail.

Meanwhile, the gangsters leave Senator Monroe with one living person less on their team. On their way, they dump his body and steal another van. On their way back, they leave the old van about twenty miles outside Denver setting fire to the interior of the vehicle to erase any evidence or finger prints. They drive for an hour without talking or discussing anything, just listening to the news on the radio. They don't hear any news about stolen or burnt vans. When they are about ten miles into the next state, with the black guy driving, Number One riding in front passenger seat, Number Two sitting in the middle of the second row and the kidnapped twin laying in the back seat, Number One says,

"Come on guys, say something…I think we are out of danger for the time being, but who knows about the future…"

The black guy replies,

"My father used to say that if you do something wrong then you are always in danger, and the wrong doer always gets caught in the end."

Number Two says,

"Number One, I think we put ourselves in big fire this time. Looks like we are in big trouble and I don't think our boss can save us if we are caught."

"Your are right, Number Two" says Number One "Our boss has connections in our city, but going into the Senator's house, who could be our next President, and killing four people and kidnapping one, where one of dead is his wife or his wife's twin sister, and then kidnapping the other is really a huge mistake to correct. Since we don't know which twin we killed, we have no idea if the twin we have kidnapped is the one who lived with Randy."

While driving, the black guys asks,

"Hey, Number One, so what is the answer? What do we do? What if we dump this twin sister as she is and get a fresh start somewhere else new?"

"Buddy, With what or where are we going to start fresh? We have no money, the boss has no money..." replies Number One. Then Number Two asks,

"So, what is our choice? We are stuck!! Our boss might turn us in for the million dollar reward that was offered!"

"I don't think he will do that. We have been with him way too long" says Number One.

Then the black guy says,

"If we don't deliver this twin to our boss, we don't get anywhere. If we deliver this twin to him, and she turns out to be our next First Lady, then we are in trouble. If this one is really the slut, who lived with our boss, but pretends to not to be her but our potential First Lady, then we are in deeper trouble!! So, Number One, you are the brainy one, so how do we get out of this mess without money?"

"I have been thinking since we left the Senator's house, and the only way, as I see it, is that we deliver this twin to the boss as the slut as ask for a million dollar each. Then we just take the money and run to somewhere in South America and hope for the best", says Number One.

Hearing this, Number Two says "I think it is a good idea. The only thing that is bugging me is what if our boss pretends not to know us and refuse to recognize us?"

"Then, I will have no choice but to kill him and take over his empire, and dump this twin somewhere" replies Number One.

To which, both the black guy and Number two say simultaneously "What about us?"

Number One says "If that happens, then we will all be together. You both will be my Number One and Number Two. But, I think, right now the best course of action is to get a million bucks each and leave our boss as quickly as possible".

"Where are we going to go?" asks the black guy.

"The only option we have is to get the money from the boss and go to South America. Then we can buy a house with tight security for one hundred and fifty grand and then go into business by opening a strip bar for a few thousand dollars. And with the remaining money and the income from the strip bar, we will be set through our old age" says Number One.

"That is a brilliant idea!" says Number Two smiling.

Number One says "It is no use killing our boss because we will not gain anything – we won't get any money. It is better to be nice to him and get the money within a week and walk out quietly. With four murders and one count of kidnapping, the prosecutors will be asking for death penalty for us since, the state does not like to spend money on people like us and give us life in prison."

The black guy gets the blues and says

"Let's talk about something else. I just want to deliver this girl to the boss, get whatever he gives and run away someplace where I can get some peace."

Number Two asks Number One "What do you think happened to the cool guy? As you heard at the Senator's house, the twin kept saying that she does not know anything about the money..."

As they continue with their discussion about the past events and what might happen in the future and keep cruising towards California, Number Two gives an injection to the girl in the back seat so that she does not wake up and cause any trouble.

Number replies "I don't know who he was or where he came from. He never smoked or drank and never went near any good looking strippers. All he did was trying to get close to the slut. In the beginning, it was very hard for him to get close to her until the day when the boss walked in with the new blonde. Then boss hurt the slut and he was there to take her to the clinic for stitches, Last Sunday, both the cool guy and the slut disappeared. Now, we found the girl, but we don't know if it is really the slut. But in the news, the slut looks like the twin of our next possible First Lady. Honestly, I don't like this twin; she is more than I can take. She hit me on my legs. The slut did not have this much guts, so this might be the next first lady, the wrong twin!"

They stop to get gas on the state highway and they pay with cash. Now, Number One takes the wheel with the black guy in the passenger seat and Number Two still in the middle seat of the van. Number Two asks Number One,

"So, you think this is not the slut, the woman the boss used to have around? This is her twin – quite possibly our next First Lady?"

"No, I don't know for sure. Maybe I am mistaken. It could very well be her, the slut, I mean. She could have reacted that way when she saw her twin, a close family member die. I don't know..." Number One says as he continues driving.

They have been driving for three hours now and still have another three hours to go. They don't want to take any risk by stopping, so they decide to go through the fast food drive through and pick up something to eat.

While eating and driving, the black guy asks Number One who is driving with one hand and eating with the other "Hey Number One, how long have you been thinking about killing the boss?"

"About two years. Ever since the Chinese Mafia started to flex their muscles in our territory, I have been telling the boss that we should get some people and get rid of the Chinese Mafia once and for all. But, he won't listen. I think he is getting old" replies Number One.

"But, the Chinese have a lot of people in this town" says the black guy.

Number One agrees "Yes, I know they have a lot of people in this town. But, once you get rid of their head honchos, they will back off".

"So, is that your plan? To take over our boss's business?" asks Number Two.

"Yes, it was, but now we need to save our skin and get money and find a safe haven...hopefully in South America somewhere with new ID's" replies Number One.

"You had a good plan to take over the business, so why have you changed your mind?" the black guy asks.

"See, people who think that they are smart and clever, also has a stupid side to them and makes mistakes. That is what the four of us did including the sharp shooter who died. We never watch TV news, listen to radio or read papers. We just followed our boss's orders..." Number One says.

Number Two laughs and says "What do we want with the news? We are too busy looking at strippers and guarding the club".

"Yes, that is the whole mistake we made" the black guy says. "We just left and went to Denver to get the slut and the stolen money. We did not think twice about where we were heading. But, the boss knew everything, he was just interested in his money, not anything else..." he realizes.

Number One intervenes, "Correct, now you guys are getting the whole picture. Our boss was getting suspicious that the slut was about to leave him. But he did not expect the cool guy and the slut to rob him. So, last Sunday when they stole his pink open top caddy and left it somewhere near town, our boss already knew from watching the news that the slut was the twin sister for our potential next First Lady, Senator Monroe's wife. So, he found our possible next President's address and sent us there thinking that the slut along with the cool guys will be there together. And it was our fate or bad luck, which I don't believe in, to go get the ten million and see how it turned out...."

Listening to this, Number Two, says

"So, we are the stupid ones!! Don't scare me any more... what are we going to do when we get back? What about this girl?"

Number One reiterates "Look, as I already said, the only way out for the three of us is to deliver this twin to the boss as the slut. We have to stick to the story and tell the boss that we could not find the cool guy or the money. But, we have the slut and he can ask her where the money is. For bringing in the slut, at least he should give us one million each. As we have been hearing, every radio station is broadcasting the news about the events at Senator Monroe's estate and his wife's murder. We were there; somebody might have seen us in the area in the last twenty four hours. Senator Monroe is powerful and has a lot of money. He will find us eventually. So, our chance is to go back to our boss, Randy, and get our money and run to South America. I don't like our justice system or the jail. Having been there once, I'd rather be dead in a shoot out than be in a jail in USA."

After listening to Number One's explanation, the other two decide that it is better to stick with Number One and his plan than with their boss. They look at each other and tell Number One that they agree with him and will all stick to the same story. Six hours later, they finally enter the gambling town and are about twenty minutes away from their own bar and club. Number Two is happy that they made it safely back to their boss's territory. He says,

"Number One, can you pull up someplace...I need some alcohol. I normally start at 7:00pm and it is 2:30am are already..."

"I need a drink too. I am dying for a beer or two" says the black guy.

"Well, I know you guys have been patient for a long time. We will be there in twenty minutes. So, let us not blow it at the last minute" says Number One trying to calm them.

They both agree with Number One. They drive through Nevada streets with its bright lights and beautiful night life, men and women singing and dancing, showing off their bodies in the comfortable night with perfect weather.

Finally, they reach Randy's club and Number One opens the door with remote control. As the van drives in, he presses another button to open another large door which leads directly into the lounge in the club. Number One says

"Let's take her to her room on the second floor. We can then come back down and enjoy ourselves."

Between the three of them, they carry the girl to her second floor room, lay her on the bed and lock the door. By the time the three of them enter the bar it is 3:00am.

As the three man sit at the bar watching the news on TV about Mrs. Monroe, the bartender, a large Hispanic man, with minimal communication skills in English brings them their usual drinks. Since it is late and they are exhausted, they gulp down drink in one shot. The bartender refills their glasses and as they finish their second drink, they start to relax that they are back in their home town. The bartender asks

"Number One, have you seen the news today?"

"No, I did not watch it on the TV but heard it on the radio" says Number One.

"Look" the bartender points to the TV where Jody, the TV reporter from Denver is reporting. All three men watch Jody continue with her broadcast.

"We have been reporting from Senator Monroe's estate all evening. The latest information we have from the police is that Mrs. Monroe had an identical twin sister. She apparently came home after fifteen years. No one knows what brought her home after all these years. After these murders took place, the twin sister has disappeared. The police are not sure as to the motive or who committed these crimes. At this time, they are still looking for evidence. We will be back at ten am with more updates" says Jody as she goes on to other news.

"Turn off that TV and give us bottle" says Number One to the bartender.

The bartender brings a bottle of their favorite drink to the table where the three men are sittings and says "Only today, boss pay. From tomorrow, you pay for your own drink. Boss has no money, .

As they fill their glasses, they look at each other and the black guys ask "We have to pay for our own drinks from tomorrow?"

"Yes, that is what the boss said. Even I have to pay for my drink. Boss has no money", the bartender says with false laughter.

"Put three large pizzas in the oven, we are all hungry. And bring us all a drink on me" says Number one and continues "Tell me, what time did the new break and what exactly did our boss Randy say?"

The bartender puts the pizzas in the oven and comes back to the bar and refills the glasses and sits on one of the high chairs and says "Now, I can talk to you senior Number One…"

Again Number One asks "What did Randy say and what time did the news break?"

"Number One, please don't get me into trouble with the boss…at 8:30pm when the news broke, the boss was here.

He was nearly drunk and with the new blonde. He sobered up for sometime, maybe till 9:30pm, and then he started drinking again. Before he left, he said that you guys blew everything. He also mentioned that if you guys came back here, he is going to kill you. He said that he was not going to get into trouble for killing the potential next first Lady But, please Number One, don't say anything to get me in trouble…" replies the bartender.

Reassuring the bartender that he will not say anything, Number One turns to the other two and says

"Did you hear what he said? The boss is worried about getting into trouble; we are the one who should be worried."

"Yes, you were right. Let us stop drinking and get some food and rest. That way we will be ready to face him in the morning" says the black guy.

Number Two says "I cannot believe that he is going against us suddenly and leaving us to deal with this".

"No, it is not sudden. As soon as he heard the news that we might have killed the Senator's wife, he realized that he could be in trouble for sending us there in the first place. He is worried about getting caught himself" replies Number One.

The black guy decides "Ok, guys, let us meet the boss here at the bar at 11:00am. Let's talk to him and collect our money as planned and get out of this mess before our face appears on the most wanted criminal list."

They eat the pizza the bartender brings them and have a couple more drinks and call it a night.

The next morning, Monday, September 8, 2008 turns out to be a nice sunny day with clear blue skies in the gambling town of Nevada. The twin sister who was kidnapped and brought here by Randy's gang starts to wake up from the effects of the injected drug. She opens her eyes slowly and looks around the room but still feels lethargic and has a headache from the drug and hunger. The girl finally sits up on the bed after a couple of attempts. She realizes that she must have been drugged and tries to figure out where she is. After half an hour, she manages to reach for the glass of water which was left beside her and slowly drinks it. She is still unable identify where she is or get up and move. As the time passes, the fog in her head starts to clear and exploring around the room, she decides to take a shower to make herself more alert.

After staying in the shower for about half an hour, she feels refreshed and much stronger. It is about eleven am. She tries to open the window but realizes that it is four inches thick and cannot be broken and the door is pretty solid too. The girl concludes that there is no easy way out of the room. She walks to the dressing table and sees and photo laying there face down. It is a picture of her twin and a bald head man. She holds the photo to her chest and comes and sits back on the bed.

Meanwhile, downstairs at the bar at eleven am, Number One, Number Two and the black guy are sitting at their regular table as agreed upon the previous evening. And Number One says,

"Guys, we need to take some food to the slut since we have not given anything to her to eat since last night".

"Since when did you start feeling sorry for someone who has not eaten?" the black guy remarks.

"Look, guys, I might be a mean and bad man. But, I don't want to starve someone who is in our custody. The cruelest thing to do is to starve somebody. It is better to kill them quickly than slowly killing them with starvation" says Number One and calls the bartender over to their table and says

"Get a couple of doughnuts along with breakfast omelet and fresh coffee to take to the girl's room upstairs right away."

Taking the order, the bartender goes to the kitchen and has a tray ready to take to the girl within fifteen minutes. He brings the breakfast tray out and along with Number Two and the black guy goes upstairs to the twin girl's room. Number Two and the black guy enter the room first with their guns drawn and the bartender enters behind them with the breakfast tray. They find the twin sitting on the bed and upon seeing the three of them, she is very angry. She stands up as the bartender brings the tray close to her and he says

"Good morning Senorita, I have brought you your usual breakfast".

"Who are you?" she asks in anger.

"I am the bartender. Don't you know me? I bring you food and drink every day" he replies.

"No, I don't know who you are! My sister did not tell me about you. I am not who you guys think I am. I am Mrs. Monroe, the Senator's wife" the girl says watching Number Two and the black guy standing by the open door. With their guns unable to escape.

Number Two and the black guy are surprised to hear her words and exchange glances. Number Two tells the bartender to leave the tray and come so that they can leave. The bartender leaves the tray and all three men leave after locking the door to her room.

It is eleven thirty am by the time they come downstairs to the bar, and they sit at their usual table discussing what the girl said upstairs about her being Mrs. Monroe and not the slut. They wait for their boss to arrive and don't have their usual morning drink as they are preoccupied with worry about their future.

The boss walks into the bar around 11:45 am with the blonde in a white suit and hat. Aware of the circumstance, he walks over to where Number One, Number Two and the black guy are sitting and takes a seat at their table. He just stares at them without saying a word for a few minutes. Then he remarks,

"So, you guys blew everything! I saw the whole thing on the news last night."

Nobody says anything. Finally, Number One says,

"Randy, I have known you for a long time. This time you have landed yourself and us in a big firry mess. You might not be able to get out and may get us burnt in the process as well. We believed you and took your word which landed us in this situation. If I had known clearly where or whose house we were going, I would have refused. Given what happened, just give each of us a million dollars in cash, in used bills, and we will get out of here and this mess. We don't want to be involved any more."

Randy is shocked to hear that his loyal gang members want to out and he says

"You know, the slut and the cool guy took all my money. So, right now, I don't have anything to give. You will have to wait a little longer. I will eventually give you three what you want. Maybe, I should go upstairs and talk to the slut and question her about my money"

Number Two and the black guy raise their hands to interrupt and when Randy asks them what they have to say, Number two replies

"Boss, we just went upstairs to give her some food. The girl upstairs is saying that she is the other twin, I mean, she is saying that she is the Senator's wife"

But Randy, who is almost fifty years old with a clean shaven head, six foot and in good shape, a person who has always been on the illegal side doing business says

"She is probably pretending. I have known her for years. She is a very good actress. She is just saying that to save herself and hopefully get out. But, I am sure she knows where the money is. I will go upstairs and ask her myself."

Randy then asks the bartender to bring drinks for everyone. Once the bartender brings the drinks, Randy gulps his down while the other do not touch their drinks. Randy is surprised and tries to pacify then and says

"Come on guys, we had a bit of bad luck. So what, we will get over it. We will get the money from somewhere"

Again Number One says,

"Boss we need to get out of this place, I have a feeling somebody must have seen us in Denver, and very soon our faces are going to appear on TV, so you have to decide how to pay us quickly"

Now Randy is getting the feeling that this might be a threat, so he tries to control his anger, and stands up and says,

"Let us go upstairs, and ask her my way, I know her better than anybody else."

So they all start going upstairs. The time is midday; the twin had to eat what was delivered to her because she was so hungry. She is now fully conscious and sitting up in bed watching the news on Jody's channel, she hears several footsteps and then a door being opened; Randy and the blonde enter first with Number One, black guy and Number Two. The twin stands up next to the bed and she recognizes the guy in the white suite from a photo with the other twin. Randy, Number One and the black guy walk towards the twin and the Number Two stays guard at the door. Randy stands in the middle between Number One and the black guy, while the blonde stays with Number Two near the door. As the three of them stand in a row, the twin walks a little closer. They are three feet apart, she tightens both her fists, and her blood pressure going up with anger, the twin now stands in directly in front of Randy. Randy asks "Where is the money."

The twin does not say anything, she just stares at him. Randy gets a little more aggressive and asks again, "Come on slut don't make me angry, where is the money. " The twin replies in a nice voice but it has anger that he does not understand and she says,

"Behind you"

Then all the three guys look behind them and see nothing. As there heads are turning back the twin lifts her right leg like karate expert with speed and hits Randy in the stomach just below the belly button. Her heal digs into his skin and makes a deep cut. He falls back on the dressing table edge and hits his back and left shoulder so hard that he falls on the floor. Everybody in the room is shocked, Number One and the black guy start pulling him up and the blonde run over and asks

"Honey are you OK."

As Randy is being lifted up he reaches for a small gun that he always carries in his right pocket, the twin says "That is for my sister, And don't you ever dare call my deceased sister that way" The twin is very angry; nobody has ever seen her like this before. Meanwhile Number One and the black guy are trying to control him; it is the first time in his life Randy is hurt and humiliated, he says "Let me kill her." But Number One and the black guy hold him back and Number One takes his gun away, "We have already done enough damage."

Randy and the twin glare at each other, like they have been enemies for centuries. Number One, the black guy and the blonde who had rushed to help Randy up try to take Randy out of the room. As they are about to move the twin says in a very angry voice, "Why did you kill my sister, what did you want? I could have given you the money; she did not steal your money; why did you kill her."

Then all of them stopped moving. Number One replied, "We did not mean to kill her, one of us panicked and he is the one who killed the security guards and the driver. When we went to your house your sister pointed the gun at the sharp shooter and he panicked. He shot her and she shot him and then you came out of the room, we were not sure which one is which and so we brought you here."

After listening to Number One the twin now feels more puzzled and says, "Let me go to my family. I am not the one for revenge who would want to see you dead. Your death is not going to bring my sister back."

"I cannot let you go" says Randy in anger, "What you just did you think you are going to forgive us later. Next time you touch me I will kill you, and I don't care if you are the next first lady or the other twin."

"Before you leave Randy, you used and abused my sister. You left her heart broken. She was very happy with me; but let me tell you one more thing, if you don't let me go back to my family today, my husband has so much power and money he will find me and your gang."

After listening to her Randy asks all his buddies to leave and as they are leaving the blonde looks at the twin giving her a dirty look and they lock the door behind and come downstairs and sit at the same table. As they are sitting down the blonde looks at the front of Randy's tee shirt and she comes close to him and say,

"Honey you are bleeding, look at your belly." He looks at the front of his shirt and sees blood. The blonde kisses him on the cheek and runs her hand on his back, and she says,

"Honey you are bleeding from the back too." Randy is already upset by the whole situation and gets up and goes to his room to change. Around the table you have Number One, Number Two, the blonde and the black guy, and they are having their first drink. After about ten minutes they see a cop coming into the bar. It was the local police chief, a long time friend so Randy's, someone who got randy out of trouble many times. Six foot tall, just over forty, and a little bit too much on the bulky side because of easy life, alcohol and fast food, he is in a different mood today, very cheerful, he likes to joke and laugh after two or three free drinks. He comes straight to the usual table near the bar, a big round table, which can take four to twelve people, he pulls a chair himself and sits next to Number One and they say "Hi" to each other. The chief cannot keep his mouth shut and says,

"Hi guys say something; it is not your funeral – is it. Where is Randy?"

Number One replies,

"He will be down in a second."

By this time the bartender has already placed a drink in front of the police chief, which he drinks in a gulp. The bartender brings him another drink, and he downs it again. Now the police chief is feeling comfortable, but nobody says anything for a couple of minutes. Randy comes down after changing his clothes. As he is walking over to the table he sees the police chief. When Randy gets close he says," Hi" like usual, because the chief is here everyday at lunch time for free food and drinks. Today is a little different, so he waits for Randy to open up.

Randy sits down and the chief keeps staring at him. Randy says to the chief,

"Why are you staring at me?"

"Well Randy", the chief laughs a little bit, "I have never seen you like this before, these boys of yours told me what happened over at the senator's house."

"Yes I know the sharp shooter blew everything, I knew there was something wrong with his head", agrees Randy

"But Randy the senator's party is offering one million dollars, either you give it to me or I shall turn you in." The chief's drinks have taken effect and he is becoming brave.

"Before you turn me in I will kill you." The chief stops smiling and he says,

"Randy you are in no position to kill anybody anymore. You and your boys need to plan something fast and get out of the country. This time you hit something that you should have not, the senator is going to come after you so hard that you will be many feet under. Look I was testing your nerve. I won't turn you in because you have helped me many times before."

Randy feels a little relaxed. Randy's gang is listening quietly because they have to decide what to do next. The chief get serious,

"Randy tell me before you sent these boys to pickup the slut. Did you not stop to think that she is the senator's wife's twin and the powerful man is going to have a lot of security everywhere?"

"Yes chief I did not think straight, when the blonde and I came back from Paris we found the room door unlocked so I suspected that something was wrong. I went to my safe. The safe door was unlocked. When I opened the safe door all the money, jewelry was gone, that is when I called Number One and Two. They told me that the cool guy and the slut were missing; they did not know that she was an identical twin of the wife of the senator from Denver. They also told me that it was certain that he was going to win the 2008 election and she was going to become next to the first lady. So I was wondering where she would go, she has nowhere to go, the cool guy is homeless too, so I thought that is where they would go, Then next day I sent my gang to the senator's house thinking that the cool guy and the slut would probably be there. You know the rest."

The chief is on his third drink. He wants to be back in control because he has the law on his side.

"OK, OK, let me give you the rest of the story from my cops head." The chief laughs a little bit to irritate Randy. "You have been treating her badly for the last six months and the cool guy was trying to get near her so he can see your bedroom where the safe is, so when you brought in the blonde she got frustrated and jealous, but she still did not care about what you did until you hit her in the belly and she cut herself in the back. That night the cool guy took her to the clinic because she was bleeding from her back. He got her stitched up and then they both started to get to know each other. Last Friday she was sitting at the bar, and this is what the bartender told me, she was crying after a couple of drinks and she started saying, why did I not listen to my mother and my sister, they were right. When her sister and her family appeared on the Ten O Clock news she was happy. She asked the bartender to turn it up and also told him that her sister was the older twin. Please don't tell anybody my sister is going to be our next first lady. She told the bartender that she was planning to see her sister. She also asked him to change the channels on all the TVs in the bar so that nobody could recognize her as the twin. She ran upstairs and Randy - you and the blonde had already left for Paris the same afternoon."

The chief motions to the bartender for another drink and tries to continue the conversation. Randy angrily interrupts him saying,

"How come these are my friends and employees and they don't tell me anything."

The chief laughs and says,

"Because you are too big headed Randy, until now you have never listened to anybody, you have put your foot in the big fire, any way let me finish the rest of the story. The twin who is your woman came back down to the bar with the cool guy. They both sat at the bar and held hands. She asked the bartender for another drink while the cool guy got a coke. She was very happy and asked the bartender to turn on the channel that her sister was on. She spoke to the cool guy so nicely that I cannot describe, they whispered to each other every now and then, holding each others hands. He left the bar around midnight and she left an hour later to go to bed. The next day she was at the bar all day, but the cool guy was missing all day. Saturday night she came back with the cool guy, and this time she was sober, she only had one drink and some food. She seemed happy and joyful. Sunday morning the cool guy broke into your pink Cadillac and drove to the national Bus Stand. The cool guy was wheeling two big bags and she was carrying a carry on and her purse."

"How do you know about the bags" asked Randy.

"Be patient Randy, I am coming to that. The cool guy was wearing your type of clothes and she was wearing very large glasses and a hat covering her forehead so she could not be recognized as the next first lady's twin. They pulled up in front of the bus stand and left your car running and dropped about three hundred dollars on the seat. Now, none of your friends and employees know about your Cadillac missing because he locked your garage from the outside, so they thought that the cool guy and the slut are missing, nothing else. That is when you called me on Thursday, when you came back from Paris, about your money and the car. I put the whole team to find it."

Now the chief is giving Randy a little bull to make himself look good.

"So we found your car at midnight on Thursday being driven by a white and a black guy in their early twenties with two white chicks. They were drinking in the car using your money. When we arrested them they told us that a man in white suit white hat and a woman went into the bus terminal carrying two large bags and the woman was carrying a small carry on bag."

"Randy look on the intelligent side, the woman did not go out at all day and the cool guy was missing all day

Saturday and your safe was opened by a professional; I think the cool guy either did it himself or he hired somebody to do it."

"Now look at the twin side, why would she take your stolen money and jewelry to the senator's house that is running for the White House. If somebody found out that his wife's sister is in their house with stolen loot he would loose the election. So in my opinion the cool guy got your money in cool robbery and the slut was just looking for a ride to the bus stand. So he dropped her their and went his way. The twin ended up in her sister's house, the cool guy got away with cool robbery and you put your cool life in a boiling pot. And you sent your boys to senator's house without any thinking or plan, everybody claps and the chief has his drink. After listening to the chief everybody takes a moment to think. Number One finally asks,

"So chief what do you think will happen to us?"

"Well boys if I were in your place I would take the money from Randy and run as fast as you can, and as further as possible. I will help you get across the border, I know a few people out there who can help you set up home and some kind of business", says the chief.

And then the three of them turn to Randy and Number One asks Randy,

"Well Randy you heard the whole nine yards, so when can we have the money."

"OK guys, don't push me, let me think, I won't let you down", says Randy.

"Chief", asks Number One again, "What do you think, how much time do we have."

"You don't have a second. The reason, the twin upstairs, whether she is The Slut as she was known in this town, or she is the next first lady. Too many people know that face and body in this town. Fifteen years ago she was America's best looking stripper, even if she did it for only six months, but someone knows", says the chief, "She is here."

The gang is getting a little sweaty with fear, again the chief says,

"I would not be surprised if the Chinese mafia, who control half the city's drugs, they might blackmail Randy to sell his side of the business to them for half the price. Because they know that the next first lady's face is often seen in the bar in the evening, having a drink. I think randy should make a deal with some body and call it a day."

"Well Randy", Number One is getting a little angry,

"OK, OK, I am beginning to get annoyed, we will do something immediately, but you guys have to give me till this evening, I have to think about this twin too. What should I do with her, if she is The Slut she knows too much, if she is the next first lady, now she knows to much too, because The Slut must have told her everything, so I have to get rid of her somehow", says Randy.

Number One is getting more upset, because randy was not coming up with any answer for their money, so he says,

"Randy, we are not doing any more killings, I have had enough. You can leave the woman locked up upstairs, just sell the club and bar to the Chinese mafia. At least we will not be facing the death penalty. The people, who will take over this bar, will take care of her, whether she is a slut or the next first lady."

Now Randy is feeling isolated, he does not have anybody on his side. He fears Number One's anger because he is much stronger than Randy, so he resigns himself to be in agreement with the gang.

"OK guys, I agree, I will get rid of our business right away and all of you will get a million each, and the chief and his cop friends will get about hundred grand. We will not cooperate with the law against each other. After this chapter is closed we do not know each other."

Everybody cheers and they ask the bartender to bring more food and drinks and even agree to pay.

The afternoon has concluded with an agreed solution among the evil. The time is just past 4:00 PM, September 8th 2008, while randy and his gang was hammering out their agreement.

On a sunny clear day in Denver it is a sad day at Senator Monroe's house. People have been coming and going all day, the children miss their mom. The senator's sister is trying to do her best to distract the children by keeping them occupied, but in vain. The whole country is sad that Mrs. Monroe is dead.

Just after 4:00 PM two police cars pull up in front of the house, A tall man about six foot one steps out of the car with a hat, suit and a tie. He has a good physique; the cool good looking man comes up to the front door of Mr. Monroe's house and rings the door bell.

A voice from the large living room calls out;

"Come in the door is open." The man opens the door; he walks in and sees about fifteen people sitting in the living room. He removes his hat.

"Good afternoon." Mr. Monroe gets up and moves towards him and shakes his hand.

"Mr. Pollack, welcome, I am sorry last night I was too upset, I was unable to talk to anybody. Let's go into the library, I will set up everything for you to look at."

They both walk to the library. Father John who has been close to the family gets up and joins them. Mrs. Jones the housekeeper walks in behind them and before the three sit down she asks,

"Gentlemen can I get you any refreshments." Mr. Monroe looks at Mr. Pollack. Detective Tom Pollack is Denver's best, maybe best in the country and has an impeccable reputation for being honest, polite and charming.

"Yes Mrs. Jones, I will have a large coffee, salad sandwich, Thank You. I have not slept a wink. I have been on this case all day today."

"I will have the same Mrs. Jones, how about you Father John", the senator looks at him.

"I am fine." Tom and Father John sit down as Mr. Monroe has pulled the chairs close to the TV.

"Mr. Pollack as I told you before we have hidden cameras in the ceilings. I made a copy, you can take one, but please don't share this with anybody, I will play the DVD see if you can make any sense of it, and I cannot."

The senator plays the DVD. "I will skip to where the killers come in through the door. As you can see it is a good clear picture." Before they opened the door, as Tom, Father John, and Mr. Monroe are watching you can see Mrs. Jones and one of the twins talking. A van pulls up, and both stand up, the twin runs into the next room, and Mrs. Jones runs to the kitchen. Three guys come in and one of the twins standing on the steps near the room on the right lifts her gun with her right hand. She is shot and he is shot.

Mrs. Jones walks into the library with a food trolley. When she sees the twin and the gangster falling down on the TV she starts shaking and says in a broken voice,

"Father John I cannot watch that anymore." She leaves the food in the library and goes back in tears. The senator, the detective and Father John however are huddled close to the TV, to find some evidence. After the first twin falls the sister appears. They put her to sleep and the gang leaves taking the dead man with them.

The senator turns the TV off gives Tom the DVD. They share the coffee and sandwich quietly. Finally Tom asks the senator,

"Mr. Monroe do you have any suspicions as to who could have done this."

"No Mr. Pollack, I don't have any enemies, however in politics one never knows. I have not tried to upset any corporations or threaten any country in my speeches", replies Mr. Monroe.

"Mr. Monroe it appears to me that it could be your political opponents who might have done this to you. They could not match your ratings in the polls, and decided this is how they were going to destroy you. From the picture I cannot tell which twin is which, I will have to go back to my office and look at the DVD more thoroughly."

Then Father John says to Tom,

"Mr. Pollack, I am sorry to interrupt, I don't think you will be able to tell them apart they are one hundred percent identical. Only their parents and I can tell them apart. Over the years the younger twin has fooled so many people including the senator a few times."

"Well Father, you are probably right, but we have to find these people first. I hope they have not left the country.

I will find them where ever they are. It is a small world because of the internet, phones and cameras. If they are still in the country and you try to apprehend these killers it always ends up in a gun fight, or they start killing each other before surrendering."

"Mr. Pollack I am not a cop or a detective, but given your experience with similar situations if there is a fire fight I am sure you will not put the twin in any danger, because she could be Mrs. Monroe for all you know."

"Father you are right, my intention is to arrest them alive at any cost. If we find the twin, if it is not Mrs. Monroe we can find out who is behind the murder, or if she is Mrs. Monroe then I am sure her sister who was here with her twin for a week, she would have told her everything. So one way or the other we will find out who the real plotters are."

The time is 5:00 PM Monday 8th September 2008, the senator and Tom has just finished eating their sandwich, the Tom's cell phone rings. He takes it out of his pocket and says,

"Hello Tom Pollack speaking." The voice on the phone,

"Hello Mr. Pollack this is the head of the DNA lab. I am sorry the DNA matches Mrs. Monroe one hundred percent."

"Are you sure?" Tom is shocked and saddened.

"Mr. Pollack we checked three or four times. It is indeed Mrs. Monroe that died."

"Is it possible that identical twins could have matching DNA's", asked Tom.

"I am not sure Mr. Pollack. This is an unusual situation; if you are able to apprehend the other twin, then we can compare her DNA. If it is a perfect match. However the other can claim that she is Mrs. Monroe. Then only way the senator can find out is this is the real Mrs. Monroe is when she makes her first mistake." Tom continued,

"Look doc I have had a lot of issues with DNA testing lately, are you sure nobody has handled the DNA besides you and your team."

"No Mr. Pollack, I was the only one, I try not to be wrong or be greedy, if you know what I mean." The doc hangs up.

Tom is sad he has to break the bad news to the senator. He looks at Mr. Monroe sitting across him with Father John and says,

"Mr. Monroe, I am sorry, the DNA belongs to your wife, looks like it was a perfect match."

"I heard the whole conversation", the senator is disappointed, and his head bows down. Father John walks up to him and rubs his back with his right hand, and looks towards Tom and says,

"Mr. Pollack, I think the only way I can be sure is, when I meet the twin. Please keep the DNA and science in your pocket, Samantha Monroe cannot die. Too many people need her, you don't know her as well as I do, I have known her since she was a child. She cannot die Mr. Pollack."

"Father John I can only follow the law, the latest DNA is very accurate."

"Mr. Pollack, I know you are an honest detective, however there are a lot of crooks out there. In the last two hundred years many innocent people have received the death penalty, because of incompetent, greedy justice officials. I need say no more, how many of these officials got any jail time, or got fired; in the meantime the people who wrongly received the death penalty are dead."

"I know what you are saying Father, my job is to apprehend the criminals and hand them to law. which I intend to do."

Father John continues to probe the detective,

"What if the twin's DNA also matches and she claims that she is Mrs. Monroe. What are you going to do?"

"Well Father you do have a point, I cannot answer until I have her in my custody."

"I can give you that answer, the DNA is human made and humans do lie, I know that if I see the twin I can tell who she is. However if somebody in the DNA lab makes a mistake or lies. And some body gets a death penalty being innocent. Would you charge that official and prosecution will seek the death penalty?

Tom replies, "Father I know your concerns regarding human life, the gang killed four innocent people and I am not sure for what, my job is to apprehend them. I am sure the prosecutors will seek the death penalty."

"Mr. Pollack my feelings and my faith tell me that she is alive, God cannot afford to take such a human being from the earth, because of the number of people she has helped and Lord only knows how many more she will be helping in the future."

"Yes I agree with you Father, I have met her couple of times. There is nobody who can match her kindness. I promise you that I will even risk my life to save her, and you will be the first one to talk to her."

"That is all I wanted to hear, now I know you care and you are not a trigger happy cop."

"Father John, Mr. Monroe I have known you for a long time, I will abide by the Lords rules of honesty. I have to leave now as I have a lot to do. Oh! I forgot to tell you, the hospital is going to call and let you know which funeral home the body is being sent to", saying this Tom gets up to leave.

"I have to go Father, Mr. Monroe and again I hope the twin is alive, and I hope it is Mrs. Monroe."

The senator sees Tom off, Tom gets into the police car and drive away.

The senator's mother and his sister who were sitting in the next room see the detective leave and come to the living room where Father and the senator are standing. The mother asks,

"Son, what did the detective say?"

The senator is heartbroken and replies,

"Mother it is Samantha who died, the DNA matched perfectly, it is almost certain."

The mother responds to her son angrily,

"I hope they catch the slut soon, I want to see her hanged with my own eyes. No wonder people called her names; she gave her widowed mom a real bad time. Our Samantha was a real lady."

"Yes mother, we need to forgive like the Lord has told us to do, may be this it had to end this way. How are the children taking this?"

The mother does not respond, the sister interjects,

"They are in a shock and miss their mother, and want to punish the killers their own way. We were so happy, why did her sister have to come and spoil our happiness."

The sister chokes and leaves the room with a napkin. The mother recalls,

"I have never seen a woman more satisfied. She never complained, or argued, even I complain some times. I don't understand why the Lord had to take her away from us and break my son's heart."

The senator gets up and leaves the room leaving his mother and Father John in the living room.

Father John says, "Mrs. Monroe, we should not bring up Samantha in your son's presence. Though he does not show it in his eyes, but his heart is bleeding, it will take him some time to recover and be normal again."

"But father, I cannot help it, I miss her too, and the house is empty without her. She was so full of life; I have never witnessed so much sadness in twenty years since my husband died. Father, who do you who think did this, is the sister part of this or do you think this is the work of my son's political opponents?"

"I don't know who or why someone did this, only time will tell, but I don't think the sister had anything to do with Samantha's death. She came here last Sunday to give up her other life and start fresh, get married and settle down. The sisters were very happy and the younger sister was keen to see the rest of the family."

The mother has her doubts about the younger twin.

"I like to believe you Father, she may just be pretending or acting, she is an excellent liar. I remember her as a very naughty child, she used to make her mom's life miserable, and her mother finally gave up."

Tom Pollack pulls up into the parking lot of the police station, he sees several reporters waiting near the door. He is now about twenty feet from the main door and he sees Jody walking towards him ahead of the others as usual. As Tom gets closer to the main door Jody catches up with him. Tom keeps walking. While the camera crew and other reporters are having him on live TV, Jody fires several questions at Tom.

"Mr. Pollack, have you made any progress, can you tell us anything, did you get the DNA analysis, and was it the next first lady or her twin that died?" Tom responds as he is walking,

"Yes we have received the phone call from the DNA lab; however I cannot tell anything until we have the official paper work in our hands."

Tom reaches the main door; he stands on the steps and faces all the reporters. Jody continues to be aggressive and asks him,

"Mr. Pollack, you went to see the senator this afternoon, did he give you any useful information as to who may have done this?" Tom replies to the gathered reporters,

"Please be patient, as soon as I get the official report my secretary will call you and give you the details." In the meantime the two cops who accompanied the detective reach the main door. One of them opens the door and says,

"Mr. Pollack get in, my buddy will handle the reporters."

Tom walks in and goes straight to his cubicle, places the DVD on the table and sits down. Then he calls his secretary on the radio,

"Barbara, could you please come in and also ask Terrence to come too."

Barbara his Tom's secretary, slightly heavy set forty year old Native American woman, married to a good loving Native American husband who drops her and picks her from work everyday.

Terrence is a computer genius, almost thirty, about five foot five, slim gay man, very loyal to his work. He likes Tom a lot because Tom Pollack is a real man, married with a daughter and a son.

Whenever Tom and Terrence are in the same room Barbara enjoys their humor. So today Tom is sitting in his usual chair, Barbara walks in first and says,

"Good evening Mr. Pollack, how did it go at the senator's house."

"Barbara sit down", and she does, "I had to break the news to him. The DNA matched his wife perfectly. He was already heartbroken, and the news about the DNA match did not help much. We can discuss this later." By this time Terrence walks in.

"Yes Mr. Pollack." Tom replies,

"I want you to drop everything." Before Tom can continue Terrence responds,

"Looks like you are in a good mood today, I thought you would never ask" and starts to unbutton his shirt. Tom gets a little irritated,

"What the hell are you talking about, I did not ask you to take your clothes off?"

"But Tom, that is what you just said. I have to obey your orders."

Barbara looks at Tom and smiles. Tom gets serious and says,

"Look Terrence I hired you for your technical skills, and not to make advances at me, besides I am not the kind of man you are looking for."

"Yes you are" replies Terrence, "You are the only real man here I fancy. How come you have not adjusted to this modern world?" Tom is really irritated,

"I am not the man you are looking for, I like a woman's skin. Stop eyeing me and find somebody like yourself. Now before I get angry please take this DVD print the pictures and make sure you don't damage the original as there is a lot of evidence on it." Tom hands him the DVD, as Terrence is leaving he says,

"There is no difference; it is only in your mind", and walks out of the cubicle with a gay walk. Terrence steps back into the cubicle and smiles,

"How desperate are you for this Tom."

"Desperate for what", getting more irritated. All this while Barbara enjoying the back and forth between Tom and Terrence.

Barbara teases Tom,

"I think that man really loves you, ever since you hired him he has his eyes on you."

"Please Barbara, not you too, I need to get to the bottom of this case, you know I get more love in my office, than I get at my home. When I get home I get more lectures than love. Here I can give orders and I get the love that I don't want. Can you please call the Attorney General, I need to talk to him personally, and you know how important this is."

"Yes I know Tom, I will call him, remember he gave us a very hard time on your last case because you are his political opponent."

"I don't think he is going to do that this time, because he and his party know that this time they are going to loose to Mr. Monroe, who is surely going to be our next president. He is afraid that a lot of people will think they had something to do with this, so he is going to help me all the way; and Barbara if the reporters or anybody else calls, please tell them I will call them back. I need to get to the bottom of this case and find the killers and the other twin."

Barbara is a little curious and asks Tom,

"You were at the senator's house, what kind of information did he give you, do you know which twin was killed?"

"Barbara while I was there I received a call from the DNA lab, it is Mrs. Monroe that died."

"Tom, how do you know it was Mrs. Monroe that died, what if both the twins have the same DNA, what are you going to do, how are you going to file murder charges against the other twin, she might very well be our next first lady?" Looks like you are going to be tested in this case, with your brain and your willpower."

"Yes Barbara this is a big one, the big heads from Washington are going to be involved. If the twin is Mrs. Monroe I will be on her side all the way. I am not going to back off under pressure from anybody. You know Barbara, Father John was saying the same thing about the DNA. He said nobody in the world can tell the difference between the two twins other than their parents and himself. I should probably invite him to watch this DVD with me and he could help me identify the twins. Let me call him." Tom dials the Father's phone number – when the Father picks up the phone Tom asks him,

"Father John, can you come over to the station, I want you to watch the DVD with me and help me identify the dead twin."

"OK, I will be there in fifteen minutes" replies Father John and hangs up. Tom asks Barbara,

"Can you let your husband know you will be an hour late?"

"Let him come in Tom and watch the DVD too, he is already on his way. Plus this way he can meet you and not accuse me of having an affair with you. This way he will get to know you better"

"Yes Barbara, it is a good idea, you know if you are married to a good looking person, the other spouse is always jealous. Don't want to loose a good looking spouse."

"Yes Tom you are right, so you think I am good looking."

"Of course you are, that is why Steve is jealous" replies Tom, and Terrence walks into the office and stands in front of Tom and drops an envelop with a bang on the table and says,

"This is the last time I am going to help you, I am never appreciated for what I do for you, from now on you are on your own." Tom opens the envelop and responds to Terrence,

"What did I do to upset you, I need one more favor."

"Tom you upset me everyday. I have been inviting you for dinner over at my place for six months and you keep make excuses that you are very busy solving this or that murder case, and now you are going to be busy with the twin's murder." Barbara looks at Tom's face for his reaction. Tom gently replies,

"OK Terrence, I promise I will come over to your house for dinner, now please set up the DVD in your cubicle, I want to watch the entire DVD. Now I am not sure what I am going to tell my wife about dinner."

"You can tell her there is another murder that needs your attention, you real men are such good liars, plus she will never leave you; she knows she will not find another man like you." Tom's radio goes off, he presses the speaker button "Yes" and the voice at the other end says,

"Mr. Pollack, Barbara's husband is here, shall I let him in."

"Yes" says Tom.

"Do you want me to search him, before I let him in? You know he does not like you."

"Who told you that" asks Tom.

"Barbara told me" says the voice on the radio. Tom looks at Barbara funnily; Barbara has also heard the conversation on the phone,

"Oh really" as tom looks at Barbra with surprise,

"Mr. Pollack Father John is here too."

"I will come and get them" Tom says and gets up, as he is leaving his office he looks at Barbra again, "Barbara already told me."

Tom walks up to the front and finds Father John and Steve standing, he shakes Steve's hand, "Nice to meet you Steve and thank you Father for coming over."

"Nice meeting you Mr. Polack." Steve follows the other two. When they reach Tom's office Tom sticks his head in and says,

"Let's go Sister Barbara" and keeps walking towards Terrence's cubicle. Barbara rushes out to follow them, Steve slows down as Tom and the Father step into Terrence's cubicle and stops Barbara and plants a kiss, "Honey I am sorry for accusing you and Tom for you know what. Looks like he is a real gentleman and even calls you sister.

"Now you know." "Don't worry we can talk about it later" and they both walk into the cubicle. They all pull the chairs and sit down to watch the Twin's last moments.

"Is it ready" asks Tom.

"I am always ready" says Terrence in his gay voice.

"I mean is the DVD ready to play." Barbara and Steve look at Tom, they knows what Terrence meant.

"Yes" Terrence replies and turns the TV on and plays the DVD. After watching the DVD for an hour, they play it again and again, and sometimes in slow motion, Tom asks everybody in the cubicle,

"Well, can anybody identify the twins?" They all shake their heads in silence. Finally Father John responds,

"The video is not enough, I want to see more. The twins do have a different walk, and somebody who has lived with them or knows them very well can tell. After their parents died I am the only one who can tell the difference?"

"Father I believe you, when the twin that is alive is apprehended, though she might have been forcibly abducted, the prosecutor may call it self kidnapping, plus since one of the twins is dead how are you going to compare their walks. The prosecutors will not believe you as a credible witness. Father I am puzzled too, even if we capture the other twin alive and she claims that she is Mrs. Monroe, only if her DNA does not match. She will be prosecuted. Mr. Monroe will not defend her either, he is going to trust the DNA like he already mentioned today."

Father John replies,

"I feel sorry for the twins, one is dead, and the other one, though she might be innocent will be in a lot of trouble. She was looking for a fresh start and now she may be accused of being an accessory to murder. To me it appears that they wanted her back and they took her against her will. The crooks ended up killing these innocent people including one of the twins. If the twin is caught alive, how she going to prove her innocence?"

"That is what I would like to know too" says Tom.

Father John replies, "Tom, she confessed to me that she had made a lot of mistakes, but now she wanted to marry and settle down, I suspect the younger twin had nothing to with all this, regardless which twin it is, she is going through hell. If Mrs. Monroe is alive, the lord is going to help her, as she has never done anything against God's will." Father John continues,

"I have known you and your family for a few years, you are a good guy, you have also known Mr. Monroe's family for a long time, if you establish that it is indeed Mrs. Monroe that is alive, and will you defend her in the name of God?"

"Yes father, I will do everything in my power to help the senator and his wife", and then Tom turns to Barbara, "What is your opinion."

"I don't know Tom, I feel sorry for the senator and his family. It is the twins who are the losers in this situation." Barbra Looks at Steve and says, "Honey, what do you think?"

"I cannot figure this case out; it is too complicated for me, I don't have the brain power. I am sure Tom will get to the bottom of this"

Terrence "Is there anything else you need Mr. Pollack." Tom replies,

"No, I don't. Thank you. Just give me the DVD." Terrence takes the DVD out and gives it back to Tom.

"OK Tom, we are leaving, he is taking me out" Barbara says to Tom. "Good to meet you Steve." Tom shakes Steve's hand and as Tom is getting ready to leave, Terrence says to Tom,

"I am leaving too, don't forget dinner." Barbara starts giggling; Steve is curious and asks her why she is giggling. I will tell you on the way out, and they start walking out of the office,

"Do you really want to know Steve; Terrence has a crush on Tom and he has been after Tom to go to his house for a candle light dinner ever since he got this job."

Steve is shocked and says, "I knew there was something wrong with that kid."

"He is no kid he is nearly thirty."

Steve says "He looks a lot younger." They hear footsteps behind them and hear Terrence saying to Steve,

"Wait for me" As Terrence comes next to Steve and says How come you didn't shake hands with me Steve?"

"Oh I am sorry we can do it now." Terrence shakes Steve's hand.

"Would you like to have dinner with me one night when you are free?"

"Sure, I would love to; I will have to get Barbara's permission. If she says OK then no problem." Steve says with a smile and looks at Barbara.

"Steve do you know any single men."

"I know plenty of single men, what did you have in mind?"

Terrence says "At this moment anybody will do"

"OK I will keep that in mind, we have to go now Terrence" Steve and Barbara exit the door leaving Terrence standing there.

As they step out Barbara tells Steve, "If you had stayed one more minute Terrence would be kissing you."

"Is he that desperate?" Barbara says "Yes".

As Terrence is standing in the hallway Tom add the Father come out of the room talking to each other and see Terrence standing.

Tom looks at him and asks, "I thought you were gone."

"I have nobody to go to" replies Terrence.

Father John has realized that Terrence is gay and suggests,

"may be you should come to church on Sundays and join the other families, you will find peace if you pray to the Lord."

"Yes father I believe you, I have money but no peace" Terrence replies broken hearted. "I need company, I want to be loved, and nobody loves me."

"Yes young man the Lord loves you, that is why you are here, probably your ties with your family are different. Come to church on Sunday and come and see me I will introduce you to some nice people."

"OK Father, I will come by on Sunday. Tom I will see you in the morning" and Terrence leaves.

"Good night Terrence. Let's go Father I will see you to your car." They walk to Father John's car.

"Goodnight", Tom goes to his car and drives home.

While he is in the car it still bugs him, how is he going to solve this case.

It is almost 7:00 PM and getting dark at the senators house. Senior Mrs. Monroe, and her son-in-law and the senator's children all gather around the big dinning table. The senator is still sitting in the library in his rocking chair looking at the picture of his wife and kids on the table. He is in a somber mood wondering, why all this had happened, and for what, and who did this and his mother comes in and stands next to him.

"Son come and join us at the dinning table, you have not eaten a proper meal since lunch on Sunday." She puts her hand under his right upper arm, "get up please, I cannot watch you burn up inside like this". But the senator does not move.

"Mother, I am not hungry. I will eat when I am hungry. Please, I want to be left alone, I will join you guys later."

The mother does not take no for an answer, "Please get up and join us."

The senator look at his mother's face and relents,

"OK let's go", he gets up walks with his mother to the dinning table, he refuses to sit in his usual chair which used to be next to his wife's chair, and decides to sit next to his brother-in-law. Everybody looks at him, but nobody says anything. The mother sits between her grand children and pours a glass of red wine for her son.

"Frank please have this wine, I know you did not get any sleep last night, I could hear your footsteps all night. Finish the wine and we will wait until you are ready to eat. I want to make sure you eat something tonight."

The senator puts the glass of wine in front of him.

The mood is very somber; the rest of the family discussed the twins and finally go to sleep.

It is Tuesday, the family wakes up at the usual time, and they freshen up and have breakfast prepared by Mrs. Jones and her assistant.

It is now 10:30 the door bell rings, Mrs. Jones opens the door, and there are two gentlemen with bowler hats standing outside.

"We are from the Funeral Home, we are the family undertakers, is the senator home".

"Yes he is home, please come in gentlemen." Mrs. Jones shows them to the guest room. "I will let the senator know you are here, please make yourselves comfortable. Can I get you anything?"

"No Mrs. Jones we are fine, Thank you." Mrs. Jones leaves the room.

The senator walks in after a few minutes, the older undertaker gets up and offers his condolences to the senator,

"Mr. Monroe we are very sorry for your loss, Mrs. Monroe was such a charming lady it is difficult to believe she is gone.

The younger one says,

"Mr. Monroe we received a call from the hospital we need your signature for permission to get the body released." He hands over the paper work, the senator reads it and signs the papers and hands it back.

"Is there anything else you need?" asks senator The younger gentleman replies,

"When would you like to have the funeral senator?"

"I need to get over this, let's do it on Friday, is that OK?"

"Yes senator Friday at 11:00 AM it is". The senator shakes hands with the two gentlemen, the two say goodbye and leave. The senator closes the door

Both of them walk towards the car and the older gentleman remarks in a rather mean spirit,

"You know this family has not had a funeral in twenty years."

The other gentleman is aghast,

"What a mean thing to say, it seems you rejoice when someone dies."

"No it is not like that, everybody has to die some day, it is not enough to do your job with a smile; we have to make money too. Not that this family has ever complained about the bill." They both get into the car and as the younger man starts to drive he looks at his companion with disgust,

"The more I know you the more I dislike you."

"Maybe you should start thinking of your own funeral and start saving, way things are going I will probably be your undertaker." says the older man.

"So you think I will die before you, you are twenty years older than me, may be it is you who should be saving money first"

"Looks like the job is getting to you, you have lost your sense of humor. You cannot take this job seriously. Do you have nightmares where dead people come into your house and dance and drink with you? Then they want to take you with them and you wake up sweating." Older man says. Their car leaves the gate and turns into the main road, the driver tells the other guy,

"No that has not happened to me yet, has it happened to you" As their car is out of senator's gate, the older man starts laughing loud as he can for at least more than a minute, and he is getting on younger man's nerves, After quieting down he replies "Yes, several times." They drive back to the funeral home.

Far away the twin who is locked up in the room, it is midday, and she is wondering what is going to happen to her. Lots of thoughts go through her head. She hears a knock on the door, sees Number Two opening the door. He has brought food in a bag. The black guy stands guard at the door. Number Two walks towards the twin who is sitting on the bed and hands her the food. The twin,

"Look I can't eat this every day; I am not used to this kind of food. I am not sure how long you intend to keep me here but I need fresh set of clothes." She picks up the TV remote and turns the TV on. Number Two replies,

"I don't know who you are; the twin who used to stay here always ate out. This is her room and everything here belongs to her. But if you can cook make me a list and I will bring you the groceries. I hope you are not pretending to be other twin. Maybe if you stick to this story Randy might let you go. He won't let you go if he does not get his money, which seems unlikely at this point."

The black guy says. "You mean you are going shopping for her?

Well I want to find out if she can cook, and maybe I will eat some home food after a long time."

While they are talking Jody is on the TV live.

"We have some breaking news, we are in front of the police station, and the detective tom Pollack will come out shortly and make an announcement about Mrs. Monroe murder case. We are told that he will be giving us an update regarding the investigation, he may have something new."

It is 12:15; Tom Pollack comes out of the door with some papers. He comes down a couple of steps and the reporters swarm him. Jody pushes and shoves her way all the way to the front and her cameraman points his camera at Tom. The reporters start hurling questions at Tom all at the same time. Tom raises his hand and requests the gathered reporters,

"Please, one at a time. Let me tell you what I know; we received the DNA report from the lab at 11:30 AM today, it is confirmed that it was indeed Mrs. Monroe that died. This is all I can tell you at this time." Jody fires away,

"Do you have any news about the other twin or her friends?"

"I don't know any thing about the other twin, all I know is that when we went to the senator's house we found his wife and three others shot. We are investigating, like I mentioned earlier, this is all I can tell you for now."

The twin, Number Two and the black guy are watching TV; the black guy takes out his phone out of his pocket and calls randy,

"Boss where are you?"

Randy "I am sitting in the bar with the police chief."

"Turn the TV on there is some shocking news"

Randy turns to the barman and asks him to the TV on, and turn up the volume. They watch **Tom** on live TV.

The twin looks at Number Two and says,

"How can this be possible, I am the senator's wife, it is my sister that was killed? How can her DNA match mine? This is impossible; this means that I could be arrested for my own murder." Her eyes are filled with tears as she tries to control her emotions, both the men in her room lock the door and leave. They walk downstairs and join the rest of the gang. They watch the report on TV as Tom tries to limit the information he gives out and tries to get rid of the reporters.

"Please, that is all I have. If anything else comes up I will let you know. Thank You."

Jody faces the camera, "This is Jody live from the police station, and we have some crime experts who maybe able to shed more light regarding this case, back to you in the studio."

As the twin watches the report on TV, downstairs in the bar all five men quietly listen to Tom and Jody on TV. The crime and DNA experts provide their views regarding the case.

The police chief turns to Randy, who is watching the news too,

"If detective Tom Pollack is personally handling the case you better find a good place to hide."

Randy asks, "Why?"

"Tom is the number one detective in the country, he will find you, it may take him a little while, but ultimately he is going to catch you. All the impossible cases that others are not able to solve, he cracks it."

"But how can he find us?" looks at the other three, "Did you leave any finger prints behind?"

"No we did not touch anything, we even ripped the cameras off the gate and took the film with us, I don't think we left any evidence behind," says Number One.

"You may not have left any evidence behind. But he will still find you." says the chief.

Randy "Ok, if he does we have you and your fellow cops right?"

"I don't know, this may be too big for me to handle, you killed the next president's wife, and the senator will do everything in his power to get to the bottom of this case.

"I know, let's see what happens in the next few days, if things start getting too hot we can sell this place to the Chinese mafia, if they make me a good offer. These guys are getting stronger by the day and vicious. Maybe it is time for me to quit and settle down in some far away place out of the country."

"Don't forget us Randy" the other three say together.

"I won't let you down; I will take care of you guys. I will go down to the bank next week and withdraw a couple of million from the bank on this property."

"Don't forget me, you can't leave town without Me." chief says

Randy "I know, let's enjoy ourselves, bartender please bring the drinks for everybody and also a pie for the chief."

"The pie takes too long, seriously, tell me something Randy, the detective said he has very little information, he is lying, and he is up to something."

"Chief, can the twins have the same DNA?"

"It is very unlikely, but one never knows, I am not God. Look even if you assume that the woman upstairs is the slut, she along with the cool guy probably dropped off the money at the senator's house; forget it you can't go there to get the money."

"Chief can you give us an advance warning if either the FBI or Tom are getting to close so that we can skip the country?"

"Sure, I will let you know. I owe you that much. You took care of my wife, she stopped bitching me. You know she almost had me locked up for getting drunk?"

Randy "Well some women are like that, they like to control their husbands, actually they can't control themselves."

While the entire gang is drinking in the bar, the woman upstairs is watching the same news playing over and over again. She only eats some of the food that was brought to her, after learning from the gangsters that this was her twin's room, she start going through her things one by one. She spends the next couple of hours looking at her twin's stuff and comes across a picture of herself and her sister along with their parents. Both sisters are sitting on their parents laps. She picks up the picture and carries it to the bed and looks at it again and again trying to remember when the picture was taken. She finally flips the picture on to the back and at the top she finds a note written by her father. It says "To my wife and daughters, Oct 15, 1975." Underneath that she finds another note written in her sister's handwriting,

"I miss my parents and my sister; I hope mom is still alive. I want to go home; I hope she will forgive me. I know I gave my mom a very hard time. Mom I love you and I want to come back home." signed Cassandra august 2008.

As she read that she becomes teary, she holds up the picture to her chest and says, "We loved you and missed you a lot and now I have lost you forever." The twin sits on the bed crying feeling helpless because she cannot get out.

The gang along with the chief are still in the bar enjoying their drinks as they plan their next move.

Number Two says "Boss, the woman upstairs wants some groceries, so that she can cook; she hates the food we give her. I would like to try her food; I have not had good home made food in a long time since I left home."

"So you feel sorry for her just like the cool guy and you want to buy her groceries. Are you out of your mind, you will ruin us, what if she escapes while you are delivering groceries to her? "Randy replies,

"Don't get me wrong, you can't hold her here forever, you can't let her go either, we are all in a lot of trouble, what is your plan?"

Randy turns to the chief, "What if we can get one of the doctors to give her drugs so that she looses her memory, we can drop her off a few hundred miles away from here in a big city. She won't remember anything about us."

"Sure you can do that, memories do come back you know, after the drug wears out. Randy you should get out of this business before all hell breaks loose. If you are not apprehended by the FBI, the Chinese mafia will surely get you, they are getting very strong. They offered you thirty million dollars about half of what your property is worth; take it because it will be worth nothing if they kill you." chief said

"Yes chief you are right."

"Randy, take the thirty million, give me one million, a million each for your boys here and a hundred thousand each to my guys for protecting you. They have been doing this for a long time and deserve something too. You will stand to net twenty five million in cash, you need about half a million to get a Canadian green card or you could go to Mexico and open a business there." The boys are happy, Number Two very excitedly says,

"I like the chief's idea, give me some money and I will get the groceries for the slut." He starts laughing, the black guy and Number One smile,

"Randy the chief is right we don't have the manpower to run this place anymore, plus we are also getting old" says Number One.

"Yes I have been thinking too, give me a day or two, we will do as the chief suggested." Randy turns to the chief and says,

"Can you arrange a meeting with the Chinese? Let's find out if we can get more than thirty million."

"I will call him in the evening; he generally does not answer his phone or see anybody during the day. He likes the dark; he seems to feel safe in the dark. Would you like to meet him tonight or tomorrow?" chief suggested.

"Let's do it tomorrow at 8:00 PM. If we talk to him today he will think we are desperate." Randy says

"OK Randy, I will fix it for tomorrow, but your sharp shooter is dead, you need to have somebody like him to accompany us."

"I know these guys are too slow" pointing to his own gangsters, you should probably bring some of your cops. Randy asks"

"I can do that but you will need to pay them a grand each." asks chief

"OK I can take care of that." Randy said

The chief replies, "I will fix it for you, how about more drinks" pointing to the bartender. "I will have the same again" as he is finishing up the pie. "Randy, this guy makes a pretty good pie." They all continue talking.

At the senator's house there is no change. Relatives and friends visit, everybody is saddened by the whole situation. This night is like the previous three nights.

Tom Pollack is sitting in his office looking at the pictures of gangsters on his computer wondering how he was going to find the killers, will he be able to apprehend them alive.

Barbara who is sitting in her cubicle receives a phone call, "I need to speak to Tom Pollack please." Barbara asks him "Who is calling."

"I can't tell you yet", Barbara replies, He is busy is there anything I can help you with."

"No it has to be him, it is very important."

Barbara "If you tell me what that is. I will fetch him."

Tom is listening to this conversation through the opening between the two cubicles. He looks away from the computer screen and turns his face in Barbara's direction and gestures to find out what is going on. Barbara puts her finger on her lips to tell him to be quiet and presses the speaker button. The caller says,

"Tom must be nearby; while you were talking to me, you had put me on speaker phone."

"No, I am sorry I hit the speaker phone by mistake." Tom appreciated Barbara's quick turn around.

The caller says, "I am in the same game, turn that speakerphone off and I will tell you why I am calling." Tom signs to Barbara to turn the speaker off.

"OK now the speaker is off, tell me who are you and what do you want?"

"I don't want anything; I think Tom want to know where the slut and the gang are." caller says. Barbara stands up and gestures Tom to pick up the phone,

"Ok, here he is, he will take the call." Tom signs Barbara to trace the call, and answers the phone,

"Hello, this is Tom, how can I help you?

"Do you want to know where the slut and killers are?" caller says

"Yes I do, but first tell me who you are." tom gets more anxious.

"I will call you tomorrow, but I need assurances from you that I will get a million dollar reward offered by the senators Party."

Tom responds "I will make my recommendations if the murderers are caught alive"

"That is not my concern, all I want is the million dollars, and otherwise I will hang up. You cannot trace this call; you might as well tell your secretary to stop wasting her time. Has anybody else called in leads before me?" caller Threaten

Tom says, "No you are the first one."

"That is why God rewards you with success because you are truthful Mr. Pollack. Give me a little more time and I will call you back."

"No, No, please don't hang up, If you are telling the truth I will make sure you get your million, and I stand by my word, just lead me to these people. If your lead takes me to the killers and the twin. Even if I have to pay from my own pocket I will give it to you."

The caller, "Are you willing to fly over here to meet with me, I have some legal papers for you to sign, then I will tell you where they are, you maybe able to pick them up live."

"Sure I am willing to sign, I have given you my word it carries more weight than any legal paper. By the way where are you?" tom said

"Mr. Pollack I will tell you everything. Come to the airport and I will take you to their hideout. You may have to disguise yourself, you are too recognizable here. You can't put their faces on the TV or internet either, because as soon as they see that, they will all go into hiding. Even if you find them they may not be alive."

"Caller you are right, call me on my cell phone, no, call me on my direct line" he gives the caller his number.

Caller "I will call you tomorrow in the afternoon"

"You are not going to let me down right? I am counting on you to apprehend the killers alive."OK tom says

"No I am not going to let you down, I want to collect the million dollars. Even after taxes I will be left with 60%, which is enough to pay off my house and other debts, and send my two kids to college. I will talk to you tomorrow" the caller hangs up.

Tom puts the phone down and turns to Barbara to ask if they could trace the call. Barbara answers in the negative, "The call was blocked in such a way we could not trace it."

"Barbara you heard the whole thing, it appears to me that the caller maybe a cop, he knows everything. After he saw me on TV he decided to get the million and save his own skin."

Tom stands near the window between the two cubicles thinking and he looks over in Barbara's direction,

'What is going on, maybe it is just the million, and it probably means a lot to the caller."

Barbara smiles, "Tom wouldn't you like to have a million too, legally and with no risk. My husband would. Now that he has met you he is no longer jealous, and he even said last night that he wished he could find the killers and collect on the million and make me happy."

"No I don't care for the money; you can only eat two meals a day, I will be satisfied if I have a small car, a small house and a couple of kids. I hope the caller comes through." Tom cannot shake the thought of the senator's situation from his head; the thought keeps going through his head again and again.

"But, Tom, when do you make your wife happy? Most of the time you are stuck with murder cases other people cannot solve. Do you really love your wife?" says Barbara.

"Oh, yes. I love her dearly. She says I got a wrong job and if somebody murders her, I would never investigate. But, every time I want to spend time with her and the kids, some thing comes up and I have to be there. Like this time with the murder at the Senator's house."

123

"Yes, I know Tom. But, your family needs you first."

"I know Barbara. After this case I am going to drive a taxi. Taxi drivers seem to have a lot of time to spare." Tom says.

And Barbara laughs and says "I would love to see you as a cabby. Pick me and my hubby up and we will have a good laugh." The phone rings and Barbara answers the phone in Tom Pollack's office.

"Honey, it is me, your husband. What time shall I pick you up?" he asks

"5:00pm like usual" she replies.

"Why, you have no work today after five?" he asks

"No" Barbara says.

"Good, I'll be there at sharp five. I need you."

She smiles and says ok and hangs up.

"Barbara, see if you can get hold of the Attorney General and put him on the speaker phone" says Tom and goes back to his chair.

Barbara calls the hot line to the Attorney General's office and his secretary answers the phone,

"Attorney General's office, may I help you?"

"This is Tom Pollack's secretary. Tom needs to talk to your boss about the Senator's wife's murder case".

"Oh, that famous cop who had some harsh words with me last time when he was on his last murder case?"

Tom is listening on the speaker phone and Barbara replies to her,

"That is because you guys never cooperated with Tom".

Then Tom intervenes "You people at the top don't really care about people in the lower level"

"Yes, I knew you were going to say something like that. I heard that you are really a man who wants to have it your way. But, right now I am not going to have any more conversation with you. I'll tell the Attorney General to call you. Give me your phone number again."

"You have it in your personal file already. Now, if he does not call me today, I'll go to the Supreme Court or House Majority Leader or to the White House and have it my way. I want to catch these killers" Tom tells her is a little aggressive way.

"Yes, I got your message, Mr. Pollack. My boss will get this within ten minutes where ever he is in the world. Is there anything else on your mind Mr. Pollack?"

"No, I am fine. I am going home. My wife and children are waiting for me. From now on, if Barbara calls, it is for a genuine reason and it is for me."

And they hand up the phone and Barbara starts laughing and says

"You know, Tom, people in power have no sympathy for anybody."

"Yes, I know" Before he says anything else, the phone rings again and Barbara answers while standing up. She presses the speaker button "Tom Pollack's office, may I help you?"

"Yes, you can" says the voice angry. "Where is that good for nothing Tom?"

"He is here" says Barbara.

"Are you sitting in his lap? Get off his lap and let me talk to him?"

"No, Mrs. Pollack, he is standing next to me in his office. And I only sit in my husband's lap"

"Oh, you do? Then why are you working for him?

Then Tom intervenes,

"Honey, what upset you today? You were in a good mood earlier. I am coming home soon. Tell me what happened?" says Tom on the speaker phone. Barbara is listening and she knows this happens often.

"Tell you what happened? These two kids of yours were fine until they needed their favorite food. Once they had that, they are making my life hell."

"But, honey, they are our kids, not just mine. I'll tell them to apologize when I get home" says Tom to his wife.

"Yes, I have heard that before. By the time you are ready to come home, there will be another murder and you won't come home."

"Honey, don't wish for that. We humans should not think like that, even though we all have to die one day."

"Yes, I know your positive logic. But if somebody killed me, you would not care, would you?" Tom's wife asks

"No, honey you are well protected. You know how much I love you. I'll be home in half an hour."

"Yes, just like I said, you will be home if there is no more murder of somebody important by that time."

"Ok honey, love you and see you in a bit."

On Wednesday morning, Tom comes to his office, sits on his chair and looks at the phone wondering if that caller is going to call or if he is a fake just after the reward. Then he says to himself that if he doesn't catch the twin and the gang, then he is not going to get the reward as the day is passing by.

At Randy's Bar, it is lunch as usual, with the Chief and the boys enjoying themselves. And the twin is upstairs watching TV with nothing else to do, just praying to God every now and then wondering if she would be let out alive or dead and the time is passing slowly.

It is just after 3 PM when Paul, the taxi driver, is driving around town picking his fares. At about 3:10 PM, he is passing the bus stand looking for a fare, but is disappointed when he doesn't find anyone and keeps on driving at the speed limit. He goes another couple of miles, a woman, about thirty, light color skin, wearing black skirt just below her knees and white blouse with a red hand bag flags down Paul's taxi. He stops his van and opens the passenger side window,

"Hi, where do you want to go?"

She leans in the window, having a full size well built body, wearing half moon shaped blouse. He first looks at her chest and quickly makes eye contact, and she hands him a paper with an address on it. He looks at the paper and tells her,

"It will be about forty five to fifty dollars."

"Ok, can you take me?" the woman says.

"Yeah, I'll take you. Do you have the money?" Paul ask

"Of course, I do have the money" she says.

"Ok get in the middle please" Paul tells her. The customer opens the middle door and she sits behind the taxi driver on the right side.

"Hi Mister, how are you? What is your name?" the female passenger asks.

"Hi, my name is Paul. I am fine. How about you? How is your day going?

"It is going ok. Now, it is even better. You seem to be a nice cabby. Most cabbies want to take money up front" she says in a nice way.

"Yeah, we can't take any risk. Some people don't pay. That is why."

As the taxi starts cruising at normal speed, the woman starts getting little friendly.

"Hey, Mr. Paul, are you married?"

"Yes, but not very happily these days. Too many arguments says Paul

"That is why I don't get married. At least, I don't have to answer to anybody when I get home" she says.

"Yes, you are right. In this country, it is difficult to be married, too many problems."

As the taxi goes along the highway, the passenger spots a big board on the right hand side which says "Frank Monroe's Estate – 15 miles on the right."

As soon as she sees that, she gets a little excited and as the taxi passes by the picture of Frank Monroe, the Senator, she says,

"Hey Paul, Is this the Senator in the news for the last 3 days? You know, I did not get the full news, but from what I heard, his wife's long lost twin came home, then one of the twins is dead and the other one is missing. I mean you taxi drivers know a lot, picking up international people."

As Paul passes the sign of the Senator's estate, he thinks to himself that he should not say anything, about him being the one who dropped one of the twins at the Senator's house. He listens to what the passenger has to say and then lies,

"I don't know what happened, I've been listening to the news for the last 3 days on the radio and TV and reading newspaper, but nobody knows anything yet. It seems that one of twins came to the Senator's house after a long time" says Paul.

"But why would a sister want to kill her own sister?" says the passenger.

"For the money. Money is the root of all evils" says Paul.

"But, if she killed her sister, then why did she not stay and pretend to be the other twin and Senator's wife. Nobody could tell them apart. She could have enjoyed his money and power" she says.

"I don't know why. But, I like to mind my own business. Sticking your nose in to something is not good these days. Police have too much power, plus I am afraid of the law. Anyway, let us change the subject" the driver says to her.

"No, Paul, tell me more. I heard the Senator's wife was very nice and that he really loved her."

Thinking to himself that he doesn't want to say anything about having been to their house and being cautious in case something slips out of his mouth, Paul again tells her to change the subject.

"Why do you want to know about something you are not related to?" says Paul.

She says "This is very interesting story, which is why." As the cab passed the Senator's gate, Paul slows down his cab and looks in to the gate. He sees two policemen guarding the gate and the gates are closed. After passing the Senator's gate, Paul gasses up his cab again and does not say anything for a little while. He remembers dropping the twin off there about ten days ago and seeing both the twins meeting and hugging each other while he waited there looking at them and wondering if somebody would love him the same way. But that is fate. Just a few days later, he had heard the bad news. But, he keeps his mouth shut and makes sure he does not get in any legal trouble.

"Hey Mister, why have gone quiet? Tell me more. I heard the Senator is a very good man and that he is going to be the next President. Are you going to vote for him?" she asks.

"Yes, I am" Paul says just to make the passenger happy. "Anyways, we are fifteen minutes from your destination. Show me the money" and he looks at the passenger.

"I don't have any money" she tells him.

"You told me that you have money" says Paul as his blood pressure goes up and he slows down to pull up to the right side of the road and comes to a full stop. He puts the lever in park and turns to face her,

"Why did you lie to me that you have money?" he says in an angry voice.

"Hey Paul" she says in a sexy voice, "I am sure I am worth more that that thirty dollars on that meter. I mean, look at me, don't you like me? I am sure I can make your day worth while."

"What are you – a hooker or something?" says Paul.

"No, I am not a hooker. I am short of money for the time being. Oh, come on Paul, I am sure you like my younger skin. I bet your wife has alligator skin. I know middle age men and women like younger ones" and she comes close to him from the middle seat. "May be, you want a closer look at me. I hope your sight is not weak."

"Yeah, my sight is not weak. You do seem to have nice skin and a good body. We older men like looking at younger skin". He melts down very quickly and says "Also, I am not getting any love at home."

"I am sure you are a real man. When a real man sees a real woman, then both can be happy" she says.

"Yes, I am a real man. I like a woman's skin. It is good that God created a woman for a man and vice versa.

"Hey Mr. Paul" she says again in a really sexy voice "is your wife making you happy at home?"

"Look, don't worry about my wife. I need to try something different. Tell me how you are going to make me happy."

"Any way you want Mr. Paul"

"Ok, let find some quiet place" he gets a little excited and drives off hoping that he will get something from this woman. He drives away cruising along the same highway.

He has been driving taxi for a few years and he knows most of streets. He keeps driving about five more minutes and he sees a street on the right. He slows down and makes a right turn and sees a sign that says "No through street". After about half a block, he sees some space on the right side. He backs his van in that space and turns off his van. He takes the key out and puts his cell phone in his upper money pocket. He is about to open the drivers door when she says

"So, this the quiet place. I suppose nobody comes in this street. Is this where you bring your lady friends?" woman asks

"No, you are the first one" Paul says to her. As he is getting out of his taxi, he says "Let me take a leak, I'll join you in the back seat."

He goes to the back of the van and stands there peeing. He looks around and there are only trees and grass, nothing else. When he is done, and looks to two yards in front of him. In the ground he sees a human hand lying there. He goes to have a closer look and it is a real hand!! Then, he sees part of the wrist in the grass which is about two feet tall. He panics and takes out his cell phone from his pocket and dials 911.

Operator says "911. Is this an emergency?"

"Yes, it is" he says.

"Your name please and what is the emergency?" says the operator.

"My name is Paul and I drive for This Cab Company. I stopped here to go to the bathroom and I think there is a dead body. I can only see a hand, but I can't see the rest of the body."

"Don't touch anything. Where are you? Just stay put. I will send the cops in two minutes" the operator says.

"Let me tell you where I am. If you go past Senator Monroe's estate, stay on the same highway, after 8 miles you'll see a sign called Last Lane. Turn right, come one block, I'll be standing there in a yellow van."

Paul finishes his phone call with the police and walks back to his driver's door and open it. He sees his cab meter is turned off.

"Why did you turn that meter off?" Paul says to the female passenger.

"Oh, you want me pay both ways – money and please you? I don't think so. You can have one or the other" she says in anger.

"No, I don't think I want either. I just called the police. There is a dead body behind the van. Looks like I am not going to get anything. I have never been lucky in love or lust."

While they are talking, one police car pulls up, and then another one. Two male and two female officers come out of the cars. One of the cops comes over to Paul as he is standing next to the driver's door.

"Did you call the police?"

"Yes, I did" Paul says

"Let me have you id" says the cop.

"Don't you want to see what is out there" says Paul

"No, give me your license". Paul takes his wallet out of his pocket and gives license to the cop. By that time, the female cop comes close to them and the male cop hands the license to her.

"Run this through. He reported a dead body. Run his whole life through" the cop tells his female colleague.

Paul is surprised to hear what the cop said and he says to the cop,

"You know I only stopped here for a leak. When I saw that hand, I called you guys. Did I do anything wrong?"

"There is a dead body out here. What are you doing here with a young female with the meter off?" the cop asks.

"Officer, she turned it off while I was taking a leak. I have to do that every hour or so."

By that time, the other male and female cops walk over while the other female cop goes to her car to check on Paul.

With the taxi driver's door open, the female cop who had just walked over, puts her head in the driver's door to look at the passenger and says,

"This is a hooker. I arrested her two weeks ago. She got out and she is doing this again."

Paul is surprised to hear her say that but controls himself not to say anything.

As the other two cops come, the one talking to Paul tells the other two,

"Go look behind the van about that hand". The other male and female cops walk behind the van and come back about 30 seconds later and tell the senior cop,

"Let me call an ambulance and murder special unit team". And he goes to his cruiser.

The cop asks Paul to open his trunk, and he walks over to the back and opens it. The cop looks in and there is nothing in the trunk. He looks thoroughly to make sure that is are no blood stains and then he walks away. Paul closes the trunk and the cop goes back to his own cruiser where the female cop was running a check on Paul. As he is stands next to his driver's window looking at the female cop, she looks from the police computer and hand back Paul's license.

"No, there is nothing on him. He is clean. His green card got renewed recently. He is ok with Homeland Security."

After taking Paul's license back, he takes his own cell phone out and is about dial a number when the ambulance pulls up. The whole team comes out of the ambulance and they ask the cop,

"Where is the body?"

He points them to the two other cops and they take the ambulance staff to the back of the taxi. When they go back there, they first see the hand. A strong male nurse bends down and pulls the hand out of the two feet tall grass. When the whole body is pulled out and turned over, the medical nurse examines the body. After some analyzing, the nurse comes to the senior cop and says,

"He has been dead for a few days. He was shot. We have to take him to where he is supposed to be – the morgue. Once we rap up, we will send you the details."

The ambulance crew starts taking pictures of the dead man and the place where they found him.

The cop goes to the other male cop and tells him

"Take full details of this cabby. I want every detail, where we can find him easily. Also, get information about the hooker. But, it is the driver we need – he is more important.

As he walks away from him to make a phone call, both the female and male cop go over to Paul and the hooker and start asking questions.

The first cop on the scene makes a call to Tom and his secretary answers the phone,

"Mr. Pollack's office"

"Let me speak to Tom Pollack. This is the Sheriff from Monroe County, 1679 Police Station".

Barbara puts him on hold and stands up and tells through the window between Tom's and her office "The sheriff wants to talk to you."

"Ask him what it is about?"

While standing, she asks the Sheriff what the call is about. He says

"We found a dead body with a gun shot, 8 miles from Senator's house. Is Tom interested?"

Barbara sighs and tells Tom to pick up the phone. Tom picks up the phone,

"Tom Pollack speaking"

"This is the Sheriff, from 1679 Police Station. Hey, I know you are a big guy, but sometime you should find time for guys like us, so we can step in to your shoes one day."

"No, no, Sheriff, it is not like that. I am waiting for a call of my life. What can I do for you?' says Tom

"We found a dead body about 8 miles from the Senator's house on the same highway. A male, shot in the chest. He looks Hispanic, 6 ft, pretty athletic. Also, found a gun next to him. Looks like he was dumped there. The other team is going to take him for examination. I will let you know."

"Thanks Sheriff. Do your regular stuff and bring me a picture of him." As Tom says that, another call comes and Barbara answers,

"Tom Pollack's office, may I help you?" As she answers she looks at the caller id, but there is no number.

"Yes, I want to talk to Mr. Pollack" says the caller. As soon as Barbara hears the familiar voice again, she quickly tells Tom to hang up and says "It is him"

Barbara then tells the caller,

"Yes, Tom Pollack is here. Let me connect you" and connects the call to Tom.

"Hello, Tom Pollack speaking"

"This is the same guy who called you yesterday" the caller says.

"Yes, I can recognize your voice" says Tom

"Ok, Mr. Pollack, let me tell you who I am. I used to be a cop, but I handed my resignation recently" says the caller.

"Let me interrupt you, if you are a cop, it is your duty to catch these murders or have them captured by law. You cannot claim that reward if you do your duty" Tom tells the caller.

"I agree with you, Mr. Pollack. I am a civilian now. But with the information I am going to tell you, you will have to move very very fast. Otherwise you will loose these killers and the twin" the caller says.

"Ok, I agree. What do you want me to do?"

"Can you get here tomorrow night?"

"What for?" asks Tom

"The club they are in, the killers and the slut, it is going to be sold tonight or tomorrow night to the Chinese gang. If you don't get here tomorrow night to see who these killers are, then by Friday or Saturday, it might be too late for you" the caller said.

"Ok, I am willing to come, but I have to be here on Friday at 11:00am for the funeral of Mrs. Monroe" says Tom.

"Well, here is the plan. You get here tomorrow evening when it is just about dark. I'll meet you at the airport. I'll pick you up, take you where the killers are and then drop you at the airport for the last flight. Go ahead and get the return ticket. Let me give you the airport name."

Tom gets a pen and paper and Tom writes the airport name and asks the caller to hold on and calls Barbara who is standing by the window between their offices and gives her the paper and says "Get me on a plane tomorrow night at six p.m. and back on the last flight at any cost. Tell the airline that it is for the Police." While the caller is listening to everything, Barbara replies,

"Yes, Mr. Pollack, I'll get you on that plane tomorrow". She goes back to her seat and starts making calls. Tom says to the caller,

"Sorry about that. Ok, go ahead, you were saying that you will pick me up. How am I going to recognize you?'

"Well, I call you Sam Denver and have that name on the cardboard when you arrive. I'll call your secretary to confirm your arrival. But, Tom, you are going to need a disguise. Do you have any?" asks the caller

"No, I don't have any, because I never needed a disguise" says Tom.

"But this time you have very little time. If you show your famous face within 5 miles of these gambling clubs and strip bars, they are going to kill you at any cost because your face was on the TV" says the caller.

"How do I know that you are not one of them?" Tom asks

"Well, then I would not be meeting you in the airport with all those cameras and security."

"Yes, you are right. I don't have any disguise. I'll meet you tomorrow. You take care of the disguise" says Tom.

"Ok, I'll take care of everything when you get here" says the caller "I will call your secretary in two hours to find out your flight time. When we get to the place, I'll introduce you to people I know as Uncle Sam Denver."

"Ok, that is good enough" says Tom. "Anyway, I'll be here till seven and it is only four now. Call us back. And I'll see your tomorrow. Thank you and bye" Tom hangs up the phone. He moves to the window between the two offices and Barbara is sitting at her desk making calls. Barbara is on the phone on hold.

"Any luck?" asks Tom. Barbara turns to Tom while on hold and says,

"No, all the airlines are busy. I am on hold with this one."

"If they give you any problem, give the phone to me and I'll talk to them" says Tom.

"No, don't worry. I'll take care of that". Tom goes back to his desk and sits on his chair to make a plan for tomorrow night.

The next two hours pass doing work, and the caller calls back again,

"Mr. Pollack's office, may I help you?" says Barbara.

"Yes, it is me again, what time is Mr. Pollack flying tomorrow?" asks the caller.

"He'll be on the 5.45 PM flight. Here is the flight number and it will be landing there at 7:00PM" says Barbara.

Barbara tells the caller which airline and flight number and what he would be wearing. She says "Oh, Thank you, I hope with your help Tom can bring these killers to justice".

"Yes, I'll do my best. Thank you too" and the caller hangs up.

Barbara stands up and goes to the window and says "Mr. Pollack, everything is taken care of, you have to be at the airport before 4.45PM."

"Thank you Barbara. I'll be there". And Tom and Barbara go back to their work.

While all this is going on at this end, it is getting a little dark at the west coast. At Randy's Club, the time is almost seven p.m. and the Police Chief and his hired cops are already in the club with Randy's three gangsters and the twin locked up. The Chief and the boys are sitting on the largest table and everybody is having a good time.

The Chief opens up,

"Well, Randy, we have an appointment with that Little Big man at eight p.m. I've got my four best cops, you got their money. Show me the money". The Chief laughs like usual and Randy pulls four envelopes out of his inner pocket and gives it to the Chief. The Chief asks again,

"Randy, you are not afraid of this Chinese Mafia, are you?"

"No, I am not afraid of anybody, only you" says Randy.

"Oh, really, why would be afraid of me? We have been pals for years. You have not cheated me and I have not cheated you. I still remember when we were younger, and I was short of money and you helped me. So, I stand by you" says the Police Chief.

"Oh, thanks Chief. It is nice to know that some people remember favors. Anyway, ask your boys not to drink too much. Once the deal is done, they can come back here and have whatever they want including hookers. I'll take care of their bill with the hookers" Randy says to the Police Chief and the Chief turns to his cops in uniform, and says

"Only one more drink boys before we go to see these new gangsters. After we are done, then we all come back here and we'll enjoy ourselves". He hands the envelope to each cop and they all thank the Chief.

The bartender comes back again with a one drink for each and leaves them on the table.

After he leaves, the Chief and Randy start explaining to all the four cops and Randy's three boys what to do once they get there. The time is almost 7:30pm and the Chief stands up and says,

"Here is the plan…"

The Chief explains the plan to everyone and tells them to be ready in ten minutes.

The Chief sits back in his chair next to Randy. The music is being played in the club and the strippers carry on with their business on one side of the bar. Even though, this room is away from the strip bar, Randy and his gang along with his cop friends can see what is going on across them.

As the time gets to be seven forty p.m., the Chief stands up again,

"Ok, boys, lets go". Every body finishes their drinks. After having had two or three drinks each, they all feel brave and ready in case there is any trouble. They all stand up and start leaving slowly. As they come out of the bar, there are five cop cars and some other cars parked in the front. All the cops get in their cars, the Chief gets in his and the other three gangsters get in their cars respectively. They are all surprised to see that Randy has a new person driving him, a person they don't even know. Randy's car is behind all of them. As they drive for fifteen minutes, they come to this huge warehouse under construction with a sign saying "Welcome to future Wal-Mart, nobody beats our prices". All the cars pull up into the partially built parking lot one beside the other.

Another two minutes later, about ten black limos pull up and they all park in front of them with their head lights on.

Randy and the Chief come out of their cars, the four cops and Randy's boys come out too. Other than Randy and the Chief, they all stand next to their cars. Randy and the Chief move forward another five feet and stop there. On the other side, eight Chinese guys come out of their cars with black suits and ties. Then, one Chinese guy six feet three, wrestler built, comes out of the middle limo and opens the back door of the limo. A little Chinese guy with black suit, tie and dark glasses come out and they both walk towards the Chief and Randy, standing in the middle of the cars. They stop when they are about three feet away from each other.

The Chief says, "Howdy, Little Big Boss. How are you?"

"I am fine" Little Big Boss answers "How are you Randy? Chief, how come you bring all these cops with you? You are in no danger from us".

"Well, you have your protection, we have ours. Ok, what is on your mind about the clubs?"

Little Big Boss says "We'll give you 20 million. Bring your lawyer tomorrow night and paper work. We will bring our lawyer and we will settle tomorrow night".

Randy speaks in a little angry voice "The clubs are worth 60 million! You offered me 30 the last time".

"That was different, now you have killed the next President's wife, sooner or later; you are going to be in trouble. Take it or leave it".

Randy tries to play innocent and says "We have nothing to do with it".

"Don't play games with us. Nobody is a fool in America. The woman everybody calls 'The Slut', who has been living with you for so many years is the Senator's wife's twin. She has been missing from your club for the last ten days. It looks like she went to the Senator's house and you wanted her back, so you sent your boys to get her and things got out of hand. Anyway, I am not here to discuss other people's crap."

"No, you are wrong; the slut is upstairs locked up because that cool guy, who was getting close to her, took my money. So, until she tells me where the money is, she is going to stay locked up" bluffs Randy.

"Look, I told you twenty million, or we are leaving" says Little Big Boss.

The Chief comes close to Randy and says in his ear "Take it, they know too much".

"OK" says Randy "We will meet you here tomorrow night, you will have all the papers."

Randy brings his hand out to shake Little Boss's hand, but his body guard moves forward and says in broken English,

"My boss doesn't shake no body's hand" and Randy moves back.

"Ok, you are a big man now, Little Man. We will see you here same time tomorrow" says Randy.

Chief says "Get in my car. We will go together in my car back to your club". Randy makes a sign to everybody "Let's go".

They all follow the Chief's car to the club with Randy sitting in the front with the Chief. The Chief says,

"Look Randy, there are too many things against. You have a chance now. Take the money and make your boys and my boys happy. And live somewhere quietly and secretly, like Mexico. You should have enough for your retirement."

"Ok Chief" says Randy, a little scared. But he does not show his weakness. Since he is nearly fifty, he feels that he does not have enough stamina left to carry on being the boss. He says "May be you are right, but once I leave how are you going to deal with the Chinese Mafia?"

"Same way like I dealt with you. If they play hard, then I am the city Police Chief, I'll make their life hard too" says the Chief.

"But you are dealing with different kind of mafia than me" says Randy.

"I'll take care of them. Half of the police force is under my control, so I am not worried about it". The Chief looks at Randy and laughs loudly like he usually does. "Anyway, Randy, I am going to spend the night here. I need one of your fresh hookers. My wife and children are gone to my in laws."

"No problem, Chief. You can have your usual suite." All the cars approach Randy's club and everybody gets out and start their usual ways and the night passes quietly.

The next day, Thursday, Tom comes to the office as usual at nine a.m. He goes straight to his office wondering what he is going to face tonight. He still can't make up his mind whether to go or not. But, he thinks that if he does not go, he might miss the killers. So, he decides to take the caller's word and go investigate. He gets up and goes to the window, slides it open and says to Barbara,

"Barbara, can you keep this trip to yourself until I get some solid proof".

"I won't say anything. You know it. This is official business; you go ahead and take this trip. I hope we can get somewhere and find these killers" she replied.

"Anyways, any reply from the Attorney General" asks Tom.

"Yes, his secretary sent an e-mail for you. You can look in your laptop. He wanted to know where the killers are. He wanted to handle it himself with the FBI, so he can get the credit. But, I refused to give them any information. So, he finally gave up. I think he is under pressure from the White House too, because they don't want to be linked to this. They already have enough scandals on their hands" said Barbara.

"Yes, Barbara you are right. We don't want the Attorney General to handle this case. Let me handle it my way. Anyway, do you think you can drop me at the airport?" asks Tom.

"Yes, my husband and I are going to drop you. He will be here earlier and I am going to tell the whole staff that we are having dinner together at my husband's parent's house, so nobody knows where you are."

"Good idea, good idea" he tells Barbara with a happy face.

"I am always learning from elders" she said to Tom to make herself look younger.

"Yes" Tom replies, "I am getting older. I need to find another job where I can relax a little bit, work a few hours a day and be with my kids and wife. Anyway, what time is your hubby going to be here?"

"He will be here at four thirty. We will take you to the airport at five. What about your gun? Do you want me to inform TSA?" she asks.

"Yes" Tom says.

"Do you need to take more rounds with you, just in case?" she asks

"Yes, Barbara, tell the co-pilot to take my bag first" he says.

"I'll tell them to meet you at the boarding gate, so they can take your bag to the pilot's cabin" says Barbara.

"Thank you Barbara, you are great!" says Tom. He goes back to his table and starts working with his laptop. He comes across an e-mail from the Attorney General saying

"Tom, you are a great detective. This time I'll give you all the help you need. But, I like to know how you have cracked this case so quickly. Just tell me where you need help and it will be done. Here is the pin number for your use only. You can go to any city in the US, the FBI will help you. But, keep me informed. And I hope you get these killers quickly."

Tom is surprised that with the change in the Attorney General's attitude.

He looks to see if there is any other information in his laptop but there is nothing else.

As Tom is sitting in his office, the phone rings and Barbara picks up the phone and says,

"Tom Pollack's office, may I help you?"

"Yes, is Tom there please?" Barbara recognizes the voice as the caller. She says "Yes, he is here, let me connect you".

Tom answers "Hello, Tom Pollack speaking"

"Mr. Pollack, my name is Brian. I've been calling you for the past couple of days. Are you coming this evening to meet me?" he asks.

"Yes, I am. I will be there between 7.00 to 7.15 p.m." says Tom.

"I will be waiting for you" Brian says.

"How come you did not tell your name before Brian?" Tom asks.

"Well, I wanted to be sure I was talking to someone genuine and truthful, who would be willing to stand by his word. Now that I have spoken to you, I feel comfortable. You will know everything once you get here tonight."

"Ok Brian. I'll see you tonight" says Tom and hangs up.

As the day goes by, people come and go to the Senator's house.

The other twin is still locked up. She continues to pray to God all the time wondering when this will end. She is so helpless and unable to do anything.

At Tom's office, he is getting desperate to fly out there to check if he is going to be lucky to find these killers. As it gets close to lunch time, he decides to call his wife. He dials the phone, puts it on speaker phone and his wife answers,

"Hi honey, this is a change, you hardly call me for at noon these days. Yeah, kids are in school. Are you coming home for your noonar?"

"Honey, how about if you meet me closer to our house and have lunch with me? Any place you prefer" said Tom. "I have about three hours to spare."

"Oh, so you going to make me happy for a short while, then you going somewhere and you won't be back for a while?"

"No, my dear, I am going somewhere for these killers of the Senator's wife. I might have to go there tonight and for the next couple of days. I have three hours to spare. I want to be with you."

"Yes, nice love talks… Come on home. I'll fix you your favorite food and your affection" wife says.

"Honey, I promise you, after this Senator's case, I am going to quit this job and do something where we and the kids are closer all the time. Ok, I'll see you in a bit. Plus, I like your cooking." And he presses the button and turns off the phone. He stands up, goes to the window and Barbara is smiling. She stares at Tom, but does not say anything and Tom stands there looking at Barbara,

"Barbara, what are you smiling for? You did not listen to our conversation, did you?"

She shakes her head saying no and then she shakes it up and down, still with a nice teasing smile on her, "Isn't that my job, Mr. Pollack?"

"Yes, it is, to keep record of all calls but not to listen to my personal calls."

"Oh, come on, come on, Tom, and go home. She is waiting for you. Then after this, you might not have time for her for a little while, once you get involved with this case till it is over."

"Yes, Barbara, I'll see you at four." Tom leaves the office, while Barbara watching him leave still has that smile on her face.

As time passes, Tom comes back to the office at 4:15 PM. He enters his own office and sees Barbara and her husband are having a laugh. But, Tom is not in a mood for a laugh. He is constantly thinking about bringing those killers to justice. He says hi to Barbara's husband through the window.

"Oh, hi, did you enjoy your lunch? She told me you went home for lunch with your wife."

"Yes, she is a very good cook. And, did Barbara tell you anything else too?"

"No, no, she didn't. Oh, did you hide anything from me, honey?" Barbara's husband turned to her. They look at each other, like they know what Tom has been up to.

"Ok, both of you cut it out. Barbara, you have my stuff ready?" Tom says.

"Yes, I do", she picks up a carrier bag and she and her husband walk around to Tom's office. She puts the bag on the table, unzips the bag and says,

"Here is your usual unloaded gun", she starts picking things out of the bag and starts putting on the table, "100 rounds of bullets, one binoculars, electric shaver, toothbrush and paste, small towel in case you have to stay there longer, super camera and e-ticket" she pulls out of the side pocket.

"Is there anything else you need? You have your cell phone and charger. I already e-mailed the airline that you are going to have a gun and rounds in a bag. Pilot is going to meet you at the check in counter and take your bag and he'll give it back when you land." She puts everything back in the back and when she is done, zips it up.

"Well, Tom, you are packed up and ready" says Barbara.

"Ok guys, lets go" Tom picks up the bad and puts his hat on. All three start walking to the exit door. They come out of the police station to the parking lot in front and Barbara's husband opens the door locks with the keys. Tom and he get in the front and Barbara sits in the back seat. They drive to the airport. They reach there in half an hour. They pull up in front of the airline and Tom gets out of the car. As he closes the door, Barbara comes out of the back seat and gets in front. As she is getting in front, Barbara and her husband say to Tom,

"Hey Tom, good luck and be careful."

"Ok, thank you both. I'll see you later". Tom walks in to the departure terminal and goes straight to the airline desk.

He takes his hat off to show respect to the airline female attendant,

"Hi, my name is Tom". Before he finishes, she says, "Yes, Mr. Pollack. I know you are Tom Pollack, give me ten seconds, I'll be back for you."

She turns right and there is an office. She knocks and opens the door and says to her manager,

"Mr. Pollack is here". As soon as he hears that, he comes out with the attendant, and stands in front of Tom and shakes his hand.

"Hi, Mr. Pollack, I am the manager. I've got your official e-mail. The co-pilot is here. Let me page him." He goes on the airport announcing speaker and calls the co-pilot, then he turns to Tom,

"Which hand bag do you have?"

Tom puts his carrier bag in front of him.

"Would you like any refreshments, Mr. Pollack, while you are waiting for the flight to board?" says the manager.

"No, thanks, I am fine" says Tom. While they are talking, the co-pilot, a young white man of slim fit, about thirties, comes. First, he looks at the manager, and then he sees Tom Pollack standing in front of him. The co-pilot turns away from the manager and turns to Tom and says,

"Hi, Mr. Tom Pollack, nice to see you, to see you nice. I am the co-pilot. I was told to take your carry on bag."

Before Tom says anything, the manager hands the bag to the co-pilot.

"Here it is. And where did you hear that – nice to see you, to see you nice. Everybody seems to like that word"

The co-pilot replies in a nice manner while Tom is listening,

"My father is English. He always used that word with women and my mother hates that."

"And where did that word come from?" says the manager.

"Oh, it came from some famous English comedian who had a lot of wives".

"No wonder. Take this bag and keep it in the pilot cabin till the plane lands and give it to Mr. Pollack" says the manager as he hands the bag to the co-pilot.

"Ok, sir." He takes the bag and goes away. Then the manager turns to Tom,

"You can sit here and relax. I'll take you to the plane ten minutes before it takes off. The flight is full. I don't want people to harass you as everybody knows you now. Anyway, any luck with the killers yet? And the slut? You think she really did kill her own sister." The manager asks as he is curious.

"You just said you don't want people to harass me about this case" Tom says to the manager.

"Yeah, you are right, Mr. Pollack. I am sorry I didn't want to ask you, but this case is so special. It is going to be the case of this century."

"Yes, I am puzzled too. I am working hard on this case, but you will hear something soon."

Tom started walking towards an empty seat, away from the public. The manager starts walking with him,

"Mr. Pollack, are you sure, I can't get you something"?

"No, no, I am fine. I just had my wife's big lunch. I won't need anything till late."

Tom goes in the corner and sits on a seat with his back to everybody and the manager walks back to his office. Tom is sitting there next to the big window glass watching the planes go by, thinking why would sister kill a sister or have her killed. He has never heard or handled a case like this before. His cell phone rings and he says "Hello"

"Tom, this is Barbara. That guy Brian called to ask me if you are coming. I told him that you are about to board the flight."

"Thanks, Barbara. He has my cell phone number. I don't know he doesn't call me directly. But, thanks for letting me know."

"Ok, Tom. Have a safe journey."

As Tom hangs up his phone, the time is approaching five thirty pm. Tom is waiting for the airline manager. He comes just after five thirty. Tom has his back to him, so he comes to the front of him and says,

"Mr. Pollack, the flight is ready to take off in fifteen minutes." Tom stands up and starts walking behind the manager. The manager slows down and Tom is now walking parallel to the manager.

"Mr. Pollack, we tried to find you a seat where you would be sitting on your own, but the flight is full. We had to cancel somebody's seat to give it to you. This is in the middle"

Before the manager says more, Tom intervenes "Don't worry, I can handle this situation. But thank you for what you did." They walk towards the gate of the plane and the manager goes right up to the plane door. Since Tom is behind the manager, the stewardess is surprised to the manager,

"You are not flying, are you?"

"No, I am not. I am just escorting this gentleman to the flight. He has a seat in the middle. Make sure he is comfortable." As Tom steps from behind the manager, the stewardess is surprised to see Tom,

"Oh, Mr. Pollack, come this way" and she takes him to his seat.

As the stewardess takes him to his seat, he takes his hat and long coat off and puts it in cabinet above. His seat C is in the middle, next to the isle. There is a middle age, little over weight lady with red hair sitting in the middle reading a magazine. The woman does not pay any attention to Tom as he putting his coat and hat away, and the man sitting next to the window has his face turned watching the planes outside. Actually, Tom is glad that nobody looked at him when he came into the plane because he had lowered his hat on his fore head as he was coming in.

Tom puts his things away and sits in his seat and two minutes later, the pilot announces for everybody to put their seat belts on as the plane is ready to take off. The plane soon starts moving towards the runway to take off. The lady next to Tom is still looking at her magazine as the flight comes to the end of the runway and takes off. As the flight gets to the cruising level at its speed, the stewardess comes with drinks. When she comes to Tom, she asks him,

"Would you like anything to drink Mr. Pollack?"

"Yes, please give me orange juice and some peanuts."

After handing him juice and peanuts, she turns to the lady in the isle,

"What would you like?" The middle age red hair lady says the same thing and she turns to Tom,

"Hi, Mr. Pollack, I saw you coming, but I wanted to make sure you are the real Tom Pollack."

"Yes, I am the real Mr. Pollack" says Tom.

As she pulls her right hand out to shake Tom's hand, she says,

"My name is Ginger, glad to meet. How far have you come with the Senator's wife's murder case? Have you had any luck?"

"No, nothing much yet. We are still searching for clues. I am hoping something will up soon. I can't say any more than that" says Tom

"You know, Tom, you are a good skilled cop. You never say anything till you are close to your target. I used to work for a private detective firm. My boss will not tell me anything till he gets his target."

"Yes, Ginger, sometimes it has to work like that" Tom replies.

"Anyway, what are you going to the gambling town for? You don't think the killers are there, do you?

"No, no, I am paying a visit to some family here. I have to go back on duty tonight. This case is very important" Tom says to the redhead again in a cool manner.

"I see you are very cool headed man, I ask you something and you give a different answer."

"Ok, what kind of answer you are looking for?" he replies in a nice soft voice.

"Ok, tell me, you know that Senator Monroe is going to be our next president, right? He is well ahead of both parities candidates. My guess is that the opposition party had it done, so Senator Monroe won't have enough will power after his wife is killed."

"Why would a sister kill a sister if she is not going to take her place? Now, she is missing. It is obvious that she had nothing to do with it. It has to be somebody jealous of Senator Monroe. You think I am right Mr. Pollack?" Ginger starts talking to Tom openly, other people sitting around them get interested in their conversation too and they are just looking at them since Ginger does not give anybody else a chance to speak.

Tom replies again to Ginger

"Ginger, you make a very good point. Why would a twin sister kill her twin if she not going to take her place? She could have it done easily if she wanted to because they were identical."

"But, what about her habits? She could have taken her place, but maybe, in their private like, you know what I mean…he would've found out that she is not his wife, but her twin. You can only fool or lie to people a couple of time, nobody is a fool these days" says Ginger.

"You know, Ginger, you are 100% right. You can't fool or lie to people too many times. After this case, I might work for your boss. I am tired of police work. Give me the name of your company. I'll talk to you first." Tom is trying to pretend and not show that he is not serious.

"No, my boss is not in business any more. He had to declare bankruptcy because he was lying and trying to fool people, and finally they sued him and he is left with nothing in the end. He is homeless now. Oh, well, I don't know Mr. Pollack, but you still haven't told me why you are here. You are after something."

"No, as I told you before, I am here to see some family friends." And he tries to change the subject with the redhead. "Well, what do you think about this case, Ginger, you've been a secretary to a detective. Maybe he failed, but you still have a good brain in that head, since I sat here, I am enjoying your conversation."

"I don't know, Tom, God gave everything to this country, but as it got rich and rich, the powerful are making mistakes and I don't know. I don't want to say any more."

As Ginger and Tom keep on sharing conversations on the flight, it keeps on cruising. After an hour and fifteen minutes, it lands at its destination and the flight comes to a full stop. After the seat belt sign goes out, every body starts standing up and gets their small carry on from above.

As Ginger gets up, Tom gets up too, and Tom says to Ginger "Let me get your carry on." As she moves from the seat to the walking isle, he opens the above cabinet and asks "Which one is yours?" and she points out "That one". As he picks her bad and hand to her, she gives him a nice smile and says,

"You seem to be a better gentleman than a cop and thank you for this, when you catch these killers. And if you catch these killers in this city, I am going to call you and say that you lied to me".

"Yes, you are right Ginger, do call me, and it has been very nice talking to you." Tom was trying to flatter her, "Well, I hope to meet you again somewhere".

"Ok, bye" as she is about to leave the flight, the co-pilot comes with Tom's carry on and hands it to Mr. Pollack.

"Here is your bag, sir. It is nice to see you, to see you nice and thank you for flying our airline."

And the young co-pilot leaves. Tom and Ginger start walking out of the flight. As they walk into the terminal, Ginger is still walking with Tom and says,

"Well, Tom, you are a nice company. Do you need any help or ride in this town? I am free; I can take you where ever you want to go. But, I know you have a lot of things on your mind." As she pulls out her business card and gives it to Tom, he says,

"No, Ginger, I will have to go back on the nine o'clock flight. My wife and children would be waiting for me till midnight. But, it is good to talk to you." As they are walking and talking to each other, going out of the terminal, Tom sees a white male, about forty, close to six foot, little on the heavy side – but not fat or with a big belly. He tells Ginger,

"I'll have to leave you. My pick up is here."

He is holding a 12 x 12 cardboard in his both hands with the name of Sam Denver. Tom starts walking towards that man and the man also recognizes Tom.

As Tom comes and stands in front, the man pulls his hand out and says while shaking hands,

"Mr. Pollack, good to see you. My name is Brian Mulhorn."

"Well, it is good to see you too Brian." And they start walking through the gate to the parking lot. As they come out of the terminal, it is getting slightly dark outside. When they come to his car, he opens the door lock with remote and Tom goes to the passenger side and puts the bag on the floor. And Brian opens the driver door and gets in and starts the car. He turns his face to Tom and says,

"Tom, we have about 25 minutes to drive. I will tell you whatever you want to know. But, I'll start with myself. We are a family of cops. Out father was a cop too, but he is retired. I quit my job last month. I have two other cousins still with the force. But, soon they will be leaving too."

As Tom is listening to Brian, the car gets out of the airport and enters the highway to the city.

"What happened a couple of months ago is," Brian continues with his conversation, "my sister's husband was shot by Chinese Mafia. According to the police, he tried to stop a car in front of him with an expired tag. As soon as he flashed his lights, the car sped away faster. He followed the car into China Town, with all the Chinese businesses and the car pulled into alley way. When he stopped behind and got out of his cruiser and was standing there, he was shot from the roof top, looks like. The driver called for help on the cell phone. They were waiting for him." As his voice got sadder, Tom intervened,

"I am sorry to hear that."

"Yeah, we are doing our best to help my sister and her children. I hope you succeed in getting these killers. If I get the reward, I'll pay my sister's house off. At least, she won't be worried about mortgage, and she can survive on his pension."

"Anyway, that is our family problem. We'll take care of that. Let me give you details about your coming problem."

"OK, Randy is the name of the owner of some gambling casinos and strip bars. Nobody knows his real name. He has been here for more than 15 years. And that woman everybody calls the Slut, she has been with him all this time. But last couple of years, they were fighting a lot. He brought another, younger, blond to take her place and she was falling for some new guy he hired recently. I believe he stole Randy's money and the slut got the blame for it. They went after her thinking she stole the money and unluckily they shot Senator's wife. They brought the slut back and she is locked upstairs."

"So, she is here too" Tom intervened.

"Yes, she is here. But since she came back, she is claiming that she is Senator's wife and her younger sister, the slut was killed. But the DNA, Mr. Pollack, shows that Senator's wife was killed. Is that true?"

"Yes, that is true. DNA matches Mrs. Monroe, so Senator has accepted that it is his wife who was killed." Tom replied and Brian continued

"Anyway, Tom where I am taking you today is something different. We will come back to this later. Let me tell you what is going on now. Where we are going tonight is where Randy is having his final bye to all his businesses. He is meeting with the Chinese Mafia and their lawyers and his own lawyers. They are going to give him 15 million dollars cash in used notes and five million on Monday when he hands over the keys to them."

As the car driven by Brian cruises on the highway, Tom is listening quietly, taking all the details in his head. After about less than half an hour driving, they are still talking and the time is coming close to ten before eight p.m. Thursday night, and Brian tells Tom,

"Let me show you what is happening tonight." As he pulls his car to a huge shopping complex under construction, which is supposed to have a lot of large retail stores, he parks his car in such a place and he turns his lights off and tells Tom,

"Let us wait about 5 to 10 minutes. They will be here."

"Who is going to be here?" asks Tom.

"The Chinese gang, Randy and our Chief, who is a crooked cop, is a member of Randy's mob and some of his cop friends. One of my cousins is in his gang too. I told him to quit, but he won't listen because he gets cash money from Randy for his gambling habit."

"But, he doesn't care. One day he is going to regret it." While they are talking, to their right about less than a quarter mile, they both see a lot of cars with high beam on. They all park in one row and other cars park in a row opposite to the first one. As they are still parking, one by one, Brian asks Tom

"Let me give you binoculars. I have two of them - one for you and one for me."

"No, I have mine" says Tom picks his bag from his foot well and pulls his binoculars out, as Brian is getting out of his car. It is dark as Brian had turned off his car's interior light earlier. Tom also picked his gun out of his bag. Which he had loaded at the airport bathroom before he met Brian. He leaves his bag on the passenger seat, carrying his binoculars and putting his gun in his holster under his left arm pit.

"OK, Tom, come this way." Brian tells Tom and Tom walks in front of the car and they stand about a quarter mile away. They are standing behind a wall which is about their waist height, and it is all dark on Tom's and Brian's side.

While Tom and Brian are watching what is going on, all the cars, about ten on each side with high beam on, and about 30 feet gap, first Randy and the Chief get out of their cars. Then Little Big man's security people come out. As Tom and Brian watch carefully, the Little Big man comes out of the big limo. He just stands there, then his other gang members, four of them, open the trunk to the limo and pull out two folding tables and six chairs. They put all those between the cars and other people come out of the Chinese gang's cars and also from Randy's side, the cops who came to help before, for money.

As the tables and chairs are being put there, only Randy, the Chief and another white male with a nice suit and a file in his hand move forward. Only Randy, the Chief, lawyer for Randy and Little Big man and their lawyer sit across each other, in the middle of nowhere. As Randy and the Chief are sitting, all other guys are standing about ten feet behind on their own.

Brian and Tom are standing a quarter mile away, watching with the binoculars, Brian says to Tom, "Look thoroughly on Randy's side on the left." As Tom runs his eyes on the whole gang, he recognizes a white male and a black guy who was in Senator's house video. But keeps his mouth shut. But Brian speaks again to Tom,

"OK, Tom, set your sight on the far side on the left. I'll tell you who every body is. Are you ready?"

Tom says, "Yes".

"OK, on the very far side, you have two cops, one of them is my cousin, and next one is our Chief's brown nose. Oh, I forgot to tell you, our Chief is the number one crook. He knows Randy for years. He is on Randy's payroll and also on the state payroll. Next one is Randy's number two guy, then the black guy. Oh, his number one guy is not here today. Then you have three of four cops and looks like he hired a new person. Tom, now you see them all. Are you happy with my call?"

While Tom is still watching them, he replies to Brian,

"Yes, I am very happy. I don't have the words to thank you. And what else is going on here?"

"See Randy, sitting in the middle, next to the Chief, across from them is little Chinese guy? They call little big man, four and half feet tall, yellow suit with yellow hat, purple tie? They are signing an agreement today. On Monday, the little big man takes over all of Randy's business. He only takes his new blond, nothing else. He leaves behind all other useless strippers and everything else. Like I told you, he gets rest of the money Monday morning, when he hands the keys to them.

As their signing ceremony is going on, Tom and Brian are still watching them; the time is quarter after eight when Tom looks at his watch. And Tom says, "Can you show me the club too? My flight is at ten."

"Ok, let us go, we should look before Randy and his friends come back to the club and all his cop friends are going to be there till very late tonight boozing and womanizing." Brian stops looking at them and turns to Tom.

"Yes Brian, I need to look at the club." And both men start moving little faster and they bet in Brian's car and start moving toward the highway.

"How far is the club from here? And, how far is the airport from there?" Tom asks.

"Well, Tom, the club is about twenty five minutes and from there, the airport is about the same. Well, you'll have about fifteen minutes to look around. As the car jumps on the highway, Brian puts his foot down, doing seventy five on sixty five. I'll try to get you there as fast as I can."

"If you can get me to the airport by 9:30 PM, I'll be ok. I got to get back and prepare the case."

"Don't worry, I'll get you there by nine thirty" says Brian. And Tom puts his binoculars in his bag and zips it.

While Brian is driving. He pulls a paper from his sun visor and turns interior light on tom's side only and gives to Tom. Tom starts reading it. After reading the paper, he gets a pen out of his pocket and signs it and gives it back to Brian. Brian puts it back on the sun visor and asks Tom,

"You did not ask any question, Mr. Pollack."

"There is nothing to ask, I gave you my word. You are only the first person to give this information, so that is why." Tom replied.

After about fifteen minutes on the highway, Brian takes the car towards the sign saying "Welcome to Happiness Town". After hitting few lights, Brian brings his car to halt on the opposite side of Randy's club with a beautiful sign, above the main door saying, "Welcome to Randy's Bar and Club."

"Well, Tom, this is it. If you can hit this place hard next day or two, after that they will be gone with the wind. Then, you will have to search the whole county."

"Yes, Brian. I cannot thank you enough." Brian had already turned his car off and he reaches with his right hand to the rear seat and he pulls something out of the bag and gives it to Tom.

"Here take this, and remove your hat." Handing what looks like a very large light red glasses, with a very big real looking nose with grey eye brows, and grey large mustache and grey looking large side burns.

"And Tom, can you walk like a fifty five year old man? I'll introduce you to the people I know as my Uncle Sam from buffalo. Nobody will ask you anything but you are way smarter than me. You know what to do. I don't have to tell you anything."

"Yes, you are right" Tom takes his hat off and puts that disguise on and the old man's hat.

Tom asks Brian what is next,

"Well Tom, we are going to go in. You will be able to see what is in there, and then you can decide what to do" so Tom says to Brian "let us go."

They both come out of the car and cross the street safely, when they come near the door, the doorman says to Brian, "Hey Brian, we haven't seen you lately where have you been and who do you have with you here?"

"This is my Uncle Sam Denver, he was passing through town, and I thought I would show him our town" says Brian

"Well that is nice of you, the place like this will make him feel younger too," and the doorman starts laughing a little and says to Tom, "It is nice of you Mr. Sam Denver to come here," as they are walking in, "Have a nice time."

"Thank you," Tom says and the doorman holds the door open for Tom and Brian. As they start going inside, Brian takes him to the right side, where lights are dimmed, so nobody can notice Tom's disguise. They go and sit in the corner, and to the right side, Tom sees a few men drinking at the bar. To his straight and left is stage for the strippers but the show hasn't started yet. On far left there, are the slot machines and some people gambling on tables. A waitress with tight blouse and very tight shorts comes towards Tom and Brian.

"Hi stranger, I haven't seen you here for a while, what can I do for you and your old man?" and she started giggling.

"Oh I'll have the usual, and this is my Uncle Sam, he is visiting," and turns to Tom, "What would you like?"

"Oh I'll have a Coke thanks" says Tom

And the girl goes towards the bar, and orders the drinks. While waiting for the drinks she starts talking to a handsome looking man, who happens to look towards Brian and Tom. He gulps his drink down and turns towards them. Brian and Tom see him walking towards them. And Brian says to Tom,

"This is Randy's number one guy; he never reveals his real name to anybody" As the tall man makes his way towards them, Tom recognizes him right away, as the third person in Senator's house, Tom has seen him on security DVD. He approaches their table and stands next to Brian and says, "Hello Brian," the man pulls his hand out to shake Brian's hand, and Brain replies, "Hi, how you doing?"

"Good, we have not seen you lately. I heard you quit your job, what do you plan to do?" "And who do you have here," asks Number One looking at Tom.

"Yes, I quit my job; I am looking for some thing to do with less tension. Anyway, this is my Uncle Sam Denver; he was passing by our town, and stopped by to visit our family.

Number One brings his hand to shake Tom's hand. As they shake hands, Tom says "Howdy," and Number One says to Tom, "You have pretty hard hand for your age" trying to insult him with smile. As Brian hears he intervenes before Tom says anything,

"My uncle used to be a coal miner and mining machine mechanic when he was younger, that is why he has hard hands and body." While Brian was saying that, waitress bring two glasses of drinks in tray and she pushes Number One with her hip and says in a cheery voice, "Hey leave these two to me, they are mine tonight."

And, Number One realizes that situation is different so he says "Ok, old man, Brian and our lovely chick; I'll leave you alone" and he walks away, and Tom looks at him through his glasses thinking hopefully you'll see this old man soon, but he has to keep quiet. The waitress pulls a chair between Tom and Brian, first she turns to Brian and says "You are married man, I don't want to hit on your money, and maybe your uncle has pension money."

"Yes you are right, I am a married man, but Uncle Sam is not married. I didn't ask him, since he came here only an hour ago, but maybe he is unattached" and Brian turns to waitress "Why don't you ask him?"

Brian and Tom pick up heir drinks and Tom toasts "Good to see you Brian, you are a decent human being. Here is to you."

And the waitress turns towards Tom as she has already couple of drinks which Tom and Brian are aware of from her behavior,

"Hey Mr. Uncle, well I can't call you uncle. I hope you are single" her voice is breaking up, "I am only worth five hundred dollars. Some of girls are worth thousand to two thousand."

"Oh really", Tom says "I don't have that kind of money. Maybe you can find someone rich later".

She gets up in anger and says to Tom

"Oh then you probably won't have money for a tip either. Yeah you are right. I will have to find someone rich." And she leaves swinging her hips, Tom and Brian smile to each other.

"OK Tom now you seen everything. What else would you like to see?" Brian asks Tom.

The time is almost nine. As they both drink their drinks, Tom says "I want to go outside and look around. Also, can you show me the streets connected to this building?"

They both stand up. Brian says "Let us go, I'll show you around then there is just enough time to get to the airport." And they both start walking to the exit door. As they come to the door, doorman opens the door and says to both,

"Well gentlemen, already leaving? You haven't seen anything yet. The nightlife does not begin till late." By this time, another bellman joins and says to Tom and Brian.

"Good evening gentlemen"

Both men say good evening and they start crossing the street. As Tom and Brian go halfway through, and Tom starts walking as he normally walks, one bellman says to the other,

"Hey, look at that old man with Brian. When he walked in, he was walking like an old man but now he is like a very strong man." Looking the other doorman says,

"Maybe he saw something inside the club or he had something which made him younger"

"I don't know, but something is fishy. I have not seen any incidences like this before. Lately there is too much going on, since that so called slut left this town. She looked like that Senator's wife. Even Randy seems worried these days" he says

"Yeah, you are right. Well we can always get another job as doormen somewhere else."

Tom and Brian both get in the car. As Brian starts the car, Tom begins to remove his disguise. But Brian notices the doormen and quickly tells Tom "Keep it on. Those doormen are still looking at us. We don't want to blow anything."

Tom thanks Brian for noticing the doorman and says that he was preoccupied looking for the building number.

"Don't worry Tom I am going to give you all info before you leave" says Brian and car moves off. "Let me show you all the side streets" says Brian and drives around for the next ten minutes.

Tom is looking around thinking about all the possible situations and when he can raid the building with a plan that won't fail. Afterwards Brian drives around the back of the bar and Tom sees that back of the building has strong walls and very thick glass on all windows, on all the floors and they are also protected by iron bars. There is no way anybody could come in or leave the building through the back.

"Well, Mr. Pollack this is it. Now you seen it all, and here is the address of this bar and my phone number." Brian hands a card to Tom and says

"You want or you need anything, let me know. I will drop you at the airport."

Tom replies "Yes I better go back. I'll have to take this flight and go back and prepare the case. And once again Brian, you made this a little easier for me and I'll make sure you'll get your reward. Just take me to the airport now. Thanks".

Brian starts driving toward the airport. And Brian gives additional details about the place. They reach the airport at 9:30 PM. Tom is dropped right in front of his airline by Brian. They shake hands and say goodbye to each other, Tom picks up his bag and goes into the airport. Watching Tom enter the airport, Brian drives off.

Tom goes into the airline check-in. There is only twenty five minutes left for the flight to takeoff. There are only a couple of passengers in front of him. By the time they get done, Tom comes to the desk and hands his e-ticket. The airline attendant without even looking at Tom since she has her eyes glued to the computer screen, says

"Sir it is too late, you'll have to fly tomorrow morning. You should've been here earlier, the flight is about to leave."

She acts like she does not recognize Tom Pollack with his hat on. Tom pulls out his badge and shows it to her and asks to speak to the manager. Seeing his ID, she says

"Oh I am sorry, we are waiting for you. Please don't tell anybody I ignored you, you can go ahead and board the flight."

Tom thanks her and starts walking towards the security gate thinking, that he has no time to complain and has too many other things on his mind. He walks to the security check and shows his badge and hands his bag to security personnel, a young white male, in his late twenties who recognize Tom and says.

"Hello, Mr. Tom Pollack, good to see you. I've seen you on TV all this week. Are you going to crack this case? I am your big fan" he says with a smile,

"Yes I am, trying my best. Let's hope. That is the only thing I can say. But take care of my bag and I'll proceed to the boarding gate" and Tom walks away from him and goes to the gate to board his flight.

Tom gets in the plane and this time does not take his hat off because he does not want to be recognized. He is shown in his seat by the flight attendant and he just sits there thinking what he has to do next. The person sitting next to him says hello and Tom acknowledges him and pretends to sleep.

About ten minutes after the flight takes off, Tom has his eyes closed thinking how he can get everything done on time when the flight attendant comes and asks him if he needed any refreshments which he declines. It reaches Denver Airport at about eleven twenty. By the time Tom comes out of the airport it is eleven thirty. He gets a taxi and calls Barbara from his cell phone. He dials the number gets the answering machine. He disconnects and he tries two minutes later. After about two rings Barbara's husband presses the speaker phone button and says

"Who is this? Can't you leave us alone at this time of the night?"

Tom realizes that Barbara and her husband are in bed and apologizes,

"Oh I am sorry. This is Tom, I need Barbara's help." Before he says anymore, Barbara's husband says,

"You know Tom, she is needed here now…more than that of your work" he replies.

"I know I did catch you at the wrong time" Tom starts to say when her husband interrupts and says,

"No, the time might be wrong for you, but it is right for us both"

Tom says again very apologetically "I am sorry to call you, but I need her help. I found these killers. I have to prepare for this case tonight."

"OK Tom. Can you give us a few minutes? I'll bring her over there myself" Barbara's husband says.

Tom thanks him for bringing Barbara back to work and hangs up. Tom reaches the station about midnight. He pays the driver and he waits at the door. After a few minutes he sees Barbara's husband pull up and Barbara comes out. And she starts walking towards Tom who is standing in the doorway.

"Hello Barbara I am sorry to call you this time of the night" Tom says to her.

"It is ok, I understand, but he was a little mad but he understands too" she says pointing to her husband driving away.

Tom rings the buzzer to the police guard who unlocks the door and lets Tom and Barbara come in. As they are passing the guard, he says to Tom

"Hi chief, this is unusual for you and Barbara to be here in the middle of the night. You must have gotten somewhere with the Senator's wife's case."

"No nothing concrete yet, I have some research to do" Tom says as he and Barbara walk towards their office and Tom tells Barbara to come to his office first.

Tom goes to his chair and presses the speaker button on his phone and dials the phone to Terrence. Barbara is standing across the table.

After a couple of rings Terrence answers

"Yes Mr. Pollack, what do you want in the middle of the night, can't you find some time earlier in the day to call me?"

"I need you here right away, I am sending you a taxi, I'll take care of the fare."

"But Tom, I'm in bed" he says

"I don't care, just get here. Taxi will be there in five minutes" Tom replies

"What made you change your mind? Why do you need me in the middle of the night? I thought you went home to your wife yesterday at lunch time" says Terrence.

"That is not your business, anyway, who told you that?" Tom looks at Barbara accusingly and she makes a sign saying that it was not her.

"Well, the whole staff knows" says Terrance

"Oh really, just get here. I need you here badly" Tom says

Terrance asks "That's nice, what time the taxi is going to be here?"

"It will be there in the next five to ten minutes" Tom says.

"Are you going to greet me at the door Tom?"

"Yes I am, with flowers and open arms" Tom answers as Barbara listens. She has an amused smile on her face as she keeps looking at Tom. Tom gives her a look that only she knows understands as a look of unhappiness and annoyance that everybody knows about where he was yesterday at lunch time.

"Are you alone in the office Tom?" asks Terrence

"Yes, I am" says Tom.

"Oh that's good. Then I'll do anything for you" Terrence says in a humorous tone and hangs up.

Barbara who was listening to the whole conversation between Tom and Terrance cannot get over what Terrance said before he hung up and continues to smile.

After Tom hangs up the phone, Barbara asks Tom,

"What do you want me to do now? Terrence is not going to be happy to see me here."

Tom does not answer her question but opens the drawer to his right side takes three photos out and hands them to Barbara.

"I don't have names for these three guys, but I want you to have the arrest warrants prepared for them. In the morning I have to attend the Senator's wife's funeral. In the afternoon, I'll have to make plans to raid the club and talk to the Attorney General so I can get FBI backing. And then I have to fly out tomorrow night to get those killers." Tom says

"So Tom you did see them?" Barbara asks

"Yes I did Barbara. They were there and so is one of the twins. She is locked upstairs. Everybody says she is acting differently than before. She is claiming to be the senator's wife all the time, but nobody believes her. Everybody over there thinks she is trying to save herself from Randy and his gang by pretending to be Mrs. Monroe." Tom replies

"But did you have a chance to go upstairs and look for yourself if she is till there?" Barbara asks.

"No I didn't. But I trust Brian. Whatever he told me turned out to be true. So I trust his word, but at least three of men who were at the senator's house that nights were there." Tom says

"OK Tom, I'll start getting the paperwork ready. It is going to take me two or three hours to do all this and put everything into computers so the Attorney General, the FBI, and the Justice Department are all aware and you should not have any problems."

While Barbara and Tom are discussing the case, the security guard rings a bell to Tom and Tom answers,

"Yes?"

"Mr. Pollack, your assistant is here in his pajamas. Shall I let him in?"

"Yes let him in. Tell him to come to my office" The guard lets Terrence in, and he walks to Tom's office. And he sees Barbara standing there about to leave with papers in her hand,

When Terrence sees Barbara in Tom's office through the glass, he gets upset and angry and he comes to the office and says in an angry voice

"I thought you were alone" he says looking at Barbara.

"She came in a few minutes ago" Tom replies

"So you knew she was coming too. Then why you ask me to come here?" Terrence asks again.

"I did not call you here for any mating game; I called you here because I need your help." Tom says getting a little irritated with Terrence. Barbara just shakes her head looking at both men.

"Yes Tom when you need technical help, you turn to me. But when I need you, you don't help."

Tom gets a little more angry and annoyed and tells Terrence,

"Look, first of all you should've come here dressed properly, not in your pajamas". Before Tom says anymore, Terrence interrupts

"Well, you told me to come the way I was dressed so I did" As Tom stands up from his chair and Terrence gets a little afraid and moves one foot away from the table and Tom drops a card on the table on Terrence's side and says

"There is an address with zip code on that card. I want you to make me 3x3 ft area map of this building and the area surrounding this building on all four sides. I want all the street names, full details about the area."

"No it is not my job to this at night. I am a 9 to 5 employee. I am leaving." Terrence gets more upset and turns to walk out of the office,

"Don't you dare leave this office? I want this work done tonight and you are going to do it." Tom says angrily. This is the first time Barbara has seen him in this mood.

And Terrence got more scared.

"OK boss, I'll do whatever you want me to do but will I get double overtime?" Terrence asks.

"Yes I will make sure of that" As Tom's voice's tone calms down. Terrence picks up the card and goes to his office cubicle, leaving Tom and Barbara behind.

After he leaves Barbara says to Tom

"This kid needs love and help from his family, Tom. He is lonely. Once this case is over, my husband and I and you and your wife and kids should invite him and try to give him some real family love. I'll go and do my work now"

"OK Barbara, I am sorry I was a little hard on him. He is very intelligent. I need both of your help. I cannot do without you and him at this point. After this case is over, I might quit the department" Tom says and Barbara leaves the office to do her own work.

And Tom just sits there thinking, very hard on what to do next.

Almost nearly two hours later, Terrence walks into Tom's cubicle with a large map 3x3 feet and hangs it on the wall next to Tom.

"Well Tom is that what you need?" Tom stands up to look at the map and location of Randy's bar. Terrence had color coded all the streets connecting to the bar.

"Yes, Terrence, thank you. That is a well done job. I am proud of you" Tom says.

"Well Tom I am not proud of you. Why did you have to get angry at me in front of Barbara? You were trying to be all macho and show your authority

"No I am not trying to be macho or wielding my authority. I am under a lot of stress and I need to solve this case. I am sorry if I offended you in anyway" Tom says to Terrence.

"OK I accept your apology"

While they are talking, Barbara walks in with a bunch of papers and hands it to Tom.

As Tom looks through these papers to see if everything is ok, Barbara says "I'll go back and take care of the computer work." And she looks at Terrence and asks "So you two gentlemen have made up?"

"Yes, we did" Terrence says. "If you leave, then we can kiss to finish the make up."

Before she can reply, Tom jumps in and says

"Barbara you had to get him started again, didn't you?" She smiles and walks back to her desk and Terrance goes back to his desk.

Tom looks at the map and starts' planning on how he is going to raid the bar, which streets to block and how many officers he is going to need. He starts putting it on the map with his own codes.

After about an hour, Barbara and Terrence come back to Tom's office and she tells him everything is complete.

"Ok. Did you send email to our judge that I am going to come to court after the funeral and to get his signature for the arrest warrants?" Tom asks

"Yes, I did. I'll also give him a call in the morning to make sure he knows." Barbara replies.

"Thank you both, Barbara and Terrence. I'll drop you home on my way. I need to get a few hours sleep" Tom says

Tom picks up the arrest warrants folder from the table and starts leading Barbara and Terrence to out of the police station. On the way out he says good night to security and they all go to the parking lot where Tom's car is parked. He unlocks the car with his remote and Barbara and Terrence get in. Tom gets in and starts driving and everyone is quiet. After ten minutes Terrence breaks the silence and asks,

"Tom who will you be dropping off first?"

"I am dropping Barbara off first, and then I'll drop you off." Tom replies

"Oh good, maybe you can come up and have a nap at my place. Why do you want to disturb your wife's sleep by going in so late or rather early in the morning?" Terrence says in a nice voice. As soon as Tom hears that, he changes direction and goes towards Terrence's house first.

"No, thank you. I think I am going to drop you off first" he says turning his head towards Terrence.

"But if you go to drop Barbara after me then you will be going out of the way to get home." Terrance says

"Yes I know" says Tom. Then nobody says anything till they get in front of Terrence's condo. As the car comes to a halt, Tom says to Terrence before he opens his side's door.

"Thank you Terrence and good morning"

Terrence comes out of the car in rage and before he closes the car he says

"God damn real men" And shuts the door very hard and walks faster towards his condo. And Barbara starts laughing and laughing. When she finally controls her laughter, Tom starts driving towards Barbara's house and she says

"Tom this guy is going to take you to his bed one day"

"Hell he will!! Barbara you really enjoy his stuff don't you?"

"Yes, it is very funny the way he comes to you" says Barbara while she is still giggling.

After about nine minutes the car is approaches Barbara's house and it is almost 4:30 in the mornings. The car pulls up in front of her house and her husband is sitting on the front stairs of the house with a beer bottle in his hand. As soon as he sees Tom's car pull up, he comes to open the car door for Barbara. While she is still sitting in, Tom opens the window on the passenger side and asks him

"Are you still awake?"

"Yes I am I couldn't go to sleep without her. So I came out here on this nice moonlight night with my own moonshine" he says showing his bottle and it is apparent that he is a little drunk. Barbara gets out of the car and closes the door and she stands next to her husband and rubs his back.

"You know Tom; he used to get jealous every time Barbara mentioned your name. He doesn't anymore. And Barbra's husband says." Every star I looked at in the sky while I was drinking, I saw her in those stars. I knew she is one of those stars I am waiting for. Now she is here. Thank your Mr. Pollack" says her husband, a bit tipsy.

"Ok, take my sister home and treat her like a star" says Tom

"And treat her like a star is what I intend to do" he says.

Realizing that he has had quite a few drinks, Tom does not say anymore. Barbara holds her husband with both her arms and says to him,

"Honey, your star is here, so let's go inside now".

And Barbara puts her husband's right arm on her shoulders and they move away to their house. Tom is still sitting there watching them to make sure they make it home safely without falling. As they get in their house and close the door, and Tom drives off to his house, has a quick drink and takes a shower and goes to bed to catch a couple of hours of sleep.

Friday morning eight AM. At Senator Frank P. Monroe's estate, people are lining up outside of his estate. The security gate is locked with lots of police presence. Families in the neighborhood are lining up on the main road. People park their cars, vans, SUVs, trucks, and all kind of vehicles. They park them on both sides of the road so they can get a glimpse of the casket of the next first lady of the USA.

In the gambling town in Nevada, the other twin who has been locked up for five days wakes up at six thirty AM like usual, goes to the bathroom and has a shower and wears her twins clothes and turns the TV on. She knows it is the day of the funeral because it was announced by the Senator had announced that that funeral would take place as soon as possible.

At nine am the twin is watching the news as Jody is standing in front of the security gate of the Senator's estate, with live news feed. She says,

"Good sad morning to the whole nation. This is Jody reporting from Denver in front of Senator Monroe's house. The senator gave us permission to broadcast this live. Our whole team is so sorry to bring this live TV broadcast. She would've been the next first lady of this nation. Due to unfortunate events, the nation and this family's heart are broken." While she is making that speech in front of the camera, the funeral cars come close. And Jody and her crew turn the camera to the funeral cars and Jody says,

"Here come all the funeral cars. In the fourth car is the next 1st lady's body. There are lots of other cars. There are so many people here. We don't know who is who, but we will keep you informed."

As all the cars are directed in by police to the senator's house, the twin sitting in locked room in Nevada is watching but is helpless and cannot do anything. She just sits there, tears coming down her eyes and she wipes them off as she sees her sister's coffin being driven into the senator's estate. She tries to recognize the people of the TV during the broadcast but is not able to do so.

Meanwhile, at the Senator's estate, Jody continues her live broadcast. She notices Tom's car in line behind numerous cars as only VIP's are allowed in. Since Jody has seen Tom's car before and she knows what he looks like, and she waits anxiously till he comes to the gate. It is almost ten AM. Since Tom as the lead detective on this case has been working late, almost till 5:00am this morning, he looks tired. As his car pulls near Jody, she comes running to Tom's driver's side followed by her camera crew.

"Hello Mr. Pollack" Jody says to Tom through his open window. He takes his hat off and says hello to Jody.

"Mr. Pollack, do you have any news about this case?" she asks

"No, not really. We are still investigating and we haven't found anything concrete yet. As soon as we know something I'll let you know."

"But you were out of town" Jody starts to say but before she can continue further, Tom puts his hand on Jody's microphone and blocks the camera by his hat on the right side and he says to Jody,

"Don't say anything on live TV about yesterday. Otherwise I'll get a gag order against you and your TV"

When Jody sees that Tom is very serious and she points to TV crew to back off.

"I am sorry Mr. Pollack. But are you on to something?" she asks

"Give me a number to reach you and I'll call you myself. I know you are hungry to be the number one reporter, so I'll let you be the first to know. Just don't say anymore" says Tom with his hand still Jody's microphone.

"OK Mr. Pollack, you made you point. I'll keep quiet for now" and she pulls a card out of her pocket and hands it to Tom.

"Jody, you will be the first one to know everything" says Tom driving off through the security gate.

Tom drives towards senator's house and notices that there is no parking. So he just parks the car on the right side on the road like a lot of the other cars and he walks the rest of the way. When he reaches the front of the house, he sees lots of people standing around. He sees Father John and the Senator with some close family members standing by the door of the house.

When he reaches them, Tom wishes good morning to the Senator and Father John, and offers his condolences. He then whispers to Father John in his ear,

"I need to talk to you and the Senator privately." Father John listens and touches the Senator's left arm and conveys Tom's request. The Senator nods and all three move near the garage which has all doors closed, and is almost thirty feet away from everybody so that nobody can hear them. Senator asks Tom

"Yes, Mr. Pollack?"

"Mr. Monroe, I have found the killers and the kidnapped twin sister. She is still alive. She is locked up in a bar/club. She is claiming to be your wife" says Tom.

"Mr. Pollack how could that be possible? I thought the DNA matched my deceased wife! Where is she and when do you intend to arrest these people?" asks the Senator.

"Tomorrow morning, but what I hear from my source is that she is claiming that it is her younger sister Cassandra who died. Even the gang who kidnapped her are puzzled. They are saying she is acting differently than the twin they had before." Tom tells the Senator

Then Father John intervenes

"Senator and Tom, you never know. Both twins could have similar DNA. First you need to save her from the gang, and test her DNA and then decide."

"Yes, Father, you are right" the Senator says and asks to Tom "How are you going to save her from this gang Mr. Pollack?

"Mr. Monroe, I have a plan. I intend to arrest her and whole gang alive. There is an ex- cop who led me to all this after your party offered the one million dollar award. Anyway, I came to inform you that one twin is still alive and she is claiming that she is your wife. When I arrest her then you or the court can decide of she is your wife or not."

"I don't know what to say Mr. Pollack. I am shocked and puzzled, whether this dead one is my wife or not. I have to take care of this one's funeral. If this one is not my wife, then she is my wife's sister and my wife's sister had nobody. I still have to take care of her funeral" says Senator to both Tom and Father John.

The Senator checks his watch and it is almost 10:30AM.

"That is very nice thought Senator" says Father John.

As he says that, he sees the funeral procession coming first. A police car then followed by a funeral limo and some other cars behind it. Even with twenty acres of land in the senator's house there are still parking problems with so many people. People stop talking and gather around as Father John starts guiding the limo to pull up near the front of door of the house. Senator and Tom are still standing by the garage talking. As the limo stops by the front door, the driver and four strong undertakers come out of the car and before they put their hat on, they turn to all the guests and bow and salute. Then they open the back door and take the coffin out and they carry it inside and the put the coffin on the stand. When the coffin is set on the stand, Father John asks undertakers to remove the lid of the casket. As they remove it, he sees the twin with a beautiful full-length dress and Father John's eyes tear up. He just stands wondering why this happened to her and also which twin is dead and where is the other twin. He just touches his forehead and crosses his chest with his hand. And he looks up to the sky and bows his head down and stands next to coffin wordless.

Meanwhile outside Tom and the Senator Frank Paul Monroe are still discussing what happened. And they both see another set of police cars with blue flashing lights come up to the senator's door. The driver and secret service get out, and the president of the USA and his wife step out. Also, the opposition party leader and his wife along and other top congressional leaders come out of their cars.

Senator Monroe and Tom are both surprised when they see President and First Lady and other top officials at his residence. They walk over to Senator Monroe and President shakes his hand and both he and the First Lady offer their condolences. The President says to the Senator,

"My whole family is with you. We are deeply saddened by her loss. She was going to be the next First Lady of the USA. Please accept our condolences. We were so shocked. The both of you would have been the most beautiful and charming first couple. Senator Monroe who is this young fellow with you?

"Thank you Mr. President for coming today. Yes, this has been the most difficult time for me. I cannot begin to understand what has happened. This is Tom Pollack, the detective who is investigating this case. You didn't see him on TV this week?" says the senator.

"No, I did not catch him on TV. There is too much crap and lies on TV" saying the President turns to Tom and shakes his hand.

"So you are Tom Pollack. The Attorney General was talking to me a couple of days ago about you. He was saying that you are close to finding the killers. He was saying you are very dedicated and thoughtful and a very smart, intelligent detective. He told me you never put the wrong person on trial."

Tom shakes hand with the President and looks straight into his eyes not showing his anger about the Attorney General' who almost frustrated him on his last case.

"Yes, Mr. President. It is an honor to meet you. That is nice of the Attorney General to say those things about me" says Tom

All the guests who are at the Senator's house for the funeral are surprised to see the President and the First Lady. They all stop talking to each other and start looking at them. Again President turns to the Senator,

"Senator Monroe, I am sure you are aware of the constraints on a president's time, but I respect you and what you stand for, and what you plan to do for this country. Personally, I wanted to meet you, but not this way. I told my secretary to cancel everything. I wanted to be here, to pay last respect to the person who would have been our nation's next First Lady. Would you please let us pay our respects? We will have to leave soon."

"Of course, Mr. President" says senator and signals his sister and her husband who are standing next to the door of the house with other family members to come over. The

Senator introduces his sister and her husband and is escorted to their living room, where twin's coffin is. All the guests go inside where Father John is standing next to coffin.

Senator and Tom are still standing by the garage. Tom asks the senator,

"Senator Monroe, should you not have accompanied the President inside?"

"No Mr. Pollack, I loved her a lot and she loved me the same way. I cannot look at her there sleeping forever. So I rather not go inside" By saying this, the senator's voice changes like he is about to cry but he controls himself. And Tom puts his hand on the senator's back by his shoulder. Being sympathetic,

"I understand Senator, losing someone suddenly like this it is very hard. I know what you are going through."

Just as Tom finishes his sentence, he sees Jody and her two companions, a cameraman and the engineer walking towards them, Jody asks the senator,

"Senator Monroe, was it the President who just came in the limo?"

"Yes he is here. He and the First lady along with some congress members are here to pay their respects. They are gone inside to have a last look at my wife. They will be out soon."

"Senator Monroe, is it possible I could have a word with the president please?"

"I don't think he has the time for a press conference, but when he comes out, I'll call him over." Tom standing next to all of them looks at Jody, wondering how a person could be so power hungry that she can be so insensitive to a grieving person.

In her effort to get close to powerful people, Jody does not ask Tom any questions because she knows the answer. As the President and the First lady step out of the front door, Jody tells her crew to start filming Live. President's security guards dressed in black suits and glasses, two of them rush over quickly to Jody before they say anything Senator intervenes,

"Please, gentlemen, the President is in no danger. I allowed her to cover this funeral; the two crew members are already cleared by our security."

Both men back off and the President and First lady followed by their companions come towards the Senator and Jody gets live shot of all. Seeing this as an opportunity to move ahead in her profession she gets more aggressive because everything is live on TV on their channel only.

Meanwhile, in Nevada, the twin who is locked up in the room for so many days is watching the whole funeral live on TV. She sits on her bed watching TV, tears coming out of her eyes wondering why her world has been turned upside down.

Again on TV, she sees the Senator as he is talking to Jody. When the President and First Lady come closer, Jody rushes near the President and asks him,

"Mr. President it is nice of you to come today, do you have anything to say?"

"Yes Jody" says the President getting her name from her ID hanging around her neck. It is a very sad day. As I was saying to the senator, this country has lost our next first lady. I just don't have the words to express why this happened to the nicest couple and our future president. But we can assure you, talking to our Attorney General a little while ago, we are going to bring these people to justice one way or another" says the President and moves over to shake Senator's hand and they all leave.

Time is approaching 11am and senator walks over to one of the security person. He tells him to start moving people so everybody can have a last view of the twin and security chief radios to the other,

"Ok guys we are ready start moving according to the plan. There are a lot of people we have to get done by twelve".

The Senator had hired extra people to make sure everything flows smoothly. As each car drives up to the front, people enter through the front door while their car is driven to the rear. They walk into the living room, pay their respects and go out of the back door. The cars that are not driven by chauffeurs are driven to the back by hired valet drivers while the people get out of their cars and go inside. This process continues for a long time, cars after cars, limo after limo, and families come to pay their respects. The scene has becomes unbelievable, there is no end of people coming some of women cry when they see a beautiful lady lying in the coffin with a most gorgeous dress. Outside, Jody covering the whole funeral keeping every body informed.

At the same time, the twin who is alive and locked up in Randy's room, is still looking at the TV, sobbing and sad and saying to herself, "Oh God, why?"

As it is getting late for the funeral, the Senator goes inside to see Father John, and motions for him to come to the side. When they are in the corner, the Senator says "Father John we have to move fast otherwise we are going to be late. There are too many people; we will have to inform them to come to Church."

"Yes Senator, do you know how many people are waiting to come in still"

"I'll go out and ask the security detail," and Senator walks out of the house and goes back to the security guard.

"Can you ask your guards in the estate and outside as to how many people are there?"

"Yes Senator, I'll call them right now."

"Hello, this is the security chief. How big is the line? We have to get done soon."

Finally someone answers, "Sir, I am a mile out of Senator's estate, but there are a lot more cars, maybe the next security person can tell you." He calls the next man on duty. He replies, "What I heard is that there is more than two mile line probably close to five miles long even passing the Church." Senator heard the conversation over the radio.

Senator walks back inside the living room and goes back to Father John. "Father John, there is a five mile long line even past the Church, can we delay the funeral for an hour or two?"

"Yes Senator, we can do that for and hour or so. But no more than that, will not be possible as all the Democratic senators and a lot of Republicans are coming to the funeral."

"Father John, let me talk to the Funeral Director, and se if he can suggest something. We can't delay longer than an hour and a half," and Senator walks out again, and he sees Detective Tom still standing at the same place, talking to another man whose back is turned to the Senator. The Senator comes up and asks the man wearing a Funeral bowler hat,

"Where is your boss? I need him right now."

"I'll get him right away Senator Monroe."

As the funeral worker runs to find his boss, Senator says to Tom, "I can't believe how many people have turned up, Mr. Pollack."

"Well Senator. It shows a lot of people in America respect you and share your pain, and that is why they are here."

As Senator and Tom are still talking, they see the funeral worker and funeral home CEO coming towards them. When they come near the CEO asks Senator,

"Yes, Senator Monroe, you need my services?"

Senator replies "Actually I do, I just talked to security, and people outside controlling the traffic. They say the line is getting longer and longer, we have to go to Church between one and one-thirty. Lots of Congress members are coming to the church and they cannot stay and wait; they have to go back to work"

"I've already heard from security. I have a suggestion which could work."

"What is that?" asks Senator Monroe

"We just bought a new Funeral Limo, it is very special, you know where the coffin lies in the middle very low, any person standing can get a glimpse in the coffin, and roof and sides are total glass. And we can drive the limo slowly, so everybody can see her on the way to Church."

"Yes that is a good idea. How long will it take for that limo to get here?" Senator asks.

"We have the limo parked at the Church. Since there are too many people here, I thought this would be the best way, so everybody can get a glimpse of Mrs. Monroe on her last journey."

"Okay, get that limo here and tell the driver and security to come through the back gate; it will be easy."

"Yes Senator, I'll take care of that right away," and he moves away from Senator, and he gets on his cell phone with the driver, telling him to bring the special limo through the back gate.

Meanwhile, Jody, the reporter, is enjoying her success at Senator's house. Any celebrities she sees or any world famous person, she interviews them on live TV, and the twin who is locked up on Randy's place keep watching what is going on. Jody sees a special funeral limo, pull up in front of the house, which is totally different from other limos. The time is almost twelve-thirty. The funeral is already half an hour late, when Jody sees the limo come to the front of the door, she and her camera crew come rushing to Father John and Tom who are standing by the garage, and she asks Father John, "Father John, we have a new Funeral Limo. Is there a plan to change the funeral time and place?"

"No, child, there is no change; a lot more people have turned up than we had expected. Yes, the funeral is getting late. This family doesn't want to disappoint anyone. We know they all want to have a last look at our next First Lady. So we decided that we are going to drive this limo slowly through the crowd to the church so everyone can get a last look."

She then goes to her radio to talk to the helicopter crew.

"Hello this is Jody. Please tell me what is happening outside."

"Yes Jody. This is the airborne crew." She hears a man's voice. "We are going to connect you to live. We have been up and down from the senator's house all the way to the church. There are thousands and thousands of people here on both sides of the road. There are children with their parents and older people with our flag. Some people have their flags attached to their car antennas and some on their windows. They are all half-mast. There are some people who have brought tables and chair. It looks like everyone wants to have a last look at the next First Lady." He continues his broadcast flying above the estate following the route to the church.

"There are too many people here. Looking down, it seems that there are a lot of SUV's with flashing lights. It seems a lot of the streets and roads are closed near the church. There might be that some VIP's are coming." He continues

"Jody, it seems like these VIP's are being escorted out of their cars to this huge church. Slowly, everybody was going in. I believe the scene was similar when the Senior Mr. Monroe, who was a congressman, died years ago. He is also buried here. What we learnt from funeral home is that the future lady will be buried almost near the senior Mr. Monroe's grave. Jody, I don't see any other change apart from it. Back to you, Jody."

Jody sees a new limo pull up. After finishing with the aircrew she takes over coverage back at the Senator's house

"This is Jody back at the senator's house. As everybody heard there are thousands and thousands of people lining up outside. I just talked to Father John. He said there is no way everyone can look at Mrs. Monroe because the funeral is 45 minutes late already. So, they will provide a new limo. It will be driven to the church slowly so everybody can get a last look at the next 1st lady." As Jody is stands in front of the senator's house, she sees the other limo move from the front of the house. The Security guards are stopping people from going inside the house to view her body. Security has also been informed that everybody should stay put and everyone will be able to see the next 1ˢᵗ lady. One person opened the back door of the limo, and four strong looking men brought the coffin out. Then two of the men removed the top. As the coffin is lying in the middle of the limo, her body is visible to anyone standing. Father John gets in the front seat with the driver. Security has informed that all people should stop where they are because the limo will start moving immediately. The limo with the coffin starts driving away from the home. Then the Senator, his mother, and the children got into the second limo. In the third limo the Senator's sister, and her husband and children follow. They are followed by other guests and Jody. She films everything live with her camera on the road and in a helicopter. This channel has everything under control, bringing live news to the whole funeral. All the limos start moving slowly starting with the one with the future 1ˢᵗ Lady. The house is left with no one but security. The limo starts moving slowly and makes a left out of the gate. There were so many people crowding the gate that there were people right next to the limo. The limo hardly had space to move. As the limo moves very slowly, the driver is very careful to not run over anybody's foot. By that time more police officers and security came to the gate to move people off. That way no one would get hurt. As the limo makes its way towards the church, it passes many people including elders, women, and children who have tears in their eyes. This chaos continues until the whole funeral procession reaches the church. All the limos park in front of the church. The limo with the coffin is driven to the back and the same strong undertakers take the coffin and bring it to the church hall for everyone to get a last glance.

By now Jody has set her camera crew up in the church in order to have live news. As this is happening, two fighter jets fly over the church. They are then followed by a slower plane, which was flying low. That plane has a banner on it saying, "America loves our future 1st lady!" The plane flies toward Senator Monroe's estate. Soon as the plane goes, a roar of helicopters start landing behind the church on the grassy ground. About eight or then people come out and the helicopter takes off and lands two blocks away on the empty ground and another helicopter lands back in the church. This keeps going on and on for 30 minutes. All the people coming out of helicopters go to the church.

Watching all this Jody says, "You have just seen two fighter jets fly by to ensure security. We have just been informed by the secret service that many of the congress members are here to attend Mrs. Monroe's funeral. Unfortunately this tragedy took her chances away from being the future first lady. She is not with us anymore. We are not allowed to film the people attending the funeral but we will keep you informed. That is all we can show on Live TV."

In Nevada, the twin who locked up in Randy's room is so sad because of what she has seen on the TV and her twin's funeral. After a few minutes she hears someone at the door. The door slowly opens and a white guy with food comes in. A black guy stands outside with a gun in his hand. The twin continues to sit on the bed with tears in her eyes. The white guy comes close to her and says

"I don't know how to say this but I've been watching the whole thing since last week. I am convinced that you are the next 1st Lady. I am glad to serve you. Here is the food for you".

The twin, who was trying to control her emotions, turns to the guy and takes the food from him.

"Look, you seem to be a very nice guy. You are the only one who helps me. You don't need this kind of life. If you two help me out of here, I have twenty million dollars in my account which both of you can have. Just take me to my family. My husband is a very powerful man. He'll get you a pardon even if you are caught. You don't know how much he loves me. Just deliver me to him."

The white and black guys are both listening to the twin. The white guy is convinced but the other one was not. He then walks in with the gun still in his hand.

"Look lady, you are very good at convincing but if we go back with you we will be arrested immediately. You know what happened at your house. It will be a long time before we get any pardon or any help from you or the senator. I'd rather be free and have less money."

"I know what you are saying", replies the twin. "You are all in trouble anyway. My husband is not just going to sit there and forget everything as soon as the funeral is over. You are all going to be hearing from him and the law. So take me back to him. I promise to protect you, all the way."

The Black guy replies to the twin.

"You are right, but I'll take my chances as it is."

He starts walking out to the door and the white guy stares blankly at him. Puzzled, he walks out of the room and locks the door behind him and the twin returns to watch the funeral.

Jody is still continuing her live coverage of the funeral.

"You just saw a lot of helicopters land here; we were told that most of senators and congressmen are here. Both

republicans and democrats are heading to the church where
the first ladies coffin is. As you know, the funeral is already
one hour late. It looks like that it is going to be delayed
even more but we don't know how long we will be here. We
will try to find out"

She walks over to one of the security officers
And asks him live on TV.
"Can you give us any hint what is going on?"
"All the congressmen and senators are inside for the
viewing of Mrs. Monroe now. I believe they will be done in
40 minutes. Then they are going to bring the coffin out for
final burial" says the security officer.

Jody thanks the officer and moves to a different location
in the church. She walks around interviewing all the
guests and people until a group of men enter. In about
40 minutes, four-dozen men, wearing black suits, come in
and ask everyone to move away from the front door. The
security clears a path starting from a half block away. They
make a path to where Mrs. Monroe will be buried.

Then the churches front doors open and the four
undertakers carry the casket outside. Following the coffin
is Father John, carrying holy water in one hand and a bible
in other hand. The Senator and his mother follow Father
John. As the casket is slowly carried towards the grave,
all the people including the congress and senators come
behind the family. After 15 minutes the casket is placed
on the side of the grave. All the visitors are asked to form a
very large horseshoe type of line.

Waiting for this moment, Jody, sets her cameras on the
front side of the church as everyone lined up. The camera
is about 40 feet from the grave so she could film everyone
lining up in that horseshoe formation. Jody starts taking

pictures, as Father John moves towards the casket. Following him is the Senator, and his family. They all stand next to the casket. Father John then opens his bible and starts the last prayer service. Next to him stands the senator, on his left side, his daughter holding his left hand. Ten minutes later, Father John is finished with the prayer and he throws the holy water on the coffin. Then Father John moves to the Senator and says, "You have to come forward and do your last duty."

As the Senator leaves his children and family, he walks with Father John to the casket. When he comes close to the casket, Father John signals the funeral workers to start preparing for the burial. Father John and the Senator go to take a last glance at the body.

The Senator looks at the beautiful twin with her eyes closed and he silently says to her "Wake up, my love, our children and family miss you. I miss you. I need you with me"

Then the casket it closed and the funeral crew begin the burial. It takes a few minutes for the coffin to be placed all the way at the bottom. Only Father John and the Senator stand next to the grave. The Senator is handed the shovel to put dust on the coffin. The Senator takes the shovel and digs some dust. As he bends down, his eyes get full of tears. With tears falling on the shovel, he then says to Father John

"I can't do this. I cannot put her under all this dirt with my hands. My heart tells me she will wake up. If I leave her where she is and if I throw this dirt on her, she is not going to forgive me. She will hate that I buried my love. I need her with me."

Father John puts his hand on the Senators' back and says, "I know what you are going through. You have to do this. Just pray to god and ask him to rest her soul in peace."

While the Senator is standing there with the shovel in his hand, deep in grief not knowing what to do, Jody gets a close up shot of the Senator's face. Whole world is now seeing Mr. Monroe's tears. And Jody says

"As you have just seen Mrs. Monroe's coffin was lowered in the grave and the Senator is unable to put the dirt on the coffin to begin the burial process. He does not want his love to be buried. He is grieving deeply.

The other twin is watching the whole funeral is crying profusely. As she is listening to Jody talking about the whole funeral and Mrs. Monroe's death, the twin says to herself "oh god…how can I watch my own funeral."

Jody continues to speak on live TV.

"It looks like Father John is trying to get the senator to put the dirt on the coffin again but the senator is still standing still. His right hand is holding the shovel and he is just staring at the coffin in the grave, he is not moving. You can see all the congress members watching in stunned silence the Senator's sadness."

Finally after thinking for a few minutes, he throws the dirt on the coffin and drops the shovel on the floor. He immediately walks back with Father John to his family.

The funeral workers start filling the grave with mud while everyone stands there watching and finally start to leave. After about a half hour the grave is covered with mud and the workers leave. All the senators and congressmen start moving slowly towards the senator and his family. Some of them just tap his shoulder and walk away while others express their condolences to him.

Slowly people pass by the senator and his family. They then all go behind the church so the helicopters could pick up the VIPs. This carries on for an hour and Jody looks at all her captured film.

Tom Pollack stayed behind the lines after the funeral was over. He just stands and watches for a while and finally gets in his car and heads to the courthouse. He gets there at 3 pm and runs to the judges chambers. He asks the clerk where he can find Mr. Kessler, the magistrate and she points him in the direction of the magistrate's office. Tom moves fast towards the magistrates' offices. He knocks on the door and hears a voice come in. Tom opens the door and he sees a fifty-five plus judge sitting on his chair behind the desk. Tom walks towards the judge with a packet in his hand.

"Hello Mr. Pollack" says the judge

"Hello Mr. Kessler, how are you?"

"I am fine. I have been watching the funeral for the last two hours and it is a very sad time for the senator. I saw him break down just before he put the dirt on her coffin. Before this, I have always seen him in good spirit but now this is too much for him to handle."

"Yes Mr. Kessler, I was there. I have been to his house a few times to make enquiries. He is totally heart broken. I don't know how he is going to carry on with his campaign. His party was counting on him. Mr. Kessler, I am here for a very important thing."

"What is it Mr. Pollack?" says the magistrate

"I believe I have found those killers, and I am going to arrest them tomorrow morning." Tom opens the packet and gets the photographs of the men and the twin, along with papers out of another envelope. They are arrest warrants. Tom puts all the paperwork on Mr. Kessler's table, including photographs. Mr. Kessler picks up the photos and looks at the arrest warrants prepared by Barbara. After looking at everything carefully, he looks at Tom and asks

"How did you find these guys so quickly because there are no names on these warrants?"

"True", Tom replies "the Senator had a hidden camera above the ceiling nobody else knew; only his close family knew it. And a good cop in gambling town he led me to them. These guys have never told their real name so as soon as I get them I'll find out whom they are."

"But Tom, the way they came to senator's house looks like they were not afraid of anything. They killed and took the twin back. What if it turns to violent and you cannot get them alive?" says the judge

"I know Mr. Kessler. This is going to be the biggest challenge of my life, I have planned in such a way that I hope to get them alive and unhurt. I can do it only if nobody leaks the news about this raid." As Tom gets serious about the plans, the judge looks at Tom's face and says

"When your cases came in my court, I felt good that I did not put wrong person in jail because you always made sure you got the right person."

Judge Kessler signs and stamps the arrest warrants and hands them back to Tom, and also puts a court stamp on the front and back of the photographs. Tom thanks Mr. Kessler for his work. Before he leaves, the Judge asks

"How sure are you about which twin was killed?"

Tom replies "I don't know both looked the same the day one of them died. That is why I want to arrest the other one alive. To make sure" Tom replies, "we will have to test her DNA too. If DNA turns out to be similar, then I don't know who is going to make the right call. What I heard from that ex cop is that the twin is claiming that she is the senator's wife."

"Yes, she would do that, even if she is the other one. Sticking to the senator is the only way she can save herself. Well Tom this case is going to make judicial history in U.S.A". Says Mr. Kessler.

"I know. We will see how it turns out. Mr. Kessler, I have to run, I am planning to arrest them tomorrow morning, when they are sleeping, and I still have to inform the FBI and arrange for flight for tomorrow morning. If I slip tomorrow morning, they will be gone, so please forgive me. I have to leave" Mr. Kessler stands up and shakes Tom's hand and wishes him good luck.

"Thank you Mr. Kessler" says Tom and takes all paper work, photos, and other documents and puts them in individual packs and leaves Mr. Kessler's office, in a hurry. He runs to his car in the parking lot.

The time is coming close to 5pm Friday. As soon as he gets in his car he calls Barbara

"Yes Mr. Pollack" she answers,

"I'll be there in twenty minutes so don't go home yet" Tom says

"Yes Mr. Pollack. I will be waiting for you" she says and Tom hangs up his phone. He pushes his pedal to the floor, and after five minutes, he jumps an almost amber red light. A cop parked on Side Street sees that car, puts his lights on and starts following Tom's car. As Tom continues to speed another cop car joins in. When Tom sees two cars following him, he puts his emergency blue light by opening his left window and on his roof. The cops behind Tom understand that it is official work, but they still follow him to the station. When Tom gets out of his car and hurries to pick up all the paperwork, the cops come out too, and one of them asks Tom,

"Chief is everything all right? You were in a hurry like you were after some killer."

"Yes you are right." Tom says and runs in to the police station. The security guard opens the door from the switch inside and Tom walks in and guard salutes him as he hurries to his office. He sees Barbara sitting in his office and says

"Hello Barbara" and he put all envelopes on the table and he sits on his usual chair.

"Hello Tom, looks like you had a rough day. It was very sad to see the senator when he was about to put dirt on her casket. That reporter Jody captured those moments so perfectly. I never had seen a man so powerful, so cool, and so strong in will power, so decisive break down like that. He did not break down the day she was shot, but on the funeral, I cried too watching him, I wonder what kind of woman she was, what made him fall for her. That kind of man could have whatever he wanted. He obviously loved her very much" she says

Tom very seriously says,

"I cannot tell you Barbara, all the wonderful things I have heard about the Senator's wife. She never got angry, she never complained. Senator's mother and sister praised her so much. She just had a beautiful mind which nobody could match. Looking at the Senator today, I wish good luck to his party in this election. They are counting on him, but after this, I don't know if he is going to carry his party to victory"

"So you think the senator is going to break down? I've seen him on TV before. But now I don't know. What is your opinion?" asks Barbara.

"Barbara I am hoping to arrest the twin alive and I hope that twin is Senator's wife. I am going to bend all cop rules to arrest those killers and the twin alive. Even if she is not his wife, his children might see her as their mom, because you just can't tell them apart we will see when the time comes. Anyways did you take care of all other arrangements?" Tom asks

"Yes Tom I did, you can log in to your computer and see all the details. Whatever you asked for, this time from Attorney General, he gave it to you" she says.

"Thanks Barbara. You have been extra helpful this time" he says

"Tom it is my job. But what you are going to do now? Are you going to sleep in the office or you going to go home to your wife? Are you sure you are going to be on that flight at six Am.?" She asks

"Yes Barbara I have to make it there by seven or seven fifteen, but have you, arranged back up in any case something happens, right?" asks Tom

"Yes Tom there is private plane and pilot ready for you. But what are you going to do now? Stay in the office or go home?

Tom replies "I think Ill stay here. It will be peaceful; at least some body can give me a ride from the station in case a taxi doesn't show up at home. I need to go through all the details."

Barbara asks "You want me to bring you some food Tom?"

"No I'll eat with these cops" Tom answers.

"Ok Tom, I'll leave now, my husband is probably out side waiting. If you need anything else, let me know, I'll keep my phone on, and I'll be here at seven. Keep me posted Tom" Barbara says

"Alright I'll do that" says Tom and Barbra leaves office and Tom sits these going through the details to how to carry this successfully. And he is hoping that nobody will inform Randy and his gang. The time is nearly nine o lock some body knocks on his door and one of the cops walk in

"Mr. Pollack, Barbara told me you are going to stay here tonight. Do you want to order any food?"

"Sure. I'll have whatever you guys going to have" he says

"Ok Mr. Pollack, but May I ask what is going on? Are you close to the killers? You hardly ever spend a night in the office" asks the cop

"I am Sam. But I can't discuss anything. Are you on duty all night?" Tom asks

"Yes I am" says Sam

"I am going to need a ride to the airport at four thirty am" says Tome

"Sure Mr. Pollack, I'll take care of that" says Sam and leaves the office.

The phone rings, Tom looks at the caller id and it is his wife. Tom presses the speaker phone and says,

"Hello honey"

"Don't you 'hello honey' me, you were supposed to be home at five after the funeral. The kids and I are still waiting. What time you going to be home?" she asks

Tom says "Remember, I told you last week that until this case is over I might have to stay out at work"

"You've been saying that for years, if you don't quit this job after this case, I am throwing you out of my life, and kids life, they need us both Tom" his wife says.

"I know honey I've found those killers and twin I am going to arrest them tomorrow morning, once they are on trial, I'll have more time for you and kids" he says

"How did you find them so quickly? You know Tom if you were not a good lover, I would have left you by now, but I have to admit that you are very good at your work too" she says in a friendlier tone and Tom replies

"So I am good for something... If I quit this job and in my next job, I may not have time to take lunch, so how are you are going to get any noonar like we used to?" he jokes

"I'll come to your work and get it" she says "you know women, if they want to get something they will get it"

"Yes I know. I should not have asked" replies Tom and he continue "Anyway I am staying here tonight; I have to wake up early to catch a flight to get those people. I have to leave at four; if I come home I won't be able to wake up."

"Tom what are you going to eat tonight? And are you going to wear same clothes tomorrow morning?" she asks

"Yes, I'll manage with the same clothes, and fellow cops have ordered food already. I'll eat with them" Tom replies

"Honey, don't eat that junk. I am going to bring you food from home and fresh clothes, It is just after nine, Kids don't got to sleep till ten thirty plus they are ok to look after themselves for little while, and I can make you happy" she laughs

"You are not serious, are you sweetie? At the police station, with all other cops on night duty? Somebody is going to suspect something. It might turn in to a scandal, especially now I am working on next First Lady's case" says Tom

"Well Darling, you have your own office don't you? All the presidents until now had mistresses in the White House, they did it. Why cant you in your own office? How could it be scandal, I am your wife."

"But you know the media is looking for something for their ratings" he says

"I don't care honey about any body's ratings, I am coming" says Tom's wife and hangs up the phone. And he sits there going over things in his head, He sits there for fifteen minutes, thinking that wife was kidding and hoping she don't show up at the police station. But a few minutes later the security guard at main door calls Tom, on his speaker phone,

"Hey Boss, there is nice looking women here to see you."

"She say she is your wife" and Tom replies with surprise "I thought she was joking, please bring her in." Tom switches off the intercom and few seconds later Sam and Tom's wife walk in. Tom's wife has two bags in her hand, one with fresh clothes in it.

She walks in first and says to Tom

"Hi honey" in a very sexy and loving voice with Sam standing there looking at Tom wife.

"Honey I thought you were kidding when you said you was coming here, Tom replies.

"You know dear that if I say something and I do it. Here's your food and your fresh clothes" Before anybody says anything else, Sam intervenes and says

"Boss, before the both of you say anymore, can I ask you something?"

"Sure" says Tom

"Where did you find this woman?" the cop asks

Tom jokingly says "With my in-laws"

"Do they have another one like this one?" he asks

"No they don't" Tom replies and Tom's wife is looking at both men listening to their conversation

"But if you find someone like her in her family would you let me know?" he asks again

"But you are married and have kids" Tom says

"Not to a woman like this, how did you brain wash her to bring home made food and fresh clothes?" Sam asks

And he continues to say "Mine does nothing like this. I have to eat junk food and that's why I am getting fat and no offense, you are older than me but in better shape! You are a very lucky man to have a woman like this!"

He then turns to Tom's wife and says "Mrs. Pollack, how much do you charge for lessons like this to my wife?"

She smiles and looks at Tom first and then at Sam and say "It comes naturally if you have it, if you don't you don't." As Sam leaves he says to Tom "She is right, I'll pick you four thirty in the morning" As he turns to leave, Tom tells Sam

"Hey Sam, if you don't mind, pick me up at my house in the morning" and looks at his charming wife "Sam, I have kept everything I need to take with me on the table, so make sure you put it all in your trunk and pick me up at my house"

"Ok Mr. Pollack" and Sam leave office. Tom stands up from his chair and holds his wife in both arms and kisses her only a touch on the lips. "Let's go home, but wake me up before four so I can get ready in time" he says

"No honey we can sit in this office till the morning then ill drop you at the airport, There is nobody here now" she says

"No, Let us go home" says Tom and starts walking out of office holding his wife's hand and as they pass by security cop and they both say good night.

Tom gets in passenger seat of his wife's car and they drive home and reach home in fifteen minutes. Tom comes inside and kids are sitting watching TV, and as soon as he sits down, his son asks Tom.

"Hey dad I heard you found those killers and the twin" Tom is surprised and asks,

"Who told you that? I hope you have not called any of your friends with that information. What about your sister?" as Tom looks at his daughter, she shakes her head saying no.

"Mom did" his son say "Dad you know, I am a cop's son, until you catch those people, I am not going to brag to my classmates, I promise"

"That is a good son" he says and looks at his wife for sharing that information with children

"Honey don't give me that cop look, our children won't say nothing till you catch those killers" she says

"What cop look? I just did not want anything leaked." Tom turns to his son and daughter and says "Anyways, children you remember I promised you that I'll be back tomorrow night or Sunday, as don't say nothing to your friends, till I get home"

"Oh dad you are great cop" and both kids get up from their chairs and hug their father.

Tom says to them

"I love you all very much; I have to get up early so let's go to bed." As Tome hugs them and kisses good night, he stands up and says to his wife "Wake me up at three forty five please."

"Ok honey" and Tom leaves, to goes to bed leaving his wife to say goodnight to the kids.

It is Saturday morning at three forty five, six days after the twin was killed and other one kidnapped and at Toms' house the alarm goes off, Toms wife switches the alarm off, and turns the bed side light on, as she sits up and she touches his right shoulder,

"Honey" before she says any thing Tom answers "Yes honey I am trying to wake up." Tom sits up too. Five minutes before four am, Tom's wife gets off the bed and asks him to get up and freshen up, while she gets his clothes and his glass of milk with honey.

As she leaves to go to kitchen Tom goes into the shower and when he comes out ten minutes later from the bathroom, he sees his suit and shirt on bed. He changes his clothes and comes downstairs to the kitchen where his wife is sitting on the dining table chair in her long night gown. Tom sits with his wife and drinks his glass of milk with honey while she has her orange juice.

Tom and his wife are still sitting in the kitchen talking to each other. At four twenty five, Tom sees a car pull up his house through the kitchen window. He knows it is Sam coming to pick him up and take him to the airport. He tells his wife,

"Honey he is here I have to leave" they both stand up and walk toward the door to go out, Tom opens the door partially and waves to Sam and he waves back, Tom and his wife hug each other and Tom's wife says to him,

"My love, I will pray to God that he will give you strength and courage to arrest those wrong doers without any bloodshed. Please come back home safe. The children and I need you. Please call me as soon as raid is over" She kisses him and her voice changes and eyes fills with tears and she says "They must be very dangerous people to come to our next president home and kill his wife. Please be careful. I love you"

Tom pulls handkerchief out of his picket and wipes his wife's tears, and kisses her on her lips and says

"Your prayer always works honey. I love you" and then opens the door and goes out. Before he gets in the car he waves to her as she is standing by the door.

Tom's wife stands there till the cop car disappears from her eye sight, she closes the door and switches off the kitchen light and goes to her bedroom and sit on their bed. She thinks about Tom, worrying about him like she always does when he is on a case like this, till he calls and tells her that he is safe. But this time, things are different; he is facing the most dangerous criminals, who had dared to kill next 1st lady.

As Sam drives to the airport, he says

"Mr. Pollack or I should I call you chief? I know you are on special mission…" but before Sam says anything more Tom replies

"I can't tell you anything. I have to keep everything a secret till I catch these killers because the police chief, the mayor and the governor of that jurisdiction are all money minded people, but by midday if all goes well, and I pray to almighty, you will see everything on TV."

"Ok chief I won't ask any more questions" and they reach the airport in fifteen minutes, by five am, since there is no traffic in the streets of Denver at this time in the morning. Before Tom gets out of the car, he says to Sam

"Oh Sam if that news reporter, Jody comes to the station asking for me make sure you let everyone know to tell her that I am home with my wife. She almost blew everything on the day of the funeral, so let her keep guessing till I get them."

"Ok chief ill take car of that" says Sam and gets out of the car with Tom opens the trunk and gets Tom his bag and map holder. Tom thanks Sam for the ride and shakes hands with Sam and goes in to terminal.

Tom goes directly to the airline check in desk and takes of his hat and shows his badge to the attendant saying hello. The attendant immediately recognizes him and gets the co-pilot.

"Hello, Mr. Pollack. It is good to see you again. We received the e-mail your secretary sent that this is official police business. Let me take you bag" says the co-pilot picking up bag with two of Tom's favorite guns and lots of ammunition. Tom asks,

"Is the flight on time?"

"Yes, it is. We are leaving exactly at 5:45am. There will be no delay. If any passenger does not show up on time, we will not be waiting. We have been directed by the CEO of this airline that this flight has to leave on time since he has received an e-mail from the Attorney General. Please go ahead through security to the terminal. We will take care of you" says the co-pilot.

Saying thank you to both the co-pilot and the attendant, Tom walks through the security and sits by the window at the terminal looking outside and wondering, as usual, how everything will end.

At 5:40am, the flight attendant comes to escort Tom to his seat and tells him that they are ready to leave. Tom sits by the window in the plane and this time there is no one sitting next to him. As the plane takes off he closes his eyes and tries to get some sleep. The plane arrives in the gambling town of Nevada at 7:00am. As the flight door opens, Tom gets his things from the overhead cabin and collects his bag from the co-pilot and gets off the plane.

By the time Tom reaches the taxi stand it is ten minutes past seven. Tom goes to the first taxi in line and gets in the back seat saying good morning to the driver. The driver says good morning and asks him his destination. Tom takes out his badge and shows it to the driver and says

"Please take me to the FBI offices. Do you know where it is?"

The driver replies

"Yes I do, Mr. Pollack. You don't have to show me your badge; I already know who you are. I will get you there within fifteen minutes without taking around the whole city."

As the taxi leaves the stand, Tom asks the driver "So, you know me?"

"Yes, everybody knows you Mr. Pollack" the driver replies in English with an accent. His English is limited since he is from the Middle East. He continues "I won't say anything to anyone. I have seen the news and I think I know why you are here."

"You appear to be an intelligent man. Can you keep seeing me here a secret till I crack this case?" Tom asks.

The driver replies "Yeah, yeah, no problem, I will not tell anyone. This county gave me a home and a good life for my children, so I will do anything to help."

Tom continues the conversation and asks "What do you think you know about this case? Do you know any of the people involved?"

"Yes, Mr. Pollack. I've been driving taxis for twenty years now. A woman who looks like the dead Senator's wife came here about fifteen years or so years ago with the gangster named Randy. Randy bought one of the bars which he turned into a strip club and casino. Initially, the business was slow until one night when the woman who came with Randy went wild after a couple of drinks. She sang in the club as she did a strip tease. She was very hot and the people in the club went crazy. Since then, Mr. Pollack, that place has been full and buzzing every night. She performed for six months; even I went to see her after another cabby told me about her. Man, she was a beauty and no one had seen a body like hers here in years! Within three months, people came from all over to watch her. At one time, Randy even had an account with our cab company to take customers back and forth to the airport" the taxi driver explained.

The driver continues "Anyway, after about six months, when she realized that Randy was just using her, she found another girl to take her place and she managed that side of the business. Eventually, she became Randy's girlfriend. They lived together and this arrangement continued for years. She wanted to get married and settle down but he had other ideas. She could not decide what to do – maybe she did not have the courage or the support to leave him. But, eventually she saw her twin sister doing well and she finally left him. Well, after that, what happened everybody knows Mr. Pollack...?"

As the taxi pulls in front of the FBI offices gates, the driver says "We are not allowed to go inside, Mr. Pollack, so I will drop you by the security gate. Good luck with case. It is thirty six dollars plus gas charge of one dollar."

Tom gives the driver sixty dollar and says

"You have been very helpful. Thank you very much." He picks up his bags and map of the town and shakes the driver's hand and walks in to the FBI offices. It is just before seven thirty when Tom walks in. The security officer recognizes Tom and comes out of his office to open the door and shakes Tom's hand and says

"Welcome, Mr. Pollack. We were expecting you. You are exactly on time. Let me walk you to the conference room where everyone is waiting for you." They walk past a few office rooms and cubicles and stop by a closed conference room. The security officer knocks the door and walks in ahead of Tom. Tom notices about forty FBI agents on the left side of the room and a raised platform on the right with table and chairs. Two FBI officers are sitting and talking to each other and another senior officer is standing behind them. As soon as the senior officer sees Tom, he walks over to him and shakes his hand and introduces himself

"I am Larry, the Chief Officer of this FBI branch office. We have everything ready as you requested."

As Tom keeps his bag on the table, he says "Thank you Larry. Before I brief everyone, I would like you to collect every agent's cell phone from them till the raid is over." Larry asks the two junior officers who are sitting at the table to collect the agent's cell phones. As they are collecting the phones, Chief Officer Larry says

"Mr. Pollack, I know you are very good at your job. The agents assembled here are also very loyal and superior officers. They all want to assist and catch these killers and bring them to justice for killing Mrs. Monroe and causing pain and turmoil to Senator Monroe and the people. What is the next step?"

Tom says "Is everyone wearing full body protection and have rubber soul shoes so that there is no noise when we enter the building like I asked?"

Chief Officer Larry replies "Yes, they are dressed as you requested". After ensuring that there have been no leaks to Randy's gang about the raid, Tom pins the map to the board and starts to brief the agents about his plan. He says,

"First of all, thank you all for being here. I apologize for asking you all to hand over your cell phones, but there is a reason for that. Next, I would like the four pilots and then teams to step forward".

As the team steps forward, Tom asks them if helicopter being used are old or new ones. Before they can answer, Chief Officer Larry says

"Mr. Pollack, these are newest ones. They are very quiet and top of line. We have very strong orders from the Justice Department to abide by your instructions."

"OK Larry. I want all four choppers to be at least three blocks away from this building." Tom points to the streets he wants blocked on the map with a stick and say "I want the four choppers to be in this area with two FBI vehicles. I want you to wait for my instructions in case someone escapes." After getting further instructions from Tom, they go back to their seats.

"Ok, next, I want the five strong agents who will be handling the battering rams to come forward" says Tom. Five agents pick up their rams and step up to stand in front of Tom and Larry. He continues with the instructions

"We are going to break the doors to get in. I want an agent with loaded guns standing on either side of the agent with the battering ram. When the agent knocks down the door, agents with the gun instruct loudly and clearly to the folks inside to freeze and put their arms up. Do not shoot unless it is absolutely necessary. I want these killers alive including the twin sister. She might be the Senator's wife.

If you have to shoot, then aim at their shoulder, leg or any other part which will immobilize them. Do your best to get them alive."

The five agents with the rams return to their seats and Tom checks his watch for the time. It is seven thirty seven. Tom concludes saying

"Chief Officer Larry and I are going to the police station in this jurisdiction to bring them on board about the raid. I want to keep them in the loop and involved. I don't want someone calling 911 and the police officers showing up at the raid and shooting at us in ignorance. Also, I want to make sure that when we approach the building without police lights or sirens. Finally, to recap, remember to block the streets quietly, and have the helicopters and two FBI cars within three blocks of the building. I want three cars with two agents at each corner of the building. Two agents will accompany the agent with the battering ram for the raid. If anybody has any question, ask me now. We are getting very short on time."

Nobody says anything. So, Chief Officer Larry says to Tom "You gave clear instructions and I am sure the agents understood it."

He turns to the agents and dismisses them by saying "Ok officers. You have your orders. Take your positions. Tom and I will meet you at the building five minutes before eight after a brief stop at the police station. Play it cool and don't let anyone get suspicious."

As the agents rush out to their cars to get into position, Tom quickly picks up his bag which contains the arrest warrants along with his guns and ammunition.

Chief Officer Larry and Tom walk at a brisk pace to the parking lot with two FBI agents. They take one car and head to the police station while the other cars and helicopters go towards Randy's club.

Driving to the police station, Tom says "Larry, the reason I asked you to collect everyone's cell phone is because the Chief of Police in this jurisdiction is a close friend of Randy's who happens to be involved in the plan to get Mrs. Monroe killed."

Chief Officer Larry is surprised and says "Oh really!! But, my boys are clean".

"I know Larry, but I did not want to take any chances" Tom replied.

As they enter the police station, it is seven forty five. Tom and Larry run in and show their badge asking to see the Police Chief.

The officer in charge answers "He is not in yet. He was supposed to be here by 7:00am, but I can call him to check…"

Tom pulls the arrest warrant out of his bag and shows it to the officer and says

"We have arrest warrants for Randy and his gang for the murders of four people in Denver. FBI agents will raid Randy's building at eight o'clock."

The officer immediately calls the Police Chief's home and says

"Chief, the famous detective Tom Pollack is here at the station with the FBI officer. They have arrest warrants and are going to raid Randy's club at eight o'clock. They want you to be present there."

Wondering how Tom found them so quickly, the Chief replies hesitantly "Tell them that I'll meet them there with the squad cars" and hangs up.

When the officer relays the information to Tom and Larry, Tom gets a little edgy and pulls Larry by the arm and says

"Let's run! I think this guy might have just blown our plan". They race to their car so that they can get to Randy's club in time.

As soon as the Chief hangs up with the officer, he immediately calls Randy's emergency line. Randy picks up the phone after about five or six rings and asks

"Why are you calling me so early Chief?"

As Randy sits up in his bed to speak, the blonde girlfriend grumbles in the background and the Chief says urgently

"Randy, you have five minutes to get out of there!!! That detective Tom Pollack is here with the FBI. They are planning to raid your place within the next ten minutes. I just got called by my officer saying that they were at the station with warrants and they asked for me to accompany them. Just get your money and leave right away! I will leave the door to my house open for you. You can stay there till it is safe and then you can leave. My wife and children are visiting my wife's family."

Hearing this, Randy panics and throws on whatever clothes he can find on. As he is rushing to get dressed, the blonde girl sits on the bed fighting her hangover and asks

"Randy, where are you going? Why are you in such a hurry?"

Randy quickly finishes getting dressed and grabs the briefcase with money and whatever other essentials he can find and replies

"We have to return this money back to the Chinese Mafia. We are going to keep the club."

The blonde believes his excuse and starts to relax. Randy takes the briefcase and runs down the stairs to the back of the building and exists through a secret emergency exit. He rushes to an old pick up truck and throws his briefcase in the back and runs to the gate to unlock it. He comes back to the truck and puts on the hat he had left in the passenger seat and drives out of there.

Randy gets out of the gate and makes a right turn and steps on the gas to pick up speed. After about two blocks, he hears and sees a helicopter making its way down. He quickly drives under it before it lands. As he continues, he sees two black cars driving in the opposite direction towards his club. He does not turn to look at them but keeps on driving straight ahead.

After a couple of blocks, he pulls into the MacDonald's parking lot from where he has a clear enough view of the activities. He notices that the helicopter landed right in the middle and the two black cars park to block off the street. FBI agents get of the vehicles with their identifying jackets and guns drawn out. They start to stop the passing vehicles. At the same time, he notices that the other three sides have been blocked in a similar manner. Randy realizes that the Chief was telling the truth and that they were about raid his club at any minute. He is just extremely relived that he managed to get out in time!

As the time gets closer to eight o'clock, the whole club is surrounded by FBI agents, the streets are blocked and no one is allowed to enter and the people leaving are being questioned and checked by the FBI.

Tom and Larry pull in front of the club and join the other FIB agents with guns and battering rams. At about the same time, the Police Chief comes racing down the street in his squad car with other cruisers following flashing lights and sirens blazing. He stops three blocks away at the barricade with the chopper and FBI cars. As the Chief gets out of his car, the agents run towards him and yell

"Turn off these lights and silence the sirens off right now and instruct your other officers to do the same!"

After the Police Chief orders his officers to silence everything, he turns to the agents and asks permission to go in. The FBI agent says

"You can walk in, but cannot drive your car in there or take your weapons or cell phone. Leave them here."

The Chief and a couple of his officers follow the agent's instructions and run to the entrance where it is a couple of minutes before eight and Tom and Larry are giving final instructions to the team. Tom puts the pictures of the gangsters and the twin sister in the side pocket of the bag which is on the hood of the car and puts on the bullet proof vest offered by Larry. As Tom is putting on the vest, the Chief comes in front of Tom, a little short of breath and introduces himself

"Hello Mr. Pollack, I am the Chief of Police and these are my officers."

"I know" Tom replies, "I know who you are Chief. We have arrest warrants for Randy and his gang" he says pointing to the papers on the hood. While the Chief picks up the papers and reads them, Tom continues to get ready by pulling one of his guns from the bag, checking if it is loaded and then puts it in his shoulder holster. He picks up his other gun and makes sure he has enough ammunition with him.

Tom then addresses the Chief and says

"Ok Chief, I am sure you are wondering how I found them so quickly…well, one of Randy's gangsters made a call to Randy from the Senator's house. That is how I traced them here."

Then Tom turns to Larry, tensed and ready to get started and says "Ok Larry, I am ready". He picks up the photos from the bag's side pocket and motions everyone to move. Tom and Larry open the front door of the club slowly without making any noise followed by the other agents. They walk in with their guns drawn and look to the left side and notice a couple of old men watching a skinny stripper performing on the stage. Tom holding his gun with his right hand, signals for four agents with his left hand and whispers to them to get rid of the old men and the stripper. When Tom looks to his right where the bar is located, he notices a large Hispanic man, who appears to be the bartender, sitting on a bar stool snoozing with his head on the counter.

As all the FBI agents move quietly in the big lounge area, Tom and Larry walk over to the bartender and Tom points his gun at the tip of the bartender's nose. The bartender wakes up in shock and before he speaks, Larry puts his finger on his lips and signals him to be quiet. Tom pulls out four pictures with his gun still pointed at the bartender and puts them in front of him and asks

"Where are they?"

The bartender is terrified and tells Tom "Second floor, four rooms to the right of the stairs or elevator".

Tom ask authoritatively "And, what about Randy? Which room is he in?"

The bartender says "Go left once you get off the elevator and he is on the first room on the right side." Tom then asks one of the agents to arrest the bartender and take him out.

Tom orders the five agents with battering rams and other agents accompanying them to head upstairs and split up and position themselves on either side of the stairs. Tom and Larry take the elevator accompanied by five agents with one of them carrying a battering ram.

When they reach upstairs, Tom signals for everyone to take position and whispers to Larry

"You take care of the twin sister and make sure she is not hurt. I will deal with Randy."

Agents with battering rams position themselves in front of the door and watch for Tom's signal accompanied by agents pointing guns at the gangster's doors. Tom is front of Randy's room and Tom counts one, two, and three with his fingers and at the count of three the agents smash the doors open.

Tom rushes in with his gun drawn along with two FBI agents. He sees a blonde girl in her nightdress sitting on the bed, her eyes wide with shock and fear. She puts her hand up as Tom goes to check in the bathroom and closet and finds it empty with no sign of Randy. He comes and stands in front of the blonde girl and points his gun at her forehead and asks

"Where is Randy?"

The girl, shaking with fear, answers

"He left a few minutes ago with a briefcase after he received a phone call. When I asked where he was going, he said that he was going to return the money he had received from the Chinese Mafia for the club. He said he wanted to give the money back and keep the club."

Tom believes her story. He looks out of the window facing the back of the club and sees no one. He runs out of Randy's room to see what is going on in the other rooms.

In one of the other rooms, Number One is sleeping with a white, middle aged woman. As soon as he hears the door smash open, he pulls his gun from under the pillow. As the two FBI agents enter and ask him to freeze, he fires at one of the agents. Since the agent has his bullet proof vest, he does not get hurt, but the other agent fires back at Number One and the bullets hits his right shoulder. Number One drops his gun in pain while the woman tries to hide under the bed screaming and yelling not to kill her. Number puts his left hand on the wound and sits on the bed in pain. The agents walk over to him and one of the agents presses his handkerchief on the wound and asks Number One to put pressure on it while the second agent calls in the medics.

As the agents break into Number Two's room, he is still groggy from the alcohol of the previous night and he just puts his hand up and surrenders. The agents handcuff him and take him into custody.

In the third room, the black guy is in bed with a fat, light skinned woman. As the FBI agents break open the door and ask him to freeze, he and the woman get up from the bed and he puts his hand up and tells the woman

"I knew this day would come. I even told Randy, that this time he has gotten himself in big trouble and that it will burn him and us along with him". They handcuff them and check under the pillow and room for weapons.

When Larry and the FBI agents break open the door and enter the fourth room, the twin sister who is just coming out of the shower is shocked to see agents in her room with guns. She recovers quickly and puts her hands up in the air and smiles to the agents and says

"What took my husband so long to send the FBI to find me? He can't do without seeing all the time. It is good to see you officers. I am Mrs. Monroe."

The agents are surprised not sure what to believe, but are sure that she looks exactly like the Senator's wife. One of the agents says

"We have orders to arrest you. Till it can be proved that you are Mrs. Monroe, we have to take you into custody."

She replies "Yes, I understand. You have to do your duty. But, can I get dressed first?"

Larry says "Yes, you can, but we have to first check the room to make sure that there is no possibility for escape".

Larry motions for the other agents to check the rooms and when he is satisfied that there is no way out, he lets her go to get dressed. Shortly afterward, the twin returns, dressed in the same outfit she was wearing the day she was the day she was kidnapped, which also happens to be the same outfit the other dead twin was wearing too. She stands in front of the agents and puts her hands out to be handcuffed.

However, one of the agents feels bad for her and says

"We'll wait for Mr. Pollack to get here before we handcuff you. Please sit there. He will be here soon."

Meanwhile, Tom leaves Randy's room and heads to the room where he thinks he heard a shot fired a couple of minutes earlier. He enters the room and finds Randy's number one man sitting on the bed with a wound to his shoulder. He asks the FBI agents

"Is he ok? Have you called the medics?"

"Yes, they should be here any minute" replies the agent.

"Ok, you guys take care of him and get him to the hospital" Tom walks over to examine the wound and realizes that it is not so bad. He says

"It does not look bad. It looks like it is just a flesh wound. Tell the medics to fix him up so that he can be transported to Denver today."

The FBI agents say ok as Tom leaves to go to the next room. As he enters, he sees Number Two sitting on the bed in his underwear, handcuffed and hardly able to open his eyes due to a hangover. Tom tells the agents

"Put him in the shower till he sobers up and make sure that he does not escape. I will check the other two rooms and come back".

As he enters the third room, he sees that the black guy and his female friend are handcuffed and in custody. He asks "Is everything under control here?" The agent says yes. So Tom says that he will return after he checks on the twin sister.

Tom rushes to the twin's room where Larry is and thinks to himself that it took only five minutes to break in and take control of Randy's club but somehow Randy got away. As Tom walks in, the twin sister is sitting on the bed with Larry and the other agent standing guard, the twin sister smiles and says,

"Mr. Pollack, I am glad to see you. This is the second time we meet. I am fortunate that you were able to rescue me". Even after being locked up all this time, she continues to be charming as always. She continues to ask "Don't you recognize me, Mr. Pollack?"

"Yes, I do. You definitely look like Mrs. Monroe, but you do have an identical twin sister. So, it is hard to tell you two apart" Tom replies.

Larry and other agents listen interestingly to their conversation as she continues,

"I am Mrs. Monroe. Let me refresh your memory. Four years ago, my husband and I had invited you, your wife and children to our daughter's seventh birthday party. Our sons got into an argument over a new toy which was just out in the market and it so happened that we had got it before you had."

Tom says "Yes, I remember that incident. However, it does not necessarily prove that you are Mrs. Monroe; your twin could have told you about it. Unfortunately, there were four murders at the Senator's house and one of them was your twin. I have to take you into custody till we can prove without a doubt that you are the Senator's real wife. The DNA testing on your twin proved that she was Mrs. Monroe and the Senator had to accept it with much grief."

"Yes, you are right. We were identical twins. Though our behavior and personal habits were different, we still looked the same, had the same skin tone and body. Being identical, we were so connected when we were young, that when I got sick, she got sick. When I lost a tooth, she lost a tooth. It was amazing. But, later as we grew older and after we turned eighteen, our behavior and personality changed completely. She and I went in different paths. She went wild and I became a lady" she said.

"Ok, I'll take your word for it for now. But I have to still take you into custody. So, I will not handcuff you behind your back. I will handcuff you to one of the FBI agents." Tom continues "I wish I had met your twin earlier. Maybe then I could tell the difference somehow."

Though his conversation with her makes him wonder if she really could be Mrs. Monroe, he still feels that he cannot take any chances till he is completely certain. Watching his expression, she says,

"Mr. Pollack, I know you are puzzled. When we were younger, no could tell us apart other than Father John or my mother. When we were high school, my sister used to pretend to be me to people who had not met me and no one could tell. But later, after people met both of us, they could tell the difference from our personalities."

"Did you tell your sister about our son's argument about the toy?" Tom asks.

She says "Yes, I think I did. She was with me for a week and we tried to catch up by discussing every thing in our lives."

"Ok, till we have concrete proof, I won't say anything." Tom replies.

Then, Tom turns to the FBI Chief Officer Larry and says

"Could you please have the agents check all the rooms and make sure everything is ok? Also, make sure that the so called 'Number One' is stitched up and ready to travel back to Denver. I will also need some air marshals for the trip back so that I can take these guys and the twin back to Denver."

As Larry leaves the room to take care of things, Tom pulls his cell phone and calls his wife while still in the twin sister's room, "Hello, honey, it's me".

His wife, who was anxiously awaiting his phone call, asks "How did everything go?"

"Everything went fine. Only one guy got hurt slightly wounded", he replies.

Tom's wife asks "Is the twin sister ok?" to which Tom replies that she is fine.

His wife continues "Which twin is it Tom? Is it Mrs. Monroe or Randy's girl?

"Honey, I can't tell. She acts like the Mrs. Monroe we met at the party." He replies.

"So she is the Senator's wife?" his wife asks

Tom says "I cannot tell the difference since I had not met the other sister. So, I have to take her into custody till we can prove that she is Mrs. Monroe"

"Tom, why do you want to lock up a nice woman? If she says that she is the Senator's wife, then she must be. Why don't you take her to her husband? I am sure you remember how well she treated us at their daughter's party. She let our son play with their son's toys even after their little argument."

"It is really not that easy to let people who are wanted for murder walk away until justice is done. It is the law. I know you like the Senator's wife, but I have to do what the law dictates." Tom says

Tom's wife replies "Yes, Tom I like her. She is one of the best woman I every met. Most Senator's wives are snobbish, but Mrs. Monroe, though she knew that there was an excellent chance that she would become the First Lady, never acted that way. She was kind and charming. Promise me that you will help her Tom. If you don't I will leave you."

Tom replies "Honey, stop this lecture. I just called to let you know that I was fine. Yes, I will help her is she is the Senator's wife. Mrs. Monroe would not have any reason to kill her twin sister. But, on the other hand, the other twin sister might have good reason to take Mrs. Monroe's place."

"Tom, why do you always have to think like a cop? Twins love each other, they have a special connection. They don't hurt each other. So, drop your damn law for once, and help this twin regardless of who she is. Don't treat her badly" his wife says.

"Ok dear, I will do what I can. I will not mistreat her. As you know, I never mistreat anyone. Anyways, I have to go now. I'll be back in town by this evening, so I will see you later." Tom says.

"Alright honey. I am really glad you are ok. I was very worried and was praying for your safety. Now, that I have heard your lovely voice, I feel better. I love you Tom. Now blow me a kiss…here is mine…" Tom's wife says.

"I can't do that since there are other people in this room with me. But I feel the same about you. I will see you later." Tom says goodbye to his wife and hangs up the phone and turns around to find the twin sister watching him. She says,

"Mr. Pollack, sorry, but I could not help overhearing, was that your wife? We keep in touch and talk to each other from time to time."

Tom is surprised and says "Oh, really. She never told me that she talks to you. I am surprised."

"Well, it is nothing. We just talk about our families and keep in touch" she says.

As Tom is talking to the twin sister, it is around 8:20am and Larry returns and reports back to Tom "Tom, everything is ok. We checked the other rooms too and found some another person who was hired recently by Randy. Other than that, we did not find anything else. The bleeding on Number One's shoulder has stopped and he is fine to fly out to Denver. Number Two is coming around too recovering from his hangover. I have directed the agents to get everyone ready so that we can take them downstairs and get them to our offices."

Tom says "Thanks Larry. But, have you seen any sign of Randy? Was there any clue in the building as to where he might be?"

"No, we searched everywhere. There is no sign of him. But there are some parts of this building we cannot get into. Once we take care of the apprehended suspects, we will come back and take care of this building and keep you posted" Larry replies.

"Ok, have your agents already taken everyone to the ground floor?" Tom asks

"Yes, they have. Are you going to escort our would-be next First Lady downstairs?" Larry asks

"Yes I will. But what makes you sure that this is our impending Fist Lady?" Tom asks.

"Well, from what I heard in the news about the First Lady after the murders, she seemed like a charming and wonderful person. And I have also heard the talk around town about the twin who lived with Randy and she was wild. Now, having met this twin, and seeing how warm and charming she is, I am beginning to believe that she is Mrs. Monroe, possibly our next First Lady!" says Larry.

Larry leaves the room and as he walks down the hall to go downstairs, he says loudly,

"Officers, if the suspects are dressed and ready, bring them downstairs." The agents bring all the four men in shackles and women in handcuffs outside and bring them down slowly. Within twenty minutes, everyone is sitting downstairs ready and Tom escorts the twin sister down and she sits in a chair away from the gangsters. Tom handcuffs the twin sister to an agent and walks over to the heavy, Hispanic bartender who is handcuffed too. He asks the agent to free him and asks the bartender to follow him to the bar.

Tom and the bartender go behind the bar counter and Tom asks in a stern voice,

"What is your name?"

"Julio" replies the bartender

"Do you have a green card?" asks Tom.

"No" replies the Julio nervously

"Do you have a family?" questions Tom

"Yes, I have a wife, two daughters and a young son" says Julio.

"Do they have green card?" Tom asks

"No" Julio replies getting really scared.

"If you help us with information, I promise not get you or your family in trouble with the INS and will help you with the green card." Tom says

"Sure, sure, I will help in anyway Senor. What do you want to know?" asks Julio eagerly since he does not want to get into trouble.

"Where is Randy? Did he leave through the front door?" asks Tom.

Julio replies "No, I did not see him leave through the front. If he had left when I was snoozing, I would have heard footsteps and the door. But, I believe he has a secret exit through the back of the club. He must have used that exit to get away."

"Thank you, Julio" says Tom and asks "Can you make some coffee for everyone? Also, do you have anything to eat?"

"Yes, Mr. Pollack, we get fresh doughnuts every morning, so we have plenty of those" says Julio and then adds "But, Mr. Pollack, if you give me forty eight hours, I will find Randy for you….if you help me and my family get green cards."

"Ok" Tom replies "If you find Randy, then I will do what I can to help you get the green card" and hands Julio his business card. Julio is very excited and tells Tom

"Mr. Pollack, please go sit down and I will take care of everyone and get the coffee and doughnuts ready." He goes behind the bar and sets the coffee to brew and gets the doughnuts and cups ready for the agents. The FBI agents start coming over to the bar to help themselves to coffee and doughnuts and Tom stands to the side looking at the twin sister, still unable to make up his mind.

As Tom stands watch her, Julio comes to Tom and asks if he can serve the twin sister fresh coffee and doughnuts, and Tom nods in the affirmative. Julio takes coffee and food to the table where the twin sister is sitting. When he reaches the table and serves her, she asks Julio to sit down for a bit and asks "What is your name?"

"Julio" he answers "How are you holding up? I am sorry that you were locked up. I wish I could have done something to help you."

The twin sister replies "Don't worry, it's over now. Soon, I will be free to go back to my family. But, tell me about my sister…."

Tom casually walks over and stands behind their table listening to their conversation.

Julio says "I don't know what to call you. The both of you look identical! You talk a little different then her, but before she left, she had started to change her way of talking too – in fact sounding more like how you sound. That is why I cannot make out the difference between the two of you. Well, last couple of years; she was sad since Randy was not treating her well. She would come and sit by the bar in the evenings and have "lunatic juice", that is what she called it alcohol. She would eat at the bar too and go to bed somewhere around eleven in the night. Some days, after a couple of drinks she would sing in a very heart broken voice. The words of the song were sad. She sang about loving her mom and her sister and how she had made mistakes in like and wondered if her mom and sister would forgive her if she came back home."

Listening to the bartender, her eyes tear up and fall on her cheeks. She quickly controls herself and says "Then what happened?"

"Then about two weeks ago, she was sitting here at the bar having her second drink and it was just after ten. She saw her twin sister with her husband and family on the news. She asked me to give her a bottle of "lunatic juice", and took it up to her room on the second floor and I think she continued to watch them on the TV."

He continued "After that night, she seemed to be at peace and happy. She told me that no matter what, family is family and that she was going back to them and apologizes for her past mistakes. She said that she would make it up to them and asked me not to tell anyone about her decision. And, you know what happened after that....but; tell me which twin are you?"

"I am Samantha Monroe, the Senator's wife" she says with certainty and confidence.

"Ok" says Julio and asks her to have her coffee before it gets cold and returns to the bar.

Tom finishes his coffee and doughnut and walks over to Number One and asks him

"Are you feeling ok, Number One? What is your real name?"

"Yes, I am fine! I cannot believe that you are asking me if I am alright after having me shot. And, I will never tell you my name. As far as you or anyone else here goes, my name is Number One" he replies rudely.

Tom says "Well, you should consider yourself damn lucky that you were not killed after you shot the agent first. Anyway, any idea where Randy would have gone after he left here?"

"I am not telling you anything. I am not going to rat on my boss. He has helped me a lot. I hate cops" says Number One.

"Yeah, I can see how your boss helped you!! He helped you by getting you the death penalty for these four cold blooded murders. You can help yourself by telling me where he might have gone and I might just save you from getting the death penalty" Tom says.

Number One says with anger "I told you that I hate cops. Get away from me. I would rather get the death penalty than help you catch him."

"Very well, you will get what you asked for then" says Tom and walks away.

He goes to Larry and says "Looks like everybody is done here. Can you get the cars closer to club so that we can get these guys to your office? I want them all transported in separate cars."

As Larry gets on his radio to have the cars brought up front, Tom adds "Before we get them to the car, can you send one of agents outside to make sure there are not TV cameras or news reports lurking around?"

Larry checks in with the FBI agents outside to ensure that there are no reporters and tells Tom that the place is clear and they are set to leave.

Tom says "Let's start moving them. But, Larry can you go to the court with me so that I can get papers signed to transport them to Denver today." Tom picks up the photos from the bar and puts it in his bag along with one of his guns and lifts his bag up ready to go. As they walk outside, they see the Police Chief and his cops standing to the left.

Tom stares at the Chief intently and the Chief realizes that Tom suspects him with Randy's escape before the raid. Larry radios the agents inside to bring the suspects out. Tom watches as Number One is brought outside in shackles and led to the police car. Number One is notices the Chief standing on the left and his blood pressure sky rockets with anger. As he passes the Chief, he spits towards him before he goes into the car.

Number Two does the same thing as he is being led away followed by another guy. Then the black guy is let outside with the new person whom Randy hired. When the black guys sees the Chief standing with his cops, he gets very angry and cannot keep his mouth shut and says,

"Chief, why don't you do something and get us out of this situation? If you don't, I am going to spill my guts. I will not spend my life in prison or on death row for murder. I had nothing to do with it. It was Randy's plan to bring the money and the twin back. I did not want to kill anyone!! And honestly, I did not fire the gun. It was the sharp shooter who killed those people including the Senator's wife."

The Chief just looks at him with shock and is worried as to its implications. But, he keeps his mouth shut. The black man is forced into the car by four FBI agents followed by the new hire.

As the next car pulls up close, the twin sister is brought out with one hand cuffed to the FBI agent. She notices Tom and Larry standing at about seventy five degrees to the left, about ten feet from the car. On the left side, she sees the Chief who thinks she is the slut, but the twin sister slowly shakes her head saying no and the Chief understands.

Since no one else is brought out, the Chief realizes that Randy got away. The FBI agents start moving away and Larry orders two the helicopters to escort the five cars with the suspects to the office and dismisses the other two helicopters back to their base.

After the club is locked up, four agents stand guard. Tom and Larry get in the car and head towards the state's Supreme Court. In the car, Larry again asks Tom

"Do you think she is the Senator's wife or the other twin?"

Tom replies "I don't know Larry. I saw the video of them from the security company just before they were shot. They both were dressed alike - the same dress, same make up, same hair style, to surprise the Senator. But the DNA on the dead sister came up as the one for the Senator's wife. Given that, the Senator accepted his wife's death with great pain. But, the state prosecutor, Melissa, and I kept up the investigation. As you know, she was aware of this raid.

Since the murders, we have been looking into the twins past and it appears that the younger twin, a.k.a. the slut, was very good at pretending to be the other one. So, honestly, I don't know which one this is. But, there is one person, the Senators preacher, who has been the family's preacher and friend for forty years who swears that he can identify the twins by the way they walk."

Larry asks in an amused tone "Since when do priests notice the way women walk?"

Tom says "No Larry, he is not that way. He has seen the twins since they were four years old. Their mother used to dress up alike and only ones who could tell them apart were the preacher and the mom. He believes that the Senator's wife is alive and he begged to not harm the twin when we arrested her. It is a good thing that we were able to get her back alive. The preacher does not believe in DNA testing. He says he believes only in God and trusts his eyes to tell the difference."

"But, Tom, look at this in a different way. What if the DNA on this twin comes up as that of the Senator's wife and the Senator still does not believe her? Since this test with DNA has already happened once... and the Senator believes his wife is dead. How will he believe that this is correct? Then again if the DNA comes up different, then he will definitely not believe that she is his wife. This woman is in trouble either way. How is she going to prove she is really his wife if the DNA of the twins is so similar? Especially now with the elections close by and in the Senator's favor, his party will not want him to get tangled in this mess" Larry says.

"Yes, you are right Larry. This has come at a very bad and inopportune time, not to say that murder ever comes at a good time! All I can say hope for is the dead twin to rest in peace and Lord have mercy on this one. Well, you know, people who have truth on their side will eventually always win in the end. From what I have heard about the Senator's wife from people around her, it seems that this one is her. How she is going to prove it and how the Senator is going to accept it, I don't have any idea" says Tom.

Their car pulls up in front of the courthouse and the time is close to 9:30 am on Saturday. At this time, both Larry and Tom realize that the court is closed since it is the weekend. Larry tells Tom "Let me try to get one of judges who live close by....." and calls his secretary.

"Hello, this is Larry. Can you try to get hold of one of the state Supreme Court judges and request if they can come over to the courthouse? This is an emergency."

His secretary says that she will try her best to get someone and hangs up.

Within five minutes, his secretary calls back to say that a judge will be there in ten minutes. Larry thanks her and tells Tom "A judge will arrive within ten minutes. Usually they have a judge on call for emergencies like this".

Larry and Tom wait in the car for the judge to arrive talking about their careers. A car pulls up behind them within a few minutes and a distinguished looking man around sixty gets out of the car. Tom picks up his bag and gets out of the car along with Larry. They walk up to the judge to introduce themselves. The judge shakes Tom's hand and says

"Mr. Pollack, it is a pleasure to meet an honest, dedicated cop such as yourself. Your fine reputation precedes you" And he turns to Larry and shakes his hand and says

"Another fine cop. I respect your work."

Tom says "Thank you, your honor. It is good to meet you too."

"What can I do for you, officers? You didn't find the killers of the Senator's wife in this town, did you? I guess you did. Otherwise, a cop like you would not here. Did you find the kidnapped twin too?" asks the judge walking towards the courthouse.

He continues "Let's go inside and discuss it. I am a little slow on these stairs, but can still talk as we climb up." The three of them climb up the stairs to the courthouse and the judge swipes his access card to enter the building. Once inside, they go into the judge's chambers and the judge sits behind his desk while Tom and Larry stand in front of his desk.

"Gentlemen, don't just stand there. Please sit down. One day, maybe you will be sitting on this side of the desk in my position!" says the judge.

After they sit down, the judge asks "So, Mr. Pollack what can I do for you?"

"Your honor, with the assistance of the FBI Chief Officer Larry and his agents, we arrested the gang who killed four people in Denver at Senator Monroe's estate and kidnapped the twin sister. Unfortunately, the boss got away. I strongly believe that he had insider knowledge of the raid and he escaped just a few minutes before we entered." Tom says and pulls out the photos along with the arrest warrants and appropriate extradition paper work for the judge's signature. The judge reviews the paper work and acknowledges that everything is in order, he says as he inputs the information into his computer

"Mr. Pollack, I don't ask good detectives such as yourself how you found these people, but I will ask if you know which twin is alive. As you as aware, this has caught national attention and the whole country in puzzled. There has never been a case such as this before."

While the judge is entering information into the computer, Tom replies

"No, your honor, I do not know who this twin is. When we arrested her, the people around there said that she acted different from the other one who used to live here. So, I have no idea. I will let the justice system decide."

Acknowledging and agreeing with Tom, the judge continues with the paperwork and about half an hour later, he signs and stamps the forms and hands them to Tom. Shaking hands with them, the judge says

"Here you go, Mr. Pollack. It was a pleasure to meet the tow of you."

"Thank you, your honor" says Tom and they all walk back to the car. As Tom and Larry are getting into their car, the judge says

"Tom, look after this twin well and treat her nicely. You never know, she could become our next First Lady and we could all be in trouble."

Tom says "Your honor, I hope she turns out to be the real Mrs. Monroe, our next First Lady, because the real Mrs. Monroe is very kind and generous and she never holds a grudge. Both the Senator and his wife are very forgiving people and I have heard from others that Mrs. Monroe very rarely got angry."

"Well, it is good to know. Anyway, gentlemen, good luck and have a safe journey back" says the judge waving goodbye and walking to this car. Tom and Larry get in their car to head back and Tom pulls his cell phone and calls his secretary, Barbara. She says

"Hello Mr. Pollack. How did it go?"

"Barbara, I got them, but Randy got way with a little insider tip I think. Anyway, can you arrange for two planes to be ready to leave around 1:00PM or so?" Tom asks

"Sure, Mr. Pollack, I will make the arrangements right away. But, what about the kidnapped twin? Did you find her too?" Barbara asks

"Yes, I found her there too." Tom replies.

A curious Barbara asks "Which twin is she?"

Tom replies "Barbara, I cannot tell. Everyone is asking me the same thing. Only DNA testing can tell if she is the Senator's wife."

"But, Tom you are a very smart detective. I thought you would have figured it out by now. I am sure you have an idea" she says.

"As I told you earlier, this case is going to go down in the history books! She definitely looks talks, acts and sounds like the Senator's wife. But, they were identical twins and I have heard that the wild twin was very good at pretending to be her sister. So, I don't know. Anyway, can you take care of the flights first?" asks Tom

"I am making the arrangements as I am talking to you Tom" she replies

Tom questions "How can you do both at the same time?"

"Tom, I am a woman. We multi-task, which means we can do a lot of things at the same time" she says.

Tom realizes that it is best not to question any further and hangs up saying "Call me back when the arrangements are final."

Barbara calls back a few minutes later and says that she has six different airlines that have flights available for Tom to pick from. Tom says

"Any airlines you are comfortable with will be fine."

"But, why do you want two planes? You only have about seven prisoners plus air marshals" questions Barbara.

Tom says "You are right and you always question just like my wife." He continues when Barbara agrees with him "I don't want the twin to travel in the same plane as the other suspects. One of them is quite dangerous, so I want a separate plane for her." Barbara realizes that Tom is really not certain about the twin's identity.

"Hey Tom, I have e-mails from airlines offering discounts if the twin sister travels in their airline" says Barbara.

Tom replies "I am sure. They all want to be involved in this story and get their fifteen minutes of fame since this is a story for the books!! I am sure some of the airlines think they will make money out of this. Anyway, use the same airline I used for my previous two trips."

"Ok Tom, it is about 10:30am, do you think you will be able to make it to the airport by 2:00PM?" she asks.

Tom puts Barbara on hold and asks Larry if they can wrap everything up by noon or shortly after. Larry says that they will be done by then. So, Tom tells his secretary

"Go ahead Barbara. We will be ready before 2:00PM."

Barbara replies, "I'll finalize the arrangements Tom. Oh, make sure to take good care of the twin, she very well could be our next First Lady."

Tom says "Yes, I will do that. Everyone is saying the same thing to me, even the judge!! I always treat every one well no matter what they are accused of. I leave it up to the justice system to punish them — that way I don't feel guilty."

"I know, Tom, you are a good person. Tom, I just got confirmation. The planes will be in hanger three. They will be ready at 1:30PM. The security at the back gate will be informed that you will be in the first car with the others following you" Barbara says.

"Thank you Barbara. You are wonderful!" Tom says

Barbara asks "You mentioned that I am like your wife, does that mean she complains a lot like me?"

"No, no, I didn't mean that. She is a good too...most of the times" says Tom in an amused tone.

"So, sometimes, we are good?" asks Barbara.

"Barbara, as much as I am enjoying this conversation, I don't have time for humor. We'll talk about this subject after this case is settled. Like always, you did an excellent job!" says Tom and hangs up the phone.

Tom checks the time and it is almost eleven o'clock. They pull into the FBI Branch office and all the prisoners have already been moved into the holding cell where they have changed and been fed. Tom and Larry go into Larry's office to discuss their next steps.

Larry asks "Tom would you like something? Is there anything on your mind?"

Tom replies that he is thinking about their flight plans and if they leave by 2:00PM then they will be back home by 4:00PM.

Larry persists "But, Tom, it seems like something else is bugging you. What is it?"

Tom answers "I wish I had met the Mrs. Monroe's twin sister earlier. Maybe caught them while they were shopping or running errands two weeks ago when the twin came.

Then, there might have been a chance that I could have figured out which one is alive today. But, my gut says that this one could very well be our next First Lady. But, once I hand them over to the Justice Department, I don't know what will happen. How will she prove that she is the real Mrs. Monroe or how the Senator who has accepted her death will believe that she is now alive?"

While they are talking, Larry's secretary walks in with fresh coffee, sandwiches, bagels and cream cheese. She is a young woman about twenty eight years old. She walks up to Tom and puts her right hand out to shake his hand. As Tom stands up to shake her hand and she says in a sexy voice

"Mr. Pollack, I had expected that an experienced detective like you would have been older, but I have been watching you on TV for a few days and now having seen you in person, I have to say you look young." Shaking his hand she continues,

"You have nice strong hands, your wife must love it" she says with a smile.

"Well, thank you. I will make sure to tell her that. It is nice to meet you." Tom says and Larry's secretary walks out slowly with her eyes on Tom.

Watching this interchange, an amused Larry asks Tom jokingly "Hey Tom, you want to take her with you? She seems ready to go with you."

"No Larry, I don't think my wife will appreciate that and I am very happy with my wife. But I can understand her sentiment of finding someone who will make her happy and provide her a secure future" says Tom.

Tom and Larry continue their conversation as they enjoy the fresh coffee and food. As they are eating, an FBI agent knocks on the door and informs them that the prisoners are ready and that the transport vans and security are standing by for them.

Larry asks Tom "Well, everything is ready. How many air marshals do you need?"

Tom replies "I need four each for the plane with the guys and two for the plane with the twin sister. I don't foresee any problems with her."

It is almost noon and Larry says that he will go take care of getting the prisoners moved and be back for Tom. Tom continues to wait in Larry office talking to agents and Larry returns thirty minutes later and informs Tom that everything set and they are ready to roll.

Tom thanks Larry for all his help and they walk out and inspect the vans with the suspects. Then Larry and Tom get into the car and head to the airport followed by the vans. As they drive to the airport, the roads are cleared of other vehicles and they reach within thirty minutes. They drive up to the back entrance of the airport and as they reach the security gate, Tom and Larry pull out their ID. Once verified, they are let in and drive up to hanger three. The FBI agents get out the vans with their guns ready and first eight air marshals go into the plane to check everything while the prisoners are waiting to be escorted into the plane. Tom and Larry are standing by the stairs when one of the marshals comes to the door and asks Tom how he wants them seated.

Tom says "Put each of them at least five rows away from each other and make sure that they are chained to metal bar on the seat."

Taking Tom's instructions, the air marshals escort and seat Number One, Number Two, the black guy and the new hire. The remaining air marshals board the plane and take their positions.

The twin is escorted out of her van and taken to the second plane followed by the air marshals. Tom and Larry walk behind them and just as they are about the climb the steps to board the plane, the twin smiles and ask Tom,

"Mr. Pollack, are these chains necessary? I am going home. There is no need to fear that I will escape. I am the Senator's wife. I will ask him to personally thank you for saving my life."

Tom looks at her and hesitates a few minutes before saying

"No, I am sorry I cannot do that. I would be breaking the law." He signals the air marshals to take her inside and get ready to take off.

Larry asks Tom which plane he will be flying in and Tom replies that he will go in the plane with the gangsters since he needs to keep an eye on them. Tom thanks Larry again for all his help and shakes his hand and climbs up the steps to board the plane and waves to Larry and gets in. Once inside, the flight attendants close the door while Tom walks through the plane for a final check. The pilot announces for everyone to take their seats and put their seat belts on. After twenty minutes, both the planes get clearance to take off.

Two hours later, they land at the Denver Airport and the planes stop at the prearranged terminal at the side of the airport. The planes are surrounded by police cars as ordered by Tom. It takes about half an hour to get everyone off the planes. Amidst heavy security, the prisoners along with the twin are escorted to Tom's precinct as previously planned and arranged.

Meanwhile, Jody, the reporter comes to the police station to get updates on the case. She has been diligently coming to the station every day to talk to Tom to get status on the case, but has not been able to talk to him and has not seen him since the funeral.

Jody walks up to the security officer and asks

"Is Mr. Pollack available to make a statement about the case? I haven't seen him in the past few days. Where is he?"

The security officer replies "Mr. Pollack is not available right now. He should be here sometime today."

Jody persists "Can you give me a hint as to where he is or when he is coming back?"

"I don't know Ms. Jody. Even if I did, I cannot divulge that information to the press. You will have to be patient and wait till he gets here. Anyways, you are here everyday for information, why are you taking this case so personally?" questions the officer.

"Well, if I am able to break this news first, then I will be the number one reporter with top billing" she replies.

The officer replies annoyed "Everyone in the press is the same; all they care about is the ratings of their show. They don't care about the fact that the Senator, who probably will be our next President and bring back respect for America in world, is heart broken and suffering a great loss. The fact that a wonderful woman, who could have possibly been our next First Lady, has been murdered does not worry them as their show ratings."

Jody backs off and walks to her news van when she sees a lot of police cars coming towards the station with just lights flashing. She gets suspicious and stands back and watches the scene from the side as lot of action appears to be going on. After about half an hour, some of the police cars leave the station and Jody hurries back to the security officer and asks

"I just saw a lot of cars at the back of the station with officers going in and out. Is Mr. Pollack here? Did he get the killers and the twin?"

Before the officer can answer, the phone rings at the security officer desk. The officer answers the phone and listens to Tom who is at the other end

"Is that news reporter Jody and her crew still out there? I saw their news van when we were driving in. Get rid of her. Tell her to come tomorrow morning at nine o'clock and I will talk to her then."

The officer hangs up the phone and without a word takes Jody's arm to escort her outside. Jody gets upset and says

"What are you doing? Let go of my arm, I can walk by myself. I will report you. Mr. Pollack is here, isn't he? That was him on the phone?"

Without answering, the officer opens the door and takes Jody outside. Her cameraman and engineer join them as them come outside and the officer says

"Ms. Jody, you will have to leave now. Yes, that was Mr. Pollack on the phone. He wants you to come back tomorrow morning at nine o'clock and he will talk to you then. But, if you continue to stay here and keep asking questions now, I will have to charge you for trespassing. Come back tomorrow and you can get your story and your ratings." The officer smiles and continues "Do not mention about what you saw today in your news because if you do, Mr. Pollack will not give you the story and you will not be able to break the news first. Do you get the point?"

Though Jody does not like it, she understands the situation and leaves with her crew. She is anxious and wants to know what is happening but realizes that she has to wait till the next morning.

By five o'clock, Saturday evening, after the prisoners are processed and in their cells, Tom walks to his office looking tired. Barbara is anxiously waiting for him. She hands him a glass of water at room temperature, just the way he prefers. As he drinks his water, he takes of his hat and sits in his chair. Barbara asks him,

"Tom you look exhausted and lost. What happened? I have never seen you look like this." She adds humorously to lighten the mood "Not even when you have had a good argument with your wife. Do you want to talk about it?"

"Yes, but first I need to talk to Brain. Can you get him on the phone for me?" Tom asks and she dials Brain's number and puts him on speaker phone.

Brian asks "Mr. Pollack, did you get them?"

"Yes, we did Brian. We got everyone including the twin sister, but Randy. He got away just a couple of minutes before we entered. My mistake was to tell the Police Chief about the raid who I am sure tipped him off. I tried to keep the information away from him till the last minute, but I had no choice. I had to notify him since it is in his jurisdiction. But, we were able to get the killers and the twin, so I will recommend that you get the reward money once the trial is over. In the meantime, can you keep your eyes open for Randy?" Tom asks

"Of course, if I find out any thing, you will be the first to know. And Mr. Pollack, what I had heard about you is true, you keep your promise and I respect you for that" Brian says.

"Ok thank you Brain. I will be in touch" says Tom and disconnects the phone.

Barbara asks again "Tom, come on, tell me what is bothering you?"

"What is bothering me is this whole situation about the twins. After we rescued her, all she has been telling me is that she is the Senator's wife and that it was her younger twin, Cassandra who was killed. But, as you know, we have proof from DNA testing, that it was the Senator's wife who was killed. The people at the club all agree that this twin was not behaving like the other one. Then again, from what I have learnt, Cassandra was very good at pretending to be Samantha, the Senator's wife, when they were young. And, we don't know exactly what the reason was for her sudden visit to the Senator's house after all these years. The bartender said that when the news broke that the Senator was the next presidential nominee and saw him and his wife on the news, Cassandra was going through a bad time with Randy. Randy was not treating her well and had taken up with a younger blonde. That is when she decided to leave him. So, the question is did she decide to leave and come to her twin in the hopes that she can redeem herself and start over or did she come with a plan to get rid of her and take her place?"

Tom continues "No matter what her reasons were for visiting Mrs. Monroe, the question still remains as to who is the twin who is alive today. How will she prove that she is the Senator's wife if the DNA comes back inconclusive or similar to the dead twin? If the Senator accepts her as his wife, but later realizes that she is not then what will he do? The only way he can find out truly if she is his wife of not is in their intimate relationship and by watching her behavior constantly. But, once he accepts her, he will be stuck with her even if she later turns out to be not her. By the time this trial will be over, Senator Monroe could very well be our next president and in the White House. His children and relatives would have accepted her. Even if it comes out that she is Cassandra at the trial, she would have become very good at pretending to be Mrs. Monroe by then and the women in this country will feel sympathetic towards her and will talk their husbands into accepting her as the Senator's wife!"

"In fact, this morning, my wife already lectured me about it, when I told her that the twin sister was safe and claiming to be Mrs. Monroe" he adds.

"What did you wife say?" asks Barbara.

"Well, she said that if she is claiming to be the real Mrs. Monroe, and has told him certain facts which are true, then I should believe her. She asked what I would do, if she was in that situation and I said that she did not have a twin, so it did not matter. And I had to hang up because I could not hear any more reasons!" says Tom

Barbara says "Oh, Tom! I don't know what to say." A cop knocks on the door and comes in and says,

"Mr. Pollack, the twin in custody keeps calling the guard from her cell and keeps insisting that she is Mrs. Monroe and wants to speak to her husband, the Senator. I told her that she cannot use the phone till she appears in court tomorrow, but she wants to know why she should go to court when she has done nothing wrong. She says that if she can talk to the Senator, he will get her out of here. What do you want me do Mr. Pollack?"

"I know I faced the same questions from her when I arrested her. Ok, wait a little while, let me call the Senator." Tom says.

Since Tom has the Senator's cell phone number, he calls him and the Senator answers,

"Mr. Pollack, how can I help you?"

"Senator Monroe, I need to see you. This is an emergency matter" Tom says.

"Ok Mr. Pollack. Why don't you come to my house around six o'clock? Perhaps you can join the family for dinner. Can you tell me what this is about?" asks the Senator.

"I don't want to get into this over the phone. Phones can be bugged. I will see you at six" answers Tom.

Tom turns to the cop and tells him inform the twin sister that he is going to meet with the Senator and will get back to her in a couple of hours. He turns to Barbara and tells her that he is going over to the Senator's estate to tell him the news. Barbara says that she is leaving for the day since her husband is waiting for her outside.

Tom arrives at the Senator's estate at six o'clock. As he drives to the security gate, the guard steps out and Tom notices the FBI agents guarding the estate. The guard tells Tom that the Senator is expecting him and opens the gate just wide enough for Tom to drive through and quickly shuts the gate.

Tom pulls up in front of the mansion and parks his car and walks up to the main door. Even before he rings the bell, the Senator himself opens the door. He walks Tom to the dining room where the whole family including the Senator's mother, children, sister, her husband and family along with a couple of party members and wives are seated.

The Senator leads Tom to the empty chair beside his own seat. Mrs. Jones brings Tom a salad and drink and as she places it in front of him asks the Senator if she could ask Tom something. The Senator agrees. So, Mrs. Jones asks,

"Have you found the twin sister?"

Tom replies "Yes, I have found the twin, but I cannot tell which one it is. That is why I am here."

The Senator immediately replies "But I can, where is she?"

"She is in custody. She is not allowed any visitors till we get statements from all the whole gang and leaves to go to the kitchen; Tom turns to the Senator,

"Senator Monroe, we have the twin in custody. She wants to talk to you; she claims she is your wife."

Senator Monroe's children all heard this, and his daughter jumped out of the chair and stands between Tom and her father.

"Please Mr. Pollack; have you found our mother yet? Bring her home, all of us miss her and so does my dad even though he never says it."

The Senator pulls his daughter to him, "I miss her too, and If Mr. Pollack says this is your mother then I shall bring her back myself."

He sees the tears rolling down her cheeks and kisses her forehead, "How about you take everyone to the play room? I'll come upstairs later."

The Senator asks his sister,

"Sister, please take them to the play room, this is just too serious, and I'll tell you everything later."

"Now Mr. Pollack, we can speak freely. You have met my wife before; who do you think she is?"

"Well Sir, she looks like your wife but I heard her sister was capable of looking just like her.

Mrs. Monroe Sr. immediately interrupts,

"Mr. Pollack let me tell you something, these two girls grew up in this house. Cassandra was a very naughty child and it was easy to tell them apart, but for some reason she started behaving and it was nearly impossible but their mother always had a way. I don't know how but she could always tell them apart."

Mrs. Jones enters the room and hears parts of the conversation,

"Excuse me, but I was with the two sisters for a week and I know the difference. When Cassandra walks she makes a little tapping sound that is the only difference."

"Now look here Mr. Pollack I told you at headquarters that the twins had different walks." Father John says.

"Well I'm willing to believe both of you, but we only have one sister, how would we compare? There isn't enough evidence to show in court that she is innocent.

"So Mr. Pollack, what is the answer to all of this? You are telling us the woman in your custody says she is my wife, but the DNA lab reports have said my wife is deceased. You said she wanted to see me."

"Senator, I know this is all very important too you but I must say that this is a very bad time for this to happen, we have an election to win." says a member of Senator Monroe's party.

"I cannot leave my wife in jail, if she is my wife. My children need their mother I have to bring her back."

"This is turning into a huge scandal and the opposition will definitely be using this against us."

"Me neglecting someone that could be my wife and letting her rot in jail is not going to help the campaign! Mr. Pollack what do you recommend."

"Well sir, I am working on getting more DNA samples and I am trying to get it as soon as possible. Court is scheduled for tomorrow and all felons must attend. If she is your wife then all charges are dropped and you can bring her home easily."

Mrs. Jones and her helper are setting up the food for everyone, Father John recites the usual prayer and they eat. Afterwards Tom decides to go home and he gets up,

"Senator Monroe, I will have to leave now, please excuse me."

Everyone says goodnight and Senator Monroe walks him to the door,

"Mr. Pollack let me tell you something, when my wife and I were dating, Cassandra used to pretend to be her and she fooled me many times. I just want to make sure that this is really my wife, if I were to take her back."

"Senator, just wait for the DNA report, until then there is nothing I can do for you."

Tom shakes hands with the Senator, "I'll keep you posted."

Tom gets into his car and makes a call to his office's operator.

"Good evening, this is Officer Pollack; I need you to pass a message to the guard watching the twin in custody. Tell her she may not see anyone until the DNA test on Monday. Thank you."

Tom drives back to his house, where Mrs. Pollack is waiting for him. When he pulls the car into the driveway she comes outside and welcomes him with a warm smile.

"It is good that you have finally come home!"

Tom's children run down and greet him too, "Dad, did you get into any fights today? Mom told us about the Senator's wife? Did you figure it all out yet?"

Tom's daughter speaks before he can answer,

"You have to tell us everything, and all our friends know you are working on the case from the news! They all want to know."

The family sits down in the living room, Tom is relaxing in the living room and the kids are all sitting by his feet while his wife stands listening. His son asks again

"What happened, all my friends are expecting a call from me! Did you find out which twin it is?"

"My dear children, this is a real case and most of the information is top secret. But we did not fight anybody nor do we know which twin it is. We have made a few arrests today; I'll tell you everything when the whole case is settled."

"But dad, shouldn't you know which twin you arrested? If you arrested the Senator's wife won't you be fired?"

"I cannot say anything until tomorrow, but I promise you will be the first ones to know."

The children get up and go back upstairs to finish their movie.

"Honey, what will you have?" asks his wife.

"I already ate at Senator Monroe's house, but let's sit and talk. Have you eaten anything?"

"No, but we can eat together later when you are hungry. I was worried about you today Tom, are you sure you have no idea who this woman is?"

"Actually I am a hundred percent sure that this is Mrs. Monroe, but I'm not quite sure what to do about it."

"Then how are you holding her in custody?"

"I have no choice, not until there is concrete proof; we have to wait for the DNA test."

The husband and wife continue their discussion and speculations until they go to bed.

Sunday morning, Tom woke up after all of yesterday's excitement. He gets ready and comes downstairs to his wife, who has prepared his usual breakfast.

Tom has his breakfast then kisses his wife before leaving home for work. He reaches the police station right before nine o'clock. He normally did not work Sundays but this case was very important. As he is walking in, he is stopped by Jody and the camera crew.

"Mr. Pollack, do you have anything to say to America regarding the Senator's wife scandal?"

"Jody, I cannot reveal any information until after twelve."

"Can't you give us a little hint Mr. Pollac?"Jody insist

"I told you, not until after twelve."

"Fine Mr. Pollack", Jody gives up for a while.

Tom goes inside the office and Barbara is already there. When he takes his coat and hat off she comes into his cubicle.

"Good morning, Tom."

"Oh good morning, Barbara, sorry to ask you to come into work today."

"It's ok Tom, it is my job and this is a big case."

"What else has happened?"

"Well Tom, cops from your team have been interrogating the suspects since seven this morning. But none of them admit they shot Mrs. Monroe. And the woman, she still insists she is Mrs. Monroe. They should be out to brief you shortly. Oh and the state's head prosecutor Melissa Wolfe is here too."

"It is sad that this has to happen to Senator Monroe now, with the election and everything. Oh Barbara is Terrence here too?"

"Yes sir, but he isn't in a very good mood."

The other officers are making their way to Tom's office,

"Mr. Pollack we need to see you in the conference room." Tom buzzes Terrence to come to the conference room as well.

When they reach the room, they see that Melissa and six other officers are already there. Tom shakes hands with Melissa.

"Mr. Pollack theses are hardened criminals, none of them are saying anything." a cop says to Tom.

"One of them is willing to cooperate but he is waiting for the others to agree too." another says.

"One of them is saying that they got hired by Randy, he is an illegal alien and needed work."

"We have also been interrogating the woman, and she keeps insisting that she is Mrs. Monroe. She isn't complaining or being difficult with any of the cops here. We don't know what to make of it."

Melissa speaks, "May I say something Mr. Pollack, this woman here in custody has a very strong will power, and I have been researching the twins past records, Cassandra was known to be able to copy her sister perfectly as children and now after spending a week with her, I am sure that she has been able to copy her now, I suppose though we must wait for the DNA."

"There is also another killer missing." says Tom.

Terrence gets up from his chair and walks towards Tom with a file in his hands; he sharply drops it in front of Tom.

"You men never look were you are supposed too."

Tom opens the file and looks at the picture.

"Where did you get this from?"

"It has been on your desk for two days Mr. Pollack, before you left to make those arrests a few other cops found this body with that taxi driver Paul's help."

"You have made your point Terrence; just find the names of these guys."

Tom turns to Melissa, "Ms. Wolfe, we have to go to court this afternoon after that we can proceed with the rest. However we have a TV conference too at noon. Will you be with us all day?"

"Yes Mr. Pollack, but let me ask you this, how are you going to present this woman in court, an accessory in murder or the Senator's wife?"

"I think in this preliminary hearing we can go ahead and charge the three men for murder, but I believe that we can persuade the judge to wait for the DNA test before putting her on trial."

Tom turns to the cops and the rest of the conference room, "Does anyone have any other questions? I know everyone was here early but we must rap this case up."

Only Terrence stands up, "Mr. Pollack, you are always a hundred percent sure on every case, why is it then you are not even zero percent sure about this?" and he walks out of the room.

After the conference Barbara orders some lunch for everyone and they discuss what else to do. Tom looks at his watch and it is almost twelve.

"Look Ms. Wolfe, Barbara, Jody and a few other reporters are outside waiting to hear any updates. Could you two please cover for me, I am not very good at public speaking."

Outside, Jody is waiting for Tom to update her on the case. It is about five minutes to twelve and Jody is occupying the stations viewers with her charm.

"We have been waiting for Mr. Pollack to come out of his conference and give us the latest updates on the Monroe scandal."

The door of the station opens and Tom comes out accompanied by Melissa Wolfe and Barbara and Jody rushes to Tom.

"Good afternoon Jody, this is Tom Pollack here and we are currently investigating the Monroe case. This here is Melissa Wolfe the state prosecutor and she has been working closely with this case. She will also be filling you in on the case."

"Good afternoon, as Mr. Pollack, one of our finest detectives has been working very hard on this case and we have already apprehended our felons." says Melissa

"What about the woman who looks exactly like Mrs. Monroe? Is it her or her twin?" Jody ask

"As of now we do not have any information on the woman in custody, we will give out more information when we get certain tests back." tom said

The other reporters swarm around Tom and start asking questions. "If the woman in custody is Mrs. Monroe what is going to happen? Won't you lose your job?"

"Well Ladies and Gentleman if that problem arises we shall deal with him. Right now I have the full support of

Senator Monroe to continue the investigation and until DNA tests return we have no way of really knowing.

Jody was getting annoyed now that the other reporters were trying to take her story and moves in closer to Tom and Melissa.

Tom says, "Please do not put this department here or Ms. Wolfe on the spot, we are really doing the best we can."

Melissa Wolfe steps in and says, "Ladies and Gentlemen, please we do not have any other information we can release."

"Ms. Wolfe, are you going to be the prosecutor for the case?" Jody ask

"I am not sure as of yet, we will let you know when we have more details on this case. That will be up to justice dept.who they pick randomly"

Tom steps in, "Alright everyone there will be no further questions at this time, this conference is over."

Tom, Melissa, and Barbara return to the office to prepare for court today.

"Well, Ms. Wolfe, any other questions you have regarding the case?"

"Mr. Pollack, the day after the murder I have just looked into Cassandra's past there is nothing else new." says Melissa

"Yes, yes I know that, but I still have further questions. The Senator won't reveal anything now so close to the elections."

"Well all we know about Cassandra is that she was known as the 'Slut'Mellisa says in aggressive.

"Ah, no one has used those terms yet, but for the sake of Senator Monroe, we should refrain from the mudslinging." tom says to Melissa

They continue to finish the paperwork for the trial before driving down to the courthouse. When they arrive the judge comes out of his chambers, his name is Richard Wolfe. Melissa and Tom go up to him and they shake hands.

"Good afternoon Melissa, I haven't seen you in a while, and Mr. Pollack, who is this lady with you?"

"Oh your honor, this is my secretary Barbara"

They all take their seats.

"Well Mr. Pollack?" The judge asks, "And I know the three felons are arriving soon, but you and Ms. Wolfe are still uncertain about the identity of the women? Ms. Wolfe how is the state going to press charges against her if they do not know which twin is which?"

"Well if it is Cassandra, then there is a lot to lose, she has nothing. But then again if she is cleared as Mrs. Monroe she has it made. The DNA test will be ready by tomorrow so she will be coming in tomorrow for her hearing."

"Even if she is the wrong twin, we may be able to let her off on probation."

"Well Mr. Pollack, Ms. Wolfe until the DNA testing is done how you have been treating her?" judge says

"We have been treating her well your honor, with certain amounts of respect. If she is Mrs. Monroe we will release her straightaway." Tom said "Alright Mr. Pollack that settles it. we will give her the hearing tomorrow, can I offer you a refreshment before we must get started?" judge replied.

"No thank you, we are all fine." says Melissa.

"Well I must finish some paperwork before the plimnary hearing. There isn't much time here but you guys should relax or get something from the cafeteria." judge says

The three get up and walk to the cafeteria to wait until the pleminary hearing. Five minutes till the pleminary hearing at four pm. Jody and her crew are waiting outside for the results. Inside Tom, Melissa, and Barbara with a few court attendants are present and waiting for the Judge to enter. He enters at exactly four pm, and everyone rises. The Judge orders the first felon in; it is Number one, one of Randy's faithful followers. He points to Melissa and tells her to come up to interrogate him.

"Are you going to tell us your real name?

The felon said nothing and Melissa continues,

"Your silence is not helping you, you are here being charged for four murders are you sure you have nothing to say?"

His silence continues.

Melissa looks at the Judge and says, "We will secure a trial for him, keep him under high security."

Number two is now brought in and his charges are read, and then Number three the Black man is also brought in and placed on the witness stand. Melissa starts speaking, "How do you plead?"

Number three starts speaking very softly and begging not to go to jail for life or get death penalty and starts blabbering nonsense,

"I want to tell you everything, the slut and her cool friend stole lot of money from my boss, we did not know she was related to Mrs. Monroe. Look I do not want to spend my life in jail, or get death penalty. I will cooperate with you."

The judge orders him to be taken away and a date for his trial is set.

The Hispanic guy is brought in next, he claims he was hired recently and had nothing to do with the murders, he also requested to be sent back to his country.

Lastly the lady who claimed to be Mrs. Monroe is brought in by a female officer, un- cuffed. She scans the room and sees a nicely dressed female woman sitting, it was Melissa. Melissa had never lost a case before and was now against her. She was ready to answer any questions Melissa asked her. Melissa gets up from her chair and walks over to the twin and looks at her eye to eye.

"Which twin are you?" asks Melissa.

"I am Mrs. Monroe" replies the woman.

"Do not try to fool us, we know that you and your sister look exactly alike and you used to fool everyone, one was known as the Slut and the other known as a lady. I have been investigating you and your twin"

Both Tom and Barbara were shocked that Melissa used that word, but she continued in an aggressive manner.

"So you decide to come to this town, followed by your gang to have your sister killed so you could try and take her place."

"I am Mrs. Monroe, and I would appreciate it if you did not use that word to describe my deceased sister." Twin pleaded nicely.

"It was a name given to one of you at an earlier age, why are you so offended?" Melissa continued harshly.

"Can you come a little closer please?" Twin says with a charming smile. And Melissa falls for that wondering what is on her mind. She comes close

"Melissa looks at the judge to your right". She does. "Now turn this way."

As Melissa turns her head to face the twin. The Twin's face shows anger for a

Second. And twin slaps Melissa so hard on her left cheek with right hand. It starts turning red and she is knocked of balance. As the twin finger points to Melissa and says in anger.

"Don't you ever dare use that word for my deceased sister" And within a split second twin has a smile and charm on her face, like she was never angry, and she says to the judge,

" Why does Govt.employs people like these"

She looks at the twin with anger, but by law she cannot hit her back. She throws her file on the table next to Tom and storms out of the courtroom. The judge was appalled and then looks back down at his paper work. Tom and Barbara are still in the front row. Tom whispers to Barbara,

"I was not expecting this." But Barbra replies. Well tom she ask for it"

Judge says."Yes, I see the DNA tests are coming in tomorrow."

He was surprised that Ms. Wolfe had dared to mention the word in front of the twin. "We shall decide your trial or release based on the tests tomorrow."

The judge raps everything up and adjourns the court for the day. The woman is taken back to the holding cell.

Tom and Barbara stand up and pick up Melissa's file and exit the courthouse and Barbara asks him,

"Mr. Pollack, what do you think is going to happen with this trial?"

"I really do not know Barbara, I know she is Mrs. Monroe, but she just blew it in there. Melissa will make sure of that, she hasn't lost a case ever." tom said while walking to their car.

"So she will break the law?" says Barbra

"Yes, most likely out of anger." tom said

"It is amazing how you can judge personality like that."

They are back on their way to the police station. "Mr. Pollack tell me what is bugging you? I will find out sooner or later."

"It isn't what you think Barbara. I am just worried about this twin" tom says

Around five, Mr. Wolfe is in his room debating the case with himself when the phone rings,

"Mr. Wolfe, two men want to speak to you, it's an emergency." says the switchboard operator.

"They say they are from the Attorney General's office and they must see you."

"Send them in." Judge tells the switchboard operator.

A few moments later two while males enter the room and they hand Mr. Wolfe an envelope. The judge reads the note inside and asks both of the men to excuse him a few minutes.

The men wait outside and start talking until the Judge comes out.

"Alright gentlemen, let us go talk." They walk outside to see a nice SUV limo, the three get inside and the limo drives off. There was silence throughout most of the ride. The limo pulls up in front of a new white building. They go inside up to the fourth floor.

"Welcome Mr. Wolfe, I am Mr. Anderson, the financial chief of the Republican party."

"Good to see you, I received your note." judge says while shaking hand with Mr. Anderson

"Ah, let us have something to drink first, make yourself comfortable, you are our special guest." says Mr. Anderson"Mr. Wolfe just relax, after we are done you will be a quarter million dollars richer."

Mr. Wolfe was a little confused. "Just wait a minute Mr. Anderson." what is on your mind?

After a one drink. Which was already on the coffee table between the judge? Mr. Anderson calls in a two other men, they sit and one of them hands a credit card to the judge.Mr. Anderson says, "This is a Republican credit card Mr. Wolfe; it has a two hundred thousand limit. And you can draw one thousand a day. And you don't have to pay a penny back"

The Judge is very taken aback, but takes the card. The other men leave the room, and Mr. Wolfe takes another drink.

"Mr. Wolfe I believe you are a republican"

"Yes, I have always been."

"Tell me then. Do you want the Senator to win the election?"Mr Anderson ask

"No, no of course not."

"The main reason we called you here Mr. Wolfe is because if you were to handle the trial dealing with the Monroe case and you can drag it along, until the election."

"How would I do that? I may not be appointed for the twin's trial." judge ask

"Oh we will make sure you are appointed, we have the Judiciary system in our hands, Plus we know all about you gambling habits, they will come in handy."Mr Anderson says

"How do you know?" judge is surprised.

"Let's just say we have some high end people working for us, so how are you gambling now. Since there is no more internet gambling?" says Mr. Anderson.

"I just buy lot of lottery tickets and expensive scratch offs?" judge say

They pour a one more drinks, and judge is getting more intoxicated than Mr. Anderson by the second. Because Anderson can tolerate more than the judge.

"Mr. Anderson, we must keep this meeting private, I could lose my job." Judge pleads.

"No of course not, we republicans are always loyal to each other."

The female server opens the door and brings in a man of about fifty, Mr. Anderson gets up and shakes his hand.

"This is Mr. Rob Carpenter, I have not seen him in a long time." and he makes Rob sit next to him, the female server knows something is up and brings an extra glass.

"Rob, meet Mr. Wolfe. He is the judge dealing with the Monroe scandal. Mr. Carpenter is a news correspondent." The Judge and Mr. Carpenter shake hands, and then take another drink. The men are pretty intoxicated now and start provoking Mr. Wolfe to tell them about the trial.

"So, you were about to say something about the hearing today." Rob ask

The Judges drinks had taken affect, "The twin claiming to be Mrs. Monroe, and she slapped State Prosecutor Melissa Wolfe." As he is talking, Mr. Anderson makes a mental note about everything he says. Bob asks Mr. Wolfe why she slapped her.

"Well Melissa is very harsh aggressive and vicious person. Today she used a poor choice of words; I would say she was

unwise. She called the twin a slut. Today she met her match"
judge don't know that rob is recording every conversation.

Mr. Anderson steps in, "So Mr. Wolfe, we have an
agreement?"

"We do, Mr. Anderson."

"We are little concerned in employing a person like you,
you may not be able to handle it." Bob says.

And judge replies even though he is pretty drunk. I can
handle anything

It is almost nine pm, and Mr. Wolfe is extremely under
the influence, and remembers nothing but the two men of
Mr. Anderson take him home and put him to bed.

Meanwhile, Melissa was extremely furious with what
happened, and being bound by the not to hit back. At
home she had had a few drinks and was switching channels
on her TV. She stops at Jody's channel who is reviewing the
case and the twins' profile.

"What you did today was your last and big mistake;
you do not know my power in court. I do not care who
you are anymore, Even if you are going to be our next first
lady. I will make sure that you are the first powerful white
woman to get death penalty from me" She says to herself
and switches channels. After another drink she heads off to
bed.

Monday morning, she wakes up usual time. So she is on
time to court. She taken time to look very well put together.
Today everything is different; she is not just the attractive
woman on the street, but a powerful state prosecutor. But
today is different. She comes out of the house at nine am
to pick her news paper. She always comes out in her short
gown well above her thighs. Because she knows that across
the street. There are some men behind the curtains want to

look at her back side. When she deliberately bends down to pick the news paper. Having her back to the street. But today when she came out. The whole neighbor hood is standing out side. She looks at every body. Wondering why every body is staring at her. So she picks up the paper and walks back to the house. When Melissa comes back in the house and takes the news paper out of plastic bag. Looking at the front page her blood goes so high that she can not control her anger. Because she was already frustrated about what happened in court yesterday. But looking at her own party paper having the news on the front page. She is too shocked. Then she turns the TV on to her favorite channel. It carries the same news. And whole world is getting more and more interested in Americas next presidency than anything else. When Melissa sees that she is the only one being humiliated. And she decides to make a call. While she is dialing. TV has the same news.

"The 'twin' in custody, slaps state prosecutor Melissa Wolfe", Melissa had turned on the TV and was on a republican favored station and was shocked. She picks up the phone and calls Barbara,

"Barbara, this is Melissa. Have you seen today's news! I want to know who leaked this."

"What news Ms. Wolfe?"

"Where is Tom?"

"At home with his children, it is a student holiday today."

"Connect me to him right away." Melissa tells Barbra in a way that looks like an order.

"Oh no, Ms. Wolfe, You do it yourself. I am not going to disturb him on his day off.

"Do you not know who I am?" Melissa yells slightly

"Excuse me, fire me if you must, my husband is waiting for me in bed. Oh do you have any body? And Barbara hangs up.

And Melissa gets more frustrated. And she finds Tom's phone number and someone answers right away.

"Hello Mrs. Pollack speaking."

"This is Melissa Wolfe; I need to speak with Tom."

"Look lady, my husband is very busy right now; it is his day off and my children's day off, so please call back some other time."

And Mrs. Pollack hangs up on Melissa. Tom had been coming down the stairs and she greets him and he asks who had called.

"Some grumpy woman, I thought you shouldn't be disturbed."

"Honey, it could be important." Tom picks up the phone looks at the in coming number.

Tom dials Melissa's number and she answers quickly, "Hello Mr. Pollack I am glad you called me. I was about to come to your house."

"What for, what happened?"

"Have you seen today's news? Someone leaked to a *republican* paper that I was slapped in the courthouse yesterday."

"I have not seen this, I normally spend mornings with my wife and kids", Tom turns on the TV to the republican known station and sure enough they were showing the story again." Tom listens to the rest of the story and turns the TV off. His children say with surprise, "Hey dad!" Tom goes into the kitchen while talking to Melissa.

"Yes, I see what you mean, though I hope you are not accusing me or my staff, none of us watch this program or read that paper" tom said

"Of course not Tom, I trust you. But find out who did, and apologize to your wife for me"

"No problem, I am very sorry to see this Ms. Wolfe." And they both hang up. Tom goes back to his wife and children sitting at the table. "Hey dad what happened yesterday in court?"

"Please children, nothing right now."

September 15, 2008 the time is 10:00 AM, Melissa is not getting anywhere, she has tried to use her power her connections she cannot seem to get any answer as to who leaked the news. She still wants to exact revenge from the twin. She calls the court clerk to tell her she won't be in today. It is not usual for Melissa to stay home, she would like to go to court and find out about the leak, however today is a dead day for her, and she decides to hang around in the house. Her phone suddenly rings; she picks up the phone but cannot recognize the number.

"Melissa speaking, who is this?"

"My name is Anderson; I am the financial chief of the Republican Party. I would like to talk to you right away."

"What is this about?"

"I can't tell you over the phone, I will have the limo meet you at the court house near the garage, and I can assure you that you will be a hundred grand richer."

"Ok Mr. Anderson you made your point, I will wait for you near the garage. I need twenty thousand cash right now; do you have that kind of money? Melissa asks

"Yes, Ms. Wolfe this is the Republican Party, there is plenty of tax payers money and soft money too out here. Please meet me and I will give you what you need."

"OK Mr. Anderson I will wait for you near the court house garage at 11:30.

In the meantime at the twin was been taken to the DNA Lab by the order of the court and it may take six hours.

Melissa gets ready, puts on her beautiful clothes and drives to the court house. She parks in her official parking spot and waits at the entrance of the garage. As she was told a brand new limo pulls up next to her and two well dressed white men step out of the limo, one of them asks Melissa

"You must be Ms. Wolfe" Melissa says "Yes", the second man opens the limo door. Melissa gets in not knowing how this is going to end. The two men get into the front seats as the limo and drive off. The man on the passenger side slides the middle glass window open and looking to his left remarks

"The TV remote is on your right, and the drinks are to your left, please help yourself."

She declines and the man closes the window. Melissa sits there shaking her feet looking outside as the limo catches speed on the highway. It is almost noon the limo the party headquarters, a nice white building. The driver jumps out and opens the door for Melissa. She is then led to the waiting Mr. Anderson on the fourth floor. Mr. Anderson greets her at the entrance of his office shaking her hand,

"Ms. Wolfe, it is my pleasure to welcome the chief attorney to the Republican Party's financial headquarters. My compliments I did not know that the state employs beautiful people like you."

They both walk to the same place where the judge visited last night. Mr. Anderson sits in his usual seat and Melissa sits across from him. Every now and the Mr. Anderson glances at Melissa's nice legs. On the table is the same news paper. Melissa looks at the new paper that has been deliberately placed on the table to irritate her.

"Mr. Anderson you wanted to see me, and I am here, how are you going to help me. Please don't waste my time because I have emergency work to get done before this evening. So please make your point quickly."

"Ms. Wolfe on the phone you said you wanted twenty thousand in cash, how is it that the states attorney is always short of money, you also drive a crappy car."

"None of you business, please get to the point." Melissa says angrily.

"Ms. Wolfe just a few seconds" Mr. Anderson pushes the button on his phone, and the same two men come in. They stand behind Mr. Anderson. The same woman from last night serves the same things. Mr. Anderson asks the man carrying the briefcase to sit next to him. He opens the briefcase. The man hands over the cash in new and used notes to Melissa. The other man sits next to her and tells her,

"This is your credit card." Melissa looks at Mr. Anderson surprised.

"What does he mean, how do you already have a credit card in my name when you don't even have my information?"

Mr. Anderson replies, "We know everything about the people in power, this card is issued by the Republican Party funded by tax payers and easy soft money. Nobody knows about it, except the people in this room. The card is worth a hundred grand. Just whisper the password in the man's ear and you are good to go."

Melissa whispers the password in the man's ear and he hands her the card gets up and joins the other man like they did last night.

Mr. Anderson "Ms. Wolfe are you happy now, you got what you wanted. What happened yesterday in court, I was surprised to see it in the media?"

Melissa tenses up she has seen the newspaper that was deliberately placed for her to see, she remarks angrily,

"You know everything about people in power, who do you think leaked this?"

"I do not know Ms Wolfe, who ever it is I can find out, I do know a lot of sources. If you want to keep this under wraps, I will find who leaked it to the media, after all I know that you and your family are loyal Republican voters and we love that, but if a scandal were to break out please keep my name out of this."

"Sure Mr. Anderson I will give you my word, as long as I know who did it. I don't care if the twin is the senator's wife, I don't care if the senator thinks he is so honest, family man, and a nationalist. I don't care that I fancied the senator at one time. The twin will pay for what she did to me in court. She is going to be the first powerful white woman to get the death penalty" Melissa says angrily. Mr. Anderson walks over to her and puts his arm around her to calm her down

"Ms. Wolfe we will back you all the way, the republican are with you, and would you care for a drink?"

"No I am fine I have a lot of things to do, I am sorry I do not have time for the drink." She puts the money in her handbag and slides the credit card into her wallet. "Mr. Anderson, can you ask the driver to drop me off."

"Sure," he dials the number on his phone and the two men come in, he asks them to take care of her and shakes Melissa's hand reassuring her,

"You have my phone number, if you need any help you can count on me."

"Thank you Mr. Anderson, it is good that I met you at the right time."

The limo drops her off at the court; Melissa disappears for the whole day, as she had called the court clerk that she was not going to be in all day.

Mean while the leaked incident in which the twin slaps the public prosecutor is a topic of discussion all over the world and sucking up a lot of attention compared to the various other scandals that also keep popping up. After all they are discussing the next first lady and the future president in trains, planes, taxis, airports, buses every where. In Denver they remember her kindness; she was always there for people in need. She helped everybody regardless color or ethnicity. When the news broke that Mrs. Monroe was alive, they wondered why the senator was not by her side, they were surprised that the senator was not able to tell the twins apart. They felt that either he should get her out of this mess or tell the nation that she is not his wife.

Everybody is waiting for the DNA results to come out. This case has garnered so much attention that even school children are discussing it and asking their teachers which one is which. Nobody is sure, in Denver the senator and his children are home, the senator's sister family left on 14th September as the children had to attend school. The senator and his children are glued to the TV watching the same news again and again. The senator is upset that the twin is claiming to be his wife. She does look like his wife, he cannot live in denial nor can he accept her as his wife given the sensitiveness due to the on going election. It certainly has come at the worst time, and he feels helpless and leaves everything to God.

It is 4:50 PM the phone rings at Tom's office, Barbara answers the phone, "Mr. Pollack's office, this is Barbara."

The caller says "I am with the DNA lab I want to talk to Mr. Pollack."

"Sure let me connect you to Mr. Pollack." She transfers the line and walks to the window between the cubicles.

Tom answers the phone, "This is Tom."

The voice at the other end "Mr. Pollack, I must regretfully say that the twin's DNA does not match Mrs. Monroe. I will have the official report for you by 10:00 AM tomorrow."

Tom is surprised he clarifies, "Are you absolutely sure?"

"Yes I am Mr. Pollack, I am a supporter of this senator, and if this woman is our next first lady why would I lie. We had our best technicians work this case like you ordered."

"Thank you; please send me the two copies of the report."

The caller hangs up. Barbara walks into Tom's office and finds him pensive.

"What's wrong?"

"Nothing, I just got word that the twin's DNA did not match. So I have to charge her for being accessory to murder."

"Tom you have charged both men and women with murder for similar crimes before and it has never bothered you so much, why now?"

"I don't know Barbara, I have never met the sister, but Father John did, I just feel guilty that I might be charging the wrong person, putting her away for a long time, far away from her husband and children."

"So you think this woman can be Mrs. Monroe?"

"Barbara, I don't know I wish I knew. I have a feeling that something is very wrong, when she slapped the prosecutor I felt she was asking for trouble regardless of who she is."

"Tom do you think the prosecutor had anything to do with this."

"I am a good judge of people, especially when they are wrong. But this time I am not so sure, my wife thinks that the woman is Mrs. Monroe and she wants me to release her, I come hear and people have a different opinion. Barbara I don't think I have enough evidence to charge her with accessory for murder. I just have the video, even with that there is no proof that it was her."

"So what are you going to do?"

It is about 5:00 PM the phone rings, Tom looks at the caller ID it is his wife, Tom motions to Barbara to be quiet and then turns the speaker on.

"Honey, how are you?"

"I am fine you were supposed to call me at 5:00 to let me know what time are you coming home. The kids missed you all day; this is supposed to be your day off. Are you going to be home soon?"

"No honey, I have to go over to the senator's house to give him the DNA results."

Tom's wife is curious about the result, "What did the result say?"

"There was no match." Tom's wife responds,

"I don't want to intrude or be judgmental, but from what I have heard on TV I believe she is our next first lady. So you better treat her right and if she goes to trial, and I know she is going to win."

"I think you made your point, I am going to stop at the senator's house for about half hour, I will see you by about 7:00. I love you."

Barbara also confirms that a lot of people seem to have doubts and are against charging the twin.

"Barbara let's go, I have to see Mr. Monroe on the way home to inform the senator about the DNA results."

Tom calls the senator and lets him know that he is on his way.

Mr. Monroe the gentleman that he is opens the door himself, and escorts Tom to the dining room. The senator's mother and Father John are also there. Father John has been visiting the Monroe's every evening to comfort the family. Tom takes his hat off and says

"Good evening." Tom sits next to Father John across from Mr. Monroe. The senator asks Tom,

"What is new, how can I help you. What is it I am seeing on TV, who leaked the news, I have a terrible feeling that my opponents are involved, because it was the Republican mouthpiece that printed this news and suggested in poor taste that it was either the slut or Mrs. Monroe that slapped the prosecutor."

"Senator I apologize, I have been trying to nab the culprit all day, and the problem is that the people who attended the court are your very strongest supporters so I am not sure who leaked it to the media. I tried to get in touch with the reporter, but I was told that he had left for Asia and that he had filed his report from there to be printed last night. It was done at the very last minute.

Mr. Pollack I tried to ask around and got the same response, the newspaper editors were not very helpful and gave me a run around."

"Senator I came here for a different reason. The DNA lab has completed the test and informed me that the twin's DNA did not match Mrs. Monroe. I will be getting copies of the official results tomorrow at 10:00 AM. I will be holding a press conference at noon, and I will be making the announcement that the woman is not your wife. Until this case goes to court you will get some breathing space and soon you will be able to leave the election behind you. She is insisting that she is your wife and she wants to see you and the children. I have been delaying that as much as I can, however when she goes on trial she will have the right to subpoena you."

"Mr. Pollack, if the DNA proves her not to be my wife I don't want to have anything to do with her."

Father John intervenes, "Excuse me Mr. Monroe, can I visit her in custody just for a few minutes, I am not a technical expert, however I have known the girls for a long time. I think I will be able to positively ID Mrs. Monroe. Ever since the beginning of time, people have been breaking the law for their own benefit, people do make mistakes."

"But Father the prosecution is not prepared to take your word for it."

"Mr. Pollack it is worth a try, on several occasions under similar circumstances one person's word has saved the innocent."

Tom agrees to let the pastor see the woman, "You can visit at 4:00 PM tomorrow."

"I will be there. Senator you should at least see her and talk to her once."

"Father, I won't have anything to do with her, after all the DNA did not match. I will not touch this until the election is over."

Father John gets little upset and says" Senator the presidency should not take precedence over Samantha's love. I think she was responsible for making you the man you are today. I am leaving, good seeing you Tom." He stands up, but Tom asks him to stay a little longer.

"Mr. Monroe, I want to tell you about what happened when I apprehended the twin. Even though she claimed that she was your wife I did not believe her. You know as well as I do that your sister-in-law left home when she was twenty one, she fell into some really bad company and let herself be used by the thug Randy. She ultimately got tiered of that lifestyle and realized her mistake. When she saw her sister and her family on TV and realized that her sister would become the next first lady, she decided to patch up with her sister that is why she was visiting your home. Randy treated the twin very badly, she sought comfort with one of Randy's men, and I think they called him cool guy. Once when Randy got very rough with the twin it was the cool guy that took the twin to the hospital to get stitches. The twin fell in love with this man and they were getting ready to get married. The twin was ready to make a lifetime commitment with the cool guy. The twin wanted to tell your wife that she was mending her ways, take a fresh start settle down and have a family.

Things did not go as planned for the twin, the cool guy stole ten million dollars in cash and jewelry from Randy's safe and ran away. Randy suspected that the twin was involved so when the twin was in your house Randy had his men come to your house to recover his property because he believed that the twin was hiding it in your house. From then onwards things went horribly wrong, the sharp shooter shot one of the sisters. The twin had nothing to do with the murder, so even if this is not your wife we may not have evidence to prosecute her. This has been corroborated by the black guy who is a member of the gang and is now cooperating with us for a plea bargain."

"Mr. Pollack, all this is great however I cannot take the twin back unless I am absolutely sure she is Samantha."

"I will leave that to you senator, I will do my job and bring charges against her, and then it is for the justice system to do their job. I have to go; my family is waiting for me."

Both Tom and Father John get up to leave. The senator sees them out, and the two walk o their respective cars. The senator is aware that Father Johns is not entirely happy with the way he is handling the situation, he watches them from the window as they leave.

Before Father John gets into his car, "Mr. Pollack, I think you are making a mistake here, you have no idea what that child is going through. Give me a few minutes to talk to her."

"Sure Father, come by tomorrow at 4:00 PM, I will make sure you get enough time to talk to the twin. After you have spoken to her please let me know what you think." Father makes a cross sign across his forehead and chest, "God bless you all". And gets into his car and drives away.

September 16th, Tuesday morning, Tom walks into his office as usual at 9:00 AM. He first take care of all pending paper work, he is waiting for the official DNA report from the lab. At 10:00 AM the DNA report is delivered by DNA lab supervisor personally. The supervisor is middle aged and a bit heavy. Tom greets him and asks Barbara to join him to take notes. She already knows what will happen.

"You have met my secretary; please forgive me like last time I will have to record this meeting. The case is too big and we cannot afford to make mistakes."

Barbara starts recording with the video camera. The supervisor hands over a sealed envelope to Tom.

"Was the test done by the same team?"

"Yes, like last time sealed and delivered. We understand the seriousness of this case involving the next first lady, we cannot afford to make mistakes, and we could land up in jail" says the Supervisor with a sly smile.

Tom asks him if he wants anything to drink.

The supervisor declines saying, "I am a beer and bourbon person, I have to go back to work in any case." He gets up and walks off slowly. Tom gives the envelope to Barbara and asks her to compare the two reports.

"Barbara I like you to arrange a news conference at noon."

"I will take care of it Tom."

"I also need to talk to the twin about the DNA report, please keep the two DNA reports in a separate envelope, and I also need to make her understand her legal rights."

"Tom, do you want me to go with you?"

"Please do."

At 11:00 AM Tom orders his deputies including female officers to bring the twin to the news conference, Tom also asks Barbara to bring photo copies of the two DNA reports. They bring her to the conference room without handcuffs. Barbara sits to the right of Tom and the twin is to his left. There are deputies behind the twin and the female officer is right next to her just in case she tries to escape. The other female officer stands next to Barbara. Tom puts the DNA reports in front of the twin.

"I am not sure where I should start; I have to inform you that your DNA did not match the senator's wife. I was with the senator last night, I told him about the DNA result, and I also passed on your request to see the family. He however wanted to wait until the end of the trial."

The twin keeps her cool in spite of her disappointment. She knows she is in a terrible situation, and she will need a cool head and all her wits to get out of this mess. She looks Tom in the eye and asks

"So what is next?"

"After the DNA results I will have to address you as Cassandra, I will be obligated to file accessory to murder charges. You will have to convince the jury of your innocence, and prove to them who you really are?"

"I understand, but I am not signing anything. I should be considered innocent until proven guilty."

"Unfortunately, as a public figure you are guilty until you prove otherwise. By the way Father John will be visiting you at 4:00 PM today; I have made arrangements for you to talk to him. He feels he can tell the two of you apart, he has a healthy disrespect for technology."

"Thank you Mr. Pollack, that was very sweet of him, since my family turned their backs to me, at least I have one person on my side. I don't know why our DNA's are different. I have told you about when you came to the senator's sister's wedding and what we said, how would my sister have known about these details, and you still won't believe me. I bet you this is the handiwork of that vicious prosecutor, but I am not worried about anything, if I pray with all my heart the Lord will save me, like he did a couple of weeks ago, and now I am going to see Father John. That is all I need."

The people in the conference room are stunned; they take the twin back to her cell. Tom and Barbara go back to their office. Tom flops into the chair in deep thought.

Barbara

"What are going to do Tom, if you have any doubts you should wait until after Father John meets with the twin."

"You are right Barbara; we should wait for the Father John."

It is almost noon, Tom and Barbara are prepared for the news conference, Melissa had already informed Barbara that she was busy in court and would not be able to make it. Jody and the other reporters are already waiting anxiously; Jody is her usual meticulous self and has everything ready. Tom and Barbara walk out and face the news cameras. Jody aggressively rushes in and sticks the microphone in Tom's face.

"Ladies and gentleman, I am Tom Pollack, I have updates relative to this case. We have received the DNA report from the lab; the twin's DNA does not match the senator's wife, so we will be charging her for being an accessory to the murder of her sister. The gang members will be charged with first degree murders of Mrs. Monroe and the three people who died at the senator's house. Do you have any questions?"

Jody is the first to go she blasts off a series of them,

"Do you know why the twin slapped the prosecutor Melissa Wolfe? Did the leak come from the prosecutor's office? How it is that only the pro republican newspaper carried the story? Where is Melissa Wolfe?"

"Jody, I can only speak for the investigation, I cannot answer questions related to the incident in the court. All I know is that the DNA report confirms the death of the senator's wife."

"Mr. Pollack why should the twin kill her own sister, leave town with the gangsters, then get arrested and claim to be the senator's wife. It does not make sense."

Tom answers, "It probably did make sense to her, this way she could fool the jury into believing that she had nothing to do with the murder and let the gang face the charges. She could then go back to the senator and pretend to be his wife."

"So you believe that you have the right twin though she is pretending to be her sister. What is going to happen if senator becomes the next president, how is he going to deal with her from the White House?"

"Jody, that concerns me as well, but based on the DNA results I will be pressing the charges, the rest is up to our justice system. That concludes the news conference, Thanks you."

While the reporters are busy news casting, and the rest of the country is wondering what next, Tom has decided not to prepare paperwork to charge the twin; he is waiting for Father John to help him make that decision.

At around 3:50 an officer escorts Father John to Tom's cubicle. Tom asks the Father if he needs any refreshments. Father John declines,

"I am fine, thank you. Have you charged the twin yet?"

Tom replies, "No not yet, I was waiting for you. Now where do you want to see her?"

"Do you have a room that is forty feet or longer?"

"I think, hopefully, our conference room will meet your expectations."

"I want to sit at one end of the room and have the twin enter from the other end and walk towards me. Your people can sit next to me or where ever you want, it does not matter."

Tom speaks on the radio and asks one of the officers to bring the twin to the conference room in ten minutes. He asks the officer to wait until the Father, Barbara, three male and three female officers are seated before bringing the twin into the conference room from the cell side.

"After she enters the conference room please ask her to walk towards us and don't say anything else." He turns towards Barbara and asks her to have Terrence turn on the camera. Terrence confirms he is ready and Tom along with the others walks to the conference room. They situate themselves on the stage side and wait anxiously for the twin to make her way into the conference room. The door on the other (cell) end opens, the twin who is wearing prison clothes enters the room. She is calm, collected and even looks pretty even in prison clothes. She scans the room and locates Father John and Tom and the other end of the room and starts walking towards them. She has a beautiful walk and a stunning presence and all the heads turn in her direction. She stops in front of Father John. The Father opens his arms to hug her and his voice starts to choke. She hugs him and fails to hold back the tears.

"I don't know why I just had to see you. I had hoped to see you next year as the First lady in the White House, and here I am meeting you in a police station. I am speechless."

The twin is now openly crying, relieved she observes, "You are the only one who has recognized me, even my husband refuses to believe me."

"I know I was there last night, I was very uncomfortable when the senator told Mr. Pollack that he did not want to see you as the DNA report had convinced him that you were not his wife."

"This is why I am here and I will stand by you Mrs. Monroe all the way, regardless of what the DNA report says."

"Thank you Father, I knew there would always be somebody who will stand for the truth. I have always had faith in God; he has stood by me these last couple of weeks, even when Randy tried to kill me."

The Father turns to speak to Tom,

"Mr. Pollack I can confirm that this twin is indeed Samantha. I am willing to stand by her all the way, what will it take to bail her out?"

"Father I don't doubt your sincerity, however just your word will not stand in court. It may take ten million dollars to bail her out. Given the slapping incident yesterday in court I am doubtful any judge will grant her bail."

Father John is a little upset, "Mr. Pollack if the prosecutor used the name against your wife or daughter what would you have done. I am sorry to say this prosecutor deserved what she got."

"Father you are right but my hands are tied, I have to follow the law and charge her."

"Let me have the phone, I want to make a call to the financial headquarters of the church." Tom offers him the phone in the conference room.

Father pulls out his phonebook, puts his glasses on and dials the number.

"This is Father John I have an emergency, I need ten million dollars to post bail."

The speaker at the other end says, "I know who you are, you must be out of your mind. Who do you want to post bail for?"

"It is for Mrs. Monroe the senator's wife."

The speaker at the other end says "Didn't she just get killed?"

"No, Mrs. Monroe is still alive; it was her sister that got killed. I need to bail her out because the senator does not think she is his wife."

"But Father if the DNA analysis says it is not Mrs. Monroe and the senator has not accepted the twin as his wife why are we taking on the headache of bailing out somebody who could be accessory to murder. I am sorry John the church has already enough law suites and we don't want another one especially when it has links to the next president."

"I am talking about helping a woman that has always stood by the church and helped the needy and now when she needs help the church is backing away, how can we have that on our conscience? I am going to take this with up with the chain of command and I will do everything possible for this woman because she deserves our support. I am sorry I wasted your time" and hangs up the phone.

Father John is dejected. The twin gives him a hug and asks him not to worry,

"I will be alright, I am happy you are on my side, and you believe me."

Father looks at the twin regaining composure, "My child, I will talk to the senator again and tell him he is making a huge mistake." Then to Tom,

"Please take good care of her; I don't want to see her harmed in any way. This woman has done so much good, the DNA analysis is a mistake, and I am sure she will prevail. I would like to visit her everyday can you please make the necessary arrangements?"

Tom agrees, and as Father John is leaving the phone rings. The operator informs Tom that a Hispanic guy has been calling here for the last half hour to talk to you."

Tom cannot contain his excitement, "Why did you not let me know earlier?" Operator, "Mr. Pollack your phone was busy and you told me not to bother you until you came out of the conference room", and connects him.

"Mr. Pollack this is Julio, the bartender from Randy's club. You had asked me to call you if I had any information and that you would help me and my family secure green cards if I had no criminal record."

"Yes I remember, I agreed to help you if you provided information to nab Randy."

"Thank you. I know where Randy is. He is hiding in the police chief's house. He has been there since the raid." Julio continues, "After getting us the green card can you help me and my family move to Denver, it will be great if you can find me a job too."

Tom agrees to help him and hangs up.

Tom is excited; he has been waiting to apprehend Randy for a long time. Randy has been wanted for robbery, deception, bribery, money laundering, and running a prostitution ring but has always managed to escape the police dragnet. But this time he had gone too far killing one of the twins and kidnapping the other. His days are numbered.

Randy had parked his truck near his club, and when he sees the FBI raid his club, he quickly ducks into a McDonald and sits there for three hours hiding his face under an old man's hat until the FBI secure the club and leave. He then makes it to the police chief's house, the door is open and he goes in with a suitcase containing about fifteen million dollars. He parks his truck in the garage and waits for the police chief. The chief comes home around noon in a squad car, opens the trunk take out takes out cases of beer and pizza and puts it on the dinning table. He opens a beer can for himself and calls out to Randy. Randy appears and glares at the chief,

"Why are you looking at me like that I just save your butt?" Randy "How come you knew nothing about the raid until the last minute"

"Randy we have been friends for a long time, we have known each other since college days, you have been always there for me and I have been there for you. I have no idea who informed the detective where the twin was being held. Now it is too late, what are you going to do, and where are you going? You are at the top of the most wanted list for killing the senator's wife."

"Randy knows that he has few options, he opens a can of beer and drinks it, "I am sorry I went off on you."

The two sit down and drink, at about 4:00 PM the chief's phone rings,

"This is the Little Big Man; I want my fifteen million dollars that you and Randy cheated me out off. If I don't get the money from you by this evening we will kill you and your family."

"Listen you foreign turd, I can get your ass arrested right now and put you on a plane back to your country, so don't mess with me."

Caller "You will see my power soon." and hangs up. Randy is worried.

A little later the phone rings again this time it is the chief's wife,

"I am leaving you, the children and I won't be coming home. You can visit them if you want I am not going to place any restrictions. The children need love, my father and brothers will take care of them, I don't want them to end up like you."

Chief to his wife, "Sure, you know, you will be back here in no time."

"Dream on." and hangs up.

After the wife's call Randy tells the chief that he cannot stay here for too long cooped up in a room, he ask the chief to suggest how he can get out. To which the chief says,

"Give a couple of million dollars cash so that I can pay this house off and I will help you get to Mexico. I can take you across the border in my cruiser as if you were an escaping Mexican convict. There are a lot of Americans living there in similar situations and it will be no problem blending with that crowd. Once you are there you are on your own."

Randy sees no other options, so he agrees. He asks,

"What if I get recognized at the border?" The chief assures Randy that as of now his picture has not been broadcast on TV, nor has he been added to the computer's wanted list. He has a couple of days to act. However once it get on the computer list and his picture is broadcast via TV he will not have a prayer.

The chief also agrees to provide Randy with some fake documents to suggest that he is a deportee, the documents however are not necessary to cross the border as Mexican authorities don't care as long because they know that dollars are going to flow in.

"I will have a couple of buddies escort you into Mexico, may even spend a couple of nights in Mexico in a hotel. I like the Mexican girls, show them a couple of hundred dollars and they don't complain.

"That is great chief didn't think you cared so much about me" sarcastically.

"Randy, I might be a lousy cop, but I always take care of people I owe favors to. I am returning your favor. I also need a break I may even call this trip a vacation thanks to the Chinese mafia."

He laughs.

"I heard on the news that Number One and Two are being charged, looks like the black guy confessed and agreed to cooperate. Even the twin is being charged as an accessory, while she continues to insist that she is the senator's wife."

"So Randy what do you think is the slut acting or is she really the senator's wife." Randy replies,

"I am not sure; she did act a bit different. I had known the slut for fifteen years and I still never understood her. She was great sometimes and at other times I did not know where she was coming from. I do know that she was the jealous type and would very easily get provoked if she thought she was had to compete with another woman and would just about do anything to beat the competition. Once I understood that it was very easy for me to exploit her weakness. But ultimately it looks like she will succeed in destroying me."

The chief gets up to go to the bathroom and come back to heat up the pizza. Ever since the chief's wife left the house has been a mess. Randy is also not used to being clean as he has never had a permanent home since he left his family at the age of twenty. Randy has tried to remain sober ever since the raid because he knows the hardship of spending time in the jail, as he had spent a few months at one point. This time he is concerned that he may get the death penalty or spend the rest of his life in jail for sending his men to recover the ten million dollars stolen by the cool guy from his safe. Randy suspected that the twin was involved with the cool guy and had the money. All Randy wanted was his money back. Lately, like all middle aged men and women he had started to prefer younger fresher skin as opposed to alligator skin and this turned out to be his biggest mistake. Given his past gangster ways he soon realizes that it is better to take the chiefs help and get out of the country so that he can sleep without any worries.

In the meantime back at the station Tom asks Barbara help him prepare for raiding the chief's house the next day.

Father John is not very upset that Tom charged the twin; he drives straight to the senator's house. The senator's kids open the door and Father walks into the living room where the senator is sitting with his mother. The senator stands up and greets Father John. Father John asks the kids if he could speak to their grandma and dad." The senator has a daughter who is almost twelve and a son who is nine. The daughter asks Father John why the police are holding her mom. She is distraught and starts crying as she misses her mom. There is silence and the daughter goes to her grandma sobbing and grandma comforts her. The son in the meantime sits next to his dad on the right side.

Father John asks to talk to the senator and his mother privately. The senator asks the kids to leave the room.

Father John opens up,

"I went to see the twin today, you may not know this but I think you are very lucky your wife is alive. I have seen both the twins, they may be identical, but the only thing different about them is their walk. The one who is in the police station is definitely your wife. Do you love your wife or are you more concerned of becoming the next president? If she is alive are you willing to give up your bid regardless of how much the country needs someone like you?"

"Yes I would any day give up power to get her back. I love her and you have no idea how much I have missed her the last several days. We were made for each other. I do not understand why it had to end this way." Senator replies,

"She is alive and if that is how you feel you must bring her home and get her out of this mess. She is waiting fro you." Father John says

"How can I do that, you have seen what is happening, my opponents are playing this political game and have made sure she is charged. The justice system is not going to let her go until the trial is over."Senator replied

Father John is disappointed; his face changes color, he is visibly upset.

"It looks like you are not going to do anything about this, it is quite apparent from your response."

"How can I, I would love to bring her back, and you don't understand nobody is above the law. They are not going to let her go until end of the trial after she proves she is my wife." says senator

"Senator I am livid, God help me. I have known your family for over forty years, for what you have done to the lovely woman you will be asking for her forgiveness very soon after she proves she is your wife in front of the entire nation. If you are a smart man you will try to get her out of this mess now. If I had the money, and believe me I tried but the church was unwilling give me the money, I would have posted bail. I am going to stand by her try as hard as I can to bail her out." Father John gets up to leave, the senator has never seen the pastor so angry before.

"You don't have to see me out; I will take care of Samantha. Goodnight."

He walks out of the door leaving the senator and his mother behind. The senator's wife sits across from her son and asks,

"I don't want to repeat what Father John just said, do you care more for the presidency than your own wife? I like to know." The senator listens to his mother waits for a few moments before answering,

"Mother, tell me what we should do?"

"If you really want to know I agree with Father John, you should do everything to bring her back. We all miss her a lot. Say mother

"Ok mother tomorrow I will do everything to bring Samantha back." The senator goes into the study.

It is almost 10:00 PM and it is very dark outside in the gambling town. In the outskirts of this lively place the police chief and Randy have been enjoying the evening. Six young men in running attire are jogging in the neighborhood. The streets are empty and hardly a soul outside. The streets are lit. a car are passes by now and then. The six young men all tall and strong look around to see if anybody is looking and approach the chief's house; three of them go behind the house and the other three take position in front of the house. They put their masks on and one man rings the door bell and the rest wait with their guns drawn. The chief is drunk by now and opens the door complaining thinking it his buddies,

"Why can't you guys leave me alone it is pretty late."

As soon as the chief comes out one of the joggers opens fire with a silencer. The chief falls down hard; Randy hears a loud thud and instinctively knows some thing is wrong. He pulls his gun out and turns the lights off in the living room. The three men who had positioned themselves at the back now break open the kitchen door and come in through the back. The three in the front know randy is in there and turn on their flash light. As two of them enter the living room. Randy shoots two of them; the third man opens fire with a machine gun from outside the living room mowing Randy falls down. The chief and Randy are now dead. The men look around the house and finally locate the suitcase in the garage. One of the men opens the suitcase to check if the money is inside, he finally says, "We have it let's go." The men take the suitcase turn the lights off in the house and escape into the night. The Little Big Guy their boss is waiting a few blocks away. The men get into their cars and drive away.

Somebody in the neighborhood hears the commotion and calls "911". A few minutes later a couple of police cars arrive. The police knock on the door but there is no answer, so the cops decide to force their way in and to their surprise they find the door is unlocked, they flash their lights inside the house and immediately see the chief lying in a pool of blood.

"Call for backup and call in the ambulance" the first cop tells his colleague and turns the light in the hall way they find Randy in the living room. By this time the backup arrives and the emergency vehicles position themselves in front of the house. The cops search the whole house, forensics is called. The neighbors are now awake and wonder what is happening, the scene is surreal like in the movies. The press is informed and the news about the murders is on all the channels.

By the next morning the cops have done their jobs, the bodies have been removed. Tom's wife wakes him up at about 5:00AM to get ready for the planned raid. Tom gets ready and waits outside as he has arranged to be picked up at 5:30. The phone rings. Tom's wife picks up it is Barbara on the phone, she tells her it is an emergency. Tom's wife,

"He is on his way I can hear his footsteps, can you tell me what is going on?"

"Mrs. Pollack I have cancelled his flight, the raid can be called off, Randy is dead, and he was apparently killed last night."

Tom's wife gives Tom the phone, "Hello, good morning, what's up?"

"Steve came home at 5:00 this morning; he heard it on the radio on the way home both Randy and the police chief were killed last night. Turn the TV on all the news channels are carrying the same story."

In the meantime Tom's wife has already turned the TV on in the kitchen.

"Mr. Pollack I have already cancelled your flight."

"Thanks Barbara, smart move." Tom hangs up and along with his wife they watch the news on the small TV in the kitchen. The news anchor,

"Good morning America, it is a lovely morning 18th September, 2008. We are here in the outskirts of Gambling City in front the police chief's house. As you can see the whole house has been taped by the police. Last night responding to a 911 call the police found several bodies with gunshot wounds in the house. The police chief was among the dead, his body was found in the hall way. Besides the chief, the police found bodies of two Asians in their mid twenties, and a balding white male of about fifty believed to be that of the night club owner Randy. The police suspect the shooting may be related to the raid that took place last week at Randy's club where they also found the missing twin who is currently in custody in Denver. The twin of course, as you know, claims to Senator Monroe's wife. It is common knowledge in this town that Randy wand the twin had been friends for a long time. The twin left Randy when she found out that her sister Mrs. Monroe was going to be the next First Lady. The mob went after the twin and killed Mrs. Monroe instead and brought the twin back. When his club was raided last week, Randy got away we believe with help from the police chief who had been buddies with him for a ling time. The latest news is that after he brought the twin back Randy was having problems with the Chinese mafia. It appears that this mafia is slowly taking control of all illegal activities in this city. We will continue to bring you updates as when they become available all through the day. The weather is next."

Tom turns the TV off, his wife looks at him, he looks at his wife and he says to her, Let s go back to bed.

"It is not just Denver, but the whole nation has been gripped by this news about the senator's wife and her wayward twin. Anybody and everybody is now digging into the twin's past so that they can make a fast buck. This has taken a toll on the twin that has been locked up, when she is trying to prove that she is the next First Lady. The senator, his children and the rest of the family have been wondering is she really who she is claiming to be or the pretending to be the older twin so that she can become the next First lady.

Tom is at a loss; he comes to the office, and goes straight to his cubicle. Barbara is already there,

"Good morning."

"Good morning tom, how are you. What do you make of what happened last night?

Tom says "I was hoping to apprehend randy alive, so we could identify the twin. Now that he is dead I am not sure what to do. If the twin is innocent I would feel guilty keeping her locked up. Unfortunately the DNA report goes against her, and the case is out of my control. Randy was my last hope, I was hoping he would help us solve the mystery about the identity of the twin. It is just a guessing game now; we will just have to wait it out until the end of the trial."

"Tom, what about Mr. Monroe?"

"Well since the DNA report does not support the twin's assertions, the senator is probably not going to take her back any time soon. His political party is not going to allow him to get involved with the twin, both the senator and the party stand to loose a lot. But is the twin is the senator's wife and she is able to prevail in court, the opposition party and the prosecutor will try to exploit this and try to embarrass the senator by even going into their sex life. The twin will do everything to save herself, but for the senator it will be difficult to answer all the questions. We are heading for a trial of the century."

"Is our role over now?"

Tom replies, "Yes it is, Randy is dead, and the other felons did not have much to do with the twin, so their testimony maybe irrelevant in court. She is pretty much on her own, so God help her, only if she tells the truth can she save herself; slightest attempt to lie could land her on death row."

"Tom, is this a hair trigger case?"

"Yes, it is a hair trigger case for Mr. Monroe too; one small slip may cost him the election."

"Barbara prepares the paperwork to charge the three felons with first degree murder and we will see how they plead. The twin will be charged as an accessory. Please send the remaining paperwork to the prosecutor's office and let them handle it from here."

"Tom what about the twin?"

"The senator refuses to stand by her and father John is unable t post bail. Let's leave it at that."

In the meantime the twin is being held in detention center for women. She passes her time walking in the detention yard and trying to remain calm and not pick a fight with the other inmates even though some of them taunt her for pretending to be the senator's wife, she shrugs it off. She believes that this is fate, and some people who have too many privileges and sometimes break the law, a little hardship is better, it reins you in and keeps you focused on your work and prevents you from engaging in criminal activities. She hopes that one day God will help her as he has done before.

Father John is allowed to visit everyday for half hour. He brings food for her, because the food in the detention center is bad. She counts seconds, minutes, hours, and days to star the trial so that she can she can prove her innocence. She cannot sleep in the night; she keeps staring in the dark. The smell, the noise from the women constantly arguing, the foul language just adds to the misery. The women in the prison don't take responsibility for their own actions, never admit fault, and always blame others. She has a big problem – nobody believes her.

She tried to get in touch with the senator, but he has refused to talk to her. She waits patiently.

In the meantime the twin is always in the news locally, nationally and internationally. Reporters keep trying to contact the senator but he refuses to talk to them. His silence is causing people to wonder if there might be something he does not want the public to know. Until now, the senator has always been well respected everywhere, but now he has become very quiet and hiding from public attention. Even though people understand that he is mourning the loss of the woman he loved, they feel that as the person who is supposed to become our next president he should at least face the public and make a statement. It has been ten days since the tragedy happened and even his party is pushing for Senator Monroe to speak to the public. His ratings in the poll seem to have dropped a couple of points though his ratings are high with the female voters. The female voters sympathize with him and are standing by him. Everyone is wondering what the outcome will be.

September 18th, Thursday morning at 10:00AM, all the felons are brought back to the court. Charges against them are read and they all plead not guilty and are provided with court appointed lawyers.

The twin is escorted back by a female police woman.

Tom and Barbara are in the court room too. The twin looks at Tom when she is being asked the prosecutor

"You, Cassandra Domenici, are being charged with being an accessory to the murder of your twin sister, Samantha Monroe, two security guards and a limo driver. How do you plead?"

"I am Mrs. Samantha Monroe, so how can you charge me with any crime?" she says

"Whether or not you are Samantha Monroe will have to be decided and you will given a chance to tell your story, but until then we need to know how you plead, guilty or not guilty?"

"Not guilty" she replies.

"Do you need the court to appoint a lawyer for you?" he asks.

"Yes, I do" she replies. She realizes that there is no use arguing with the law and since she does not have any support, she decides to take the help of a court appointed lawyers.

The prosecutor signs the papers and hands it to the judge. The judge reviews them and approves it and says to the twin,

"I will authorize a lawyer to come to see you and a date for the trial will be set soon afterward. Please take her back" says the judge.

As she is being taken away, she looks at Tom and smiles in a way to express how a man like Tom or her husband could make a mistake like this. The court is adjourned.

Tom and Barbara leave the courtroom and walks towards the parking lot. When Barbara asks

"Tom why do you think the twin kept looking and you?"

"I don't know Barbara. I just don't know. I would like to send her in for a second DNA testing, but it is not in my control now. I don't think my superiors or the Justice Department will be pleased with my interference in this case any more. I think the incident with the twin slapping the prosecutor has caused a lot of powerful people to get involved. We will just have to wait and see."

Tom and Barbara return to the station and attend to their duties. After a while, Tom buzzes Terrance and Barbara to come in. As Barbara sees Terrance pass her cubicle to go to Tom's office, she follows him to Tom's. Terrance stands in front of Tom, looks at Barbara as she comes and stands by Tom's desk with a notepad and asks.

"Mr. Pollack, what do you want from me?"

Tom says "Nothing from you"

Terrance asks "Then, what do you need from me?"

Tom says "Nothing" realizing that Terrance is back to his usual gay attitude. But Tom is not in the mood for it, so he asks in an annoyed tone

"I asked you find out about these felons, have you found anything out?"

"Yes, I did" says Terrance banging a large envelope in front of Tom on his desk and continues

"I am leaving this job! I am not going to stay where I am not respected!" and he leaves them.

After Terrence walks out, Barbara looks at Tom and smiles,

"Looks like you and him have a husband and wife relationship. You upset him few days ago and now it is his turn. Why don't you take him to dinner one day?"

"Yes, Barbara, I will do that after you take him home and have him sleep between you and your husband."

Tom opens his envelope and he sees all the information he needs.

"Looks like Terrance got everything we need against those guys. If his temperament were only like Brian's he would be wonderful."

Barbara walks out of Tom's office asking Tom to go Terrance and ask not to leave his job, so Tom replies

"Yes, I will do that Barbara, but you come back and prepare the charges with their names on them."

Barbara walks back to Tom and takes the envelope and walks out to do her work.

It is Friday, September 19th and the twin is in the Detention center that was appointed by the court. She has sent back her awful breakfast, and was getting a lot of attitude from the other women.

The lady was feeling very alone, like no one kind existed on earth. After being interviewed for almost two hours by the court she feels like in order to have a fair trial she has to go in front of a jury. Father John comes around four pm.

When Father John is escorted in and they are watched by a female officer as they have their conversation.

"Father John, why do you do this for me every day?"

"Well, I have felt like your own father since you were little and your father passed away. Since I have no children, it makes me feel happy to be cared by someone who is like a daughter to me."

The twin was enjoying the food he had brought her, and they continued their conversation like a father and daughter. The female officer wonders why she does not call the senator. She asks Father John

"Have you gone to our house again? What did my husband and family say?"

"Well your mother in law did not say much, but your children want you home. For some reason your husband has turned cold. I tell him you are Samantha but he will not believe me. I have stopped speaking to him, but I am sure deep down he misses you badly."

"Father I have never known you to be angry, please speak to him. You have always taught me to be forgiving"

Father John replies "But, my child, things are different now. You are locked up here and suffering. For the first time since I have known him, he does not trust my word. Just because he thinks he is going to the next President?"

"No Father John, I know him more than any one else, we have our secret when he finds out he will surly take me back. You know when my sister and I were younger, how many problems my mother had? Even you know the trouble in the church. Though my sister was always wild I do not think she meant harm. She probably could not restrain herself like me. I learnt a lot of self control from my parents. Then I met Frank, and he and his family thought me how to maintain a calm outlook."

She was almost finished with her food.

"The day my sister came home was one of the happiest days in my life. She had decided to turn her life around and settle down with a family. I would like to meet the man who helped her make that decision and who wanted to marry her."

"Don't worry; I'm sure the man who she was going to marry will come forward now that Randy's dead. He is our last chance to prove that you are real Mrs. Monroe and your name will be cleared."

"How do I thank you Father for all that you have done for me over the years? You guided us to take the right path. Even though my sister made some mistakes, she eventually came back to the right path. But unfortunately, she ended up dying in my arms" she says with tears in her eyes. Wiping her tears, she continues "Father John before she died she said that she loved me."

Father John replies "I know you are brave and strong and won't give up, you can fight this, and my prayers and faith are with you. God is always on the side of truth".

The twin says "Father, I miss my family."

"I know you do. My heart goes out for you. I will pray to the Lord to give you strength so that this ordeal passes quickly for you" says Father John.

Listening to their conversation, the female officer looks at her watch and she tells Father John "I am sorry, your visiting time is over."

Father John turns to the officer and says politely "I know, but thank you for reminding me. Time is set by the Lord and it is his will when visiting time will be over." He pulls his card from his pocket and gives it to the officer and says

"Maybe you should visit our church sometime, you will find peace."

Taking the card, the female officer replies "Yes Father. Listening to your conversation, I don't know what to think. My feeling is that she is our next First Lady. The law is sometimes wrong. Anyways, if I was the supervisor, I would let you talk to her all night."

She continues "But, Father John, I heard that the younger twin was very good at pretending to be the older one, so you never know. I don't want to get into any trouble with my supervisors by letting you stay longer. I will give her company till I have to leave."

Father John stands to leave while the twin puts the containers Father John brought with food in the bag for him to take back. Taking the bag, he says goodbye to her and tells the officer,

"Please keep my daughter's spirit up. She is going to need it through the trial."

He walks to the door and looks back and waves goodbye to the twin.

Once Father John leaves, the female officer stands by the twin, but there is no conversation. The twin looks around the visiting room wondering how many people here have committed crimes and how many are innocent. She sits there till eight pm watching the visitors leave.

She then goes back to her cell and lays down on the bed with her eyes open and watches her life go by. She thinks back on everything that has happened in her life. She wonders why God has put her in this situation. Thinking of all the people in here, she wonders why there is not quick justice where only the guilty are punished and the innocent are set free. The clock ticks by and she thinks that no matter how much she thinks or wishes for, it is the same thing every day. Father John comes to visit every day and comforts her but once he leaves it is the same loneliness, same prison smell, same verbal abuse from fellow inmates.

She thinks of the days and nights that have passed with no word from her family. She feels like a lioness, locked up and helpless. There is nobody to talk to except God. Like always, she prays for justice and the time passes slowly.

One day she is informed by her court appointed lawyer that her trial date is set for September 29, 2008. She is happy to hear that, at least she will be able to spend time away from here in the courtroom and maybe see her family.

As the trial date gets closer, she starts to get anxious. She is hoping that the Senator will be in the courtroom and it will give her a chance to see him at least five days a week. But, she cannot help thinking why the Senator did not visit her when she needed him the most. She thinks that even if he thought that she was his wife's twin, he could have visited her to say something. She is very disappointed that he did not come to see her. But there is nothing she can do but wait.

Finally, Monday, September 29, 2008 comes. Though it has been only three weeks, she feels like she has been locked up for centuries. She waits anxiously for her day in court.

The Trial Of the twin,
   Next first Lady's Bad Twin" Part Two Will be out on sep29, 2008

Printed in the United States
121873LV00004B/14/P